The Fish

JOANNE STUBBS

Fairlight Books

First published by Fairlight Books 2022

Fairlight Books
Summertown Pavilion, 18–24 Middle Way, Oxford, OX2 7LG

A CIP catalogue record for this book is available from the
British Library

1 2 3 4 5 6 7 8 9 10

ISBN 978-1-914148-19-4

www.fairlightbooks.com

Printed and bound in Great Britain

Designed by Holly Ovenden

MIX
Paper from
responsible sources
FSC® C018072

For Madeleine, who famously loved books

Chapter One

Cathy

We are going to plant the back garden up as a rice paddy. There is a stream running down the left side of the plot, and when we moved here nearly seven years ago, it was always a trickle. Now, with every storm, it bursts its banks and swamps the garden. And there are a lot of storms. My wife's beloved vegetable patch has become too waterlogged to bear fruit, so we're giving up on the carrots. Perhaps we'll start something – maybe rice will be the future of Cornwall.

Ephie is half in and half out of the back door, a tray of rice seedlings in each hand, squinting upwards. 'It's the perfect day for it, Cathy,' she says.

Picking up two more trays, I follow her out. The sky is leaden, air close. All May we have had no rain, an awkward prelude to our experiment with water plants, and then June started with thunder. Today the clouds are pregnant and fit to erupt. I feel the sea in the air, too, damp and sticky.

Her veg patch, which took up half the garden, is now a shallow pool, with mud oozing at the edges of long water-filled channels. The earth that came out of each channel is heaped at the borders of the paddy, to keep the water in. She dug the bed over two weeks, in the long summer daylight hours after work. I used that time to focus on getting ahead of a wedding commission for autumn: three bridesmaid dresses with cap sleeves and fishtails, in a raw silk the colour of Victoria plums. I've been running my own dressmaking business for five years now; wedding work is the most demanding, the most delicate and the most potentially dramatic. Those two weeks gave me three toiles, though, so that I'm ready for three bridesmaids to try them on before I cut the silk.

Now I look at Ephie's creation, which is messy and full of mud.

'It's been a lot of work,' I say. 'I hope it's worth it.'

She catches me in her gaze, brown eyes smiling. 'It will be. And, yeah, it really has. I got blisters from the shovel.'

'You poor thing.'

We grew the seedlings with care on the south-facing window-sills of our cottage. They have started life as they mean to go on, beside the sea. Ephie watered them daily from the stream, until their green stems each had two leaves. They look like new grass, vibrant and spindly. I wonder how they will take to the salty air. Will their leaves cloud over, like blackberries on a bluff? Will the rice have a seaweed tang?

In between going back and forth for plants, Ephie tells me her calculations – how many seedlings will fit in each row of the paddy and what the distance between each plant must be. The rice patch is all her experiment: from the research into which variety to grow, down to the number of biodegradable starter trays we needed to buy at the garden centre. I think her favourite app on her phone is the calculator; that or the to-do list. I'm intrigued and happy to help, and looking forward to cooking the rice, but we both know who the project manager is in this endeavour.

'How long before we have rice, then?' I ask.

She scrunches her nose, remembering the facts. 'This is a late variety – I think it said around 130 days after sowing.' She ticks off four months on her fingers. 'We should be able to harvest in mid-September, just before the season turns. I hope I've got the timings right. Is that like most cereals, a late summer harvest?'

I shrug, thinking of a field of wheat. 'Will I get to drive the combine?'

She raises her eyebrows – either I'm not taking this seriously enough or she thinks it's a terrible joke. I try again. 'And will we save some of the seed for next year? Or doesn't it work like that?'

She tells me that's exactly how it works. That she ended up buying enough *Halorice* seed – that's the variety, some kind of salt-resistant hybrid – for two years, because she wasn't sure how good our germination rate would be, but that we should also keep back some seed. 'Don't cook it all just yet, Cathy,' she says. She carries on talking, but I get distracted by the piping call of two oystercatchers flying overhead and watch them, white and black, until they disappear over the top of the house. They'll be heading down to the rocks now that the tide is low, searching for whatever it is they eat. I've never seen an oyster down there.

'These plants are small. Do you think the water will keep the slugs away?' Ephie says, holding up a seedling.

We have a brief discussion about the swimming ability of slugs. Ephie reminds me that they drown in beer traps, but I think that's because they're drunk, rather than because they can't swim. She grimaces. 'Let's hope British slugs don't have a taste for rice,' I offer, and she makes a joke about them being nationalists that only like native food. I remind her they always made short work of our pak choi. 'Damn slugs,' she says.

She makes two more trips and then all the trays of seedlings are on the patio, crowding next to each other like pots at a church fete. I try to ignore her bare feet, which I know are trailing muddy footprints through to the kitchen. My wellies are by the back door, and I pull them on, hoping they're tall enough for the deepest part of the paddy.

Hands on hips, Ephie stares out at the water.

'So, you just scoop out a handful of soil, stick the seedling – including its compost pot – into the hole and then push the soil back round to secure it. Then a ten-centimetre gap, then the next. Should be easy enough.'

She's wearing her gardening shorts, navy linen with deep pockets, and a cotton shirt so threadbare that one of her tanned shoulders is peeking out. She's only done up four of the buttons across her front so that her soft, lean belly shows beneath a V of open fabric. When she bends, the whole thing falls forwards and her breasts come into view. I know she'd take the shirt off entirely, unabashed, if it were a little warmer. She has an ease with her body I've been envious of since the moment I met her.

'You're not going to wear those?' she asks, pointing down at my wellies.

'It's muddy.'

'You are such a girl,' she says, a smile showing at the corners of her mouth.

I tilt my head up. 'Proud of it. Don't use "girl" in a derogatory sense.'

She reaches out a hand and tugs me towards her. My wellies squeak on the way and she kisses me: a coaxing, gentle sort of kiss that ends as soon as it begins. She lets me go. 'Honestly, I think you should take the wellies off. I don't want them stomping all over my carefully laid paddy.'

I bow my head, bending to tug off the boots. I take three steps over the damp grass to the edge of the paddy, my toes spreading wide, enjoying the earth. I stop at the brown water, looking into its murky depths. Ephie plunges in like a child in a paddling pool, splashing her way to the centre and then grinning back at me. I follow slowly, raising a foot over the earth wall and plunging it down, into the paddy. Over my head, gulls squawk.

It's not cold, and the soil at the bottom isn't gritty like I expected, but a smooth gunge that oozes between my toes. My feet sink as though in soft sand, and I feel at home, like I'm down on the beach and not in a muddy pool. I imagine the soft footprints

I leave behind, the little clouds of brown that will disperse every time I take a step. I move towards Ephie, nearly falling over as I stretch from one trench to another -- they're only thirty centimetres apart, but hard to see with the water lying across the top of them all. The paddy suctions my toes, begging me to be still. I flail my arms to catch my balance. Ephie watches me like a cat.

'Stay where you are,' she says. 'I'll put a tray at the end of that row for you.'

She skips out of the paddy, three steps to the back door, and I see the shimmer of sun lotion across her cheekbones. She doesn't need it – she tans at the first hint of spring sun, to the colour of acorn cups. She wears sun protection in solidarity with me, though, because I live each summer beneath the sheen of Factor 50. I have the skin of a jellyfish, semi-translucent. I could burn on this overcast June day.

When my tray of seedlings is waiting at the end of the row, I wade towards it, enjoying the squelch. I pick up the first little plant and run my fingers through its leaves. It is luscious, flat-edged and sharp-tipped, and it smells like earth. The pot it's in has turned mushy from all the water it's soaked up, like cornflakes left in milk.

'We should be able to get forty-five plants in one row,' Ephie says, looking about her. Everything is calculated, everything organised right to the end. We'd have a wild bog, no more planning than that, if it were left to me.

I hold the plant up. 'How do I do this, then, just stick it in the channel?'

'Use your fingers to make a little hole for it to go into... There, at the start of the channel.' She points, directing me, and I hover the plant above the surface of the water, picking our spot. 'The earth should be soft enough to scoop out and then just, well, plant it.'

It's a tricky business. I put the plant down again so that I can use two hands to dig, but water and mud seep back into the hole as soon as I make it, and I feel like a child on the beach trying to stop waves from washing away the walls of my sandcastle. I squat down to get a better angle, and feel the cold of water soaking into the bum of my shorts. Reminding myself there's a hot shower at the end of this, I sink a little lower, getting balanced, pants soaking in water now, and decide on a two-pronged attack – scoop then shove. I pick the seedling up again and ram its squashy little pot into the half-formed hole, mud squeezing between my fingers. The leaves are wonky, but the thing is in earth. Ephie says it's perfect and that I should get on with the next. The second one is just as hard to plant, but the third seedling is better. By the fourth, I feel I'm getting the hang of it. The water is cool on my wrists, the mud soft, and the smell of soil is in my nose. The gulls have gone quiet, perhaps out at sea, and Ephie starts to sing as she works. She has a terrible, monotonous voice, which makes me smile. I really love the few things she's not excellent at.

I am scraping out a hole halfway down the row when I feel something move against my foot, like an eel or a python or a water-borne spider, and I scream.

'Something touched me,' I shout, noisy and hysterical, convinced I will die. I splash my way through the water, desperate for dry land. 'There's something in the water. What is it?'

Ephie frowns and I let out a stream of nervous laughter, breathing hard, panting over the safety of green grass. She bends down, looking into the trench I've just evacuated. She waits. Nothing.

'Maybe a frog? Or you might have just imagined it?' she says.

I shake my head. 'You had to make me take off the wellies.'

'Don't be a baby. Go and put them back on if you're that upset about it.'

'I guess a frog is OK.' I hate the way she challenges me. I step gingerly back into the water.

She smiles, to win me back. 'Yeah, I'm sure it was just a little frog. Probably had the fright of its life. Bit of a shock for everyone,' she says.

I nod and tell her she's probably right. I believe that she's right for another thirty centimetres of planting. Then I see it: a silver flicker in the brown water.

'It's a fish!' Its metallic tail disappears among the brown and green.

Ephie moves closer. 'A fish? Really, are you sure?' She bends low and I can feel her mind whirring, like an electric charge.

For a minute, and then another, we both stare into the paddy. 'It can't be,' she mutters. I will the thing to make an appearance. Just a little hint of a fish body. This mysterious thing that has slithered past me, that has piqued my wife's scientific brain, that is living in our garden, needs to show itself.

I'm ready to give up looking, about to turn and retreat to the comfort of my rubber boots, when she grabs my arm and points. Her fingers are a vice.

'Did you see it?' she says in a stage whisper.

I shake my head and keep watching the water.

'Where did it come from?' I ask.

'It must have swum up the stream from the sea. Can fish even do that? This is really cool. Although it probably means our paddy is brackish.' Her words tumble out, partly to me but mostly to herself. 'Good job we got the salt-resistant rice variety. I don't know how a coastal fish could survive, unless it was brackish. Although salmon... They do both, don't they?'

I stand up straight and ease myself out of the paddy, pulling the wet wedge of shorts from between my bum cheeks. My discovery is now Ephie's and she rushes on, one thought after another. 'You know it's a thing, having fish in rice paddies? I was reading about it the other day. It's common in China – the farmers raise fish among their rice. I think it keeps everything sort of clean and tidy. And it supplements their income.'

She lowers to her hands and knees, nose close to the water like a dog in a puddle. The belly of her shirt hangs low, into the water, and I see the linen start to soak through, navy turning to the colour of space. She stares into the water and I think of the view that fish would get if it did come out of hiding. I'd stay put.

'Come on out – I want to see you again,' she says. 'Maybe this little lady can invite her friends. How great would that be? We could have a shoal.'

I tell her it would be lovely, and that I'm going inside to make a cup of tea. I take my time over it, feeling somehow unsettled by our visitor, wondering if it was the wrong thing to do, to fill our garden with water. I feel left out, too. I'd never be able to delight in the fine details of this fish the way my wife can.

I stir the teabags, staring out of the kitchen window. A Cornish fishing village with a rice paddy. A fish living in my garden. What next? I put the packet of teabags back in the cupboard and wonder how long before we'll be growing tea ourselves.

Beyond the kitchen window, clouds roll over the harbour, and the first drop of rain falls against the pane.

A month later, when June's longest day has come and gone, and the July rainstorms are falling regularly on us, Ephie and I step out of the back door to catch a few moments under an unusually dry sky. We admire our handiwork. The plants have grown over half a metre in height, nourished by the rains that have kept their paddy full. Between the lime-green stems and the flat, sharp-edged leaves, the water shimmers soft brown. It's like looking into the edges of a jungle. There is no seed yet, not for another month or so, but the plants already look delicious.

We sit on the back step, each with a cup of tea. It is a Tuesday morning and Ephie is working from home while I begin to put my plum silk patterns together. She wraps her free arm around me and I close my eyes for a minute, feeling the warm sun through my lids.

'It's a bit scary, isn't it?' I say, opening my eyes to look at the paddy.

She raises her eyebrows.

'Scary that we've got to this point. That we're fundamentally changing what we grow because of the weather?'

She replies quickly. 'But we can't just sit around and worry about it.'

I nod, unconvinced.

'We're adapting to a new situation,' she continues. 'And while we do that, we're trying to fix some of the shit that's gone wrong.'

'Are we, though?'

She smiles. 'We are, in the lab. Or we're trying to understand it, so that then it can be fixed.'

'Good for you.' I'm half-proud, half-jealous.

She drains her tea and stands, holding out her hands to pull me up, but I shake my head, mug still mostly full.

She steps towards the paddy with her hands out, running careful fingers through the leaves, then bends down close to the water's edge and pokes a finger into the pool. The water ripples and she grins back at me.

'They're doing fine,' she says.

She means the herring that whistle back and forth along the trenches. She identified what flavour of fish it was that first day, when we still thought there might only be one. We now have a whole shoal. We're like real grown-ups, with a pond.

She beckons me over to her, and her wedding ring flashes in the sun. 'Come and look, Cathy.'

Chapter Two

Ricky

Ricky stares out at the ocean, grinning.

'Absolutely brilliant. An orca,' he says to his friend.

Kyle lifts his head from his hands and looks up. He's sitting on the beach, dark-brown sand all around him. An hour or two before, he saw his ex-girlfriend kissing some guy outside the school gates.

'Pretty cool,' he mutters.

Ricky sits down, too. He looks at his best friend – sees melancholy.

'Don't think about it, eh?' he suggests.

Kyle grunts and wipes his nose with the back of his hand. 'Sure.'

'We saw an orca just now.' He pokes Kyle in the ribs. 'Hey, we're having a whale of a time. Eh?'

Kyle moans. 'Terrible,' he says. But there is a smile in his voice. 'Surely we're having a killer time?'

Ricky snorts. 'That sounds like something a surfer would say.'

In front of them the waves break against the beach and the sun struggles out from behind grey clouds. They've both grown up with this view, there on the western edge of the South Island. The beach, the Tasman Sea, the endless, open waves. The sandflies. There's a salty tang to the air and it settles on them, damp and sticky, like it has done every day of their lives.

Kyle sighs, lying back in the sand. 'At least it's the weekend,' he says.

They decided at school not to bother trying to go to the party that some people in the year above were talking about. It's in Hokitika, a thirty-minute drive, and neither of them has a car or knows anyone going who would give them a lift. They hung around in town a bit after school, eating hot chips, and then started home along the beach. Ricky spotted the whale.

'Let's go,' he says.

'Don't you wanna stay longer? Look for more whales?' Kyle asks.

Ricky shakes his head, satisfied. 'They'll be back.'

Kyle peels off first, heading up the beach towards his house. Ricky's is a bit further on. They both live a couple of kilometres north of town, on the coast road, so they've been walking to and from school together – sometimes on the road, sometimes on the beach – for years.

Ricky takes a path through the dunes and out to the road, then through his front gate. The house, standing on flat ground just behind the sand, has sky-blue wooden walls. Two palm trees, old and battered by years of coastal rain, huddle in a corner of the front yard. The screen door at the front porch drags on rusty hinges.

He goes to the kitchen to make a drink and looks out of the window to the back yard, where a pair of rabbit hutches stand side by side. He can just see the fluffy end of one bunny. Above the sound of the TV coming from the other room, there's the roll of the waves on the beach. Drifts of sand stack up on the outside windowsills, blown there off the dunes.

Ricky feels a hand slot into his and looks down at Janie, his little sister. She still has her school uniform on and her black hair is falling in a straight mess around her face.

'The other girls said I look stupid,' she mumbles, eyes cast down.

'Why?'

'Because I wear shorts instead of a skirt. Because they're your old shorts, not even mine. I'm nearly ten – I want my own clothes.'

Ricky goes to the fridge. He pulls out a bar of Whittaker's and breaks off a piece.

'They sound like idiots,' he says to Janie, handing her the chocolate.

'They think I'm weird.'

Ricky reminds himself not to swear, but he wants to tell Janie to tell her friends to fuck off.

'They just don't understand yet that it's good to be able to think for yourself. Why do you wear shorts?' he asks.

She smirks. 'I always win the handstand competitions. Because my skirt doesn't fly up.'

'There you go, then,' he says, laughing.

She still looks uncertain. 'But maybe I could get a skirt.'

'Maybe.' He shrugs. 'I could buy you one, if you really wanted.'

She looks happy. How much do girls' school skirts cost? Maybe he can get one second-hand. Maybe Mum will pay. He breaks off another piece of chocolate and passes it to her.

Mum appears from the laundry room, carrying a load under her arm, still in her uniform from the care home. She says they're having pizza for dinner – they just have to wait for Dad to get home.

Later, full of mozzarella, Ricky sits on the sofa with Janie next to him. She has Checkers, one of the family's two cats, on her lap. Dad sits on the end and Mum's in the armchair. The room smells like pizza crusts. They are halfway through a movie when Kyle messages. Just a short one: *Come over, mate.* Ricky protests, replying to say he's comfortable and that his friend should come round to him. It doesn't work. *Everything's gone wrong here*, Kyle's next message says.

Janie looks disappointed when he gets up from the sofa and says he's going out. Dad sends a casual 'Don't get too pissed' after Ricky. The sky outside is dark and the air's cold. He pulls his hood up and his sleeves down over his hands.

His feet sink into the soft sand on the walk to Kyle's, and when he pushes open the back door, his sneakers trail the grains inside with him, across the kitchen tiles. Kyle and his mum are sitting side by side at the counter, sculling shots out of egg cups. A half-empty bottle of vodka sits in front of them.

'What's going on?' Ricky asks.

'Come and join us,' says Mary, Kyle's mum.

Ricky likes her. She gives them lifts places and often buys them beer. She always cooks great food and never lets him leave the house without being fed. A motherly mum, but she's cool about it. Ricky has seen her with a glass of wine on plenty of occasions, but he's never seen her drunk. The way her eyes are squinting now, as she sits with egg cup in hand, he can tell she's well on the way.

Kyle slides off his stool and opens a cupboard, returning with a third egg cup. 'Mum couldn't find shot glasses. Here you go, mate,' he says, filling the cup and handing it over.

Ricky shakes his head, peering down at the liquid. 'Come on, I hate vodka.'

Mary snorts. 'Don't be silly. What is it you young men say? Man up.'

'Actually, no one says that anymore, Mary. Toxic masculinity and all that,' Ricky says, half-smiling.

'Sorry, dear. Can't keep up.'

Ricky looks at Kyle, who's sitting slumped, eyes boring a hole into the counter in front of him.

'How did you two end up like this?' he asks. 'Where's Hannah?'

Hannah – Kyle's younger sister, thirteen and insufferable – is nowhere to be seen. Mary flaps a hand in the air. 'She's with friends. Sleepover.'

Kyle picks up the vodka and pours himself another shot. He has a miserable look in his eyes as he waves the bottle in front of his mum, who nods and pushes her cup closer to him for a refill. Ricky frowns. This can't just be about Kyle's ex.

'Why did you two decide to get wasted?' Ricky asks again.

Mary tosses back her shot and grimaces. 'Disgusting,' she declares. Then she sighs and looks up at Ricky. 'Tony left. He's fucked off, and he won't be coming back,' she says.

She shrugs. Ricky looks at Kyle, who shakes his head a little and then goes back to staring at the counter.

'Oh, right,' Ricky says, wondering what it means when a dad fucks off and doesn't come back. 'Here goes, I guess.'

He looks at his egg cup. 'All Blacks' is emblazoned on the side, beneath the fern. Kyle's dad is a diehard rugby fan. Ricky stares at the colourless liquid, summoning courage, then downs the shot.

'You two are crazy,' he says, shuddering at the aftertaste.

Mary pulls her cup towards her and looks down at her hands. 'I'm heading straight for a nervous breakdown, love,' she says.

Ricky joins them at the counter and the shots go on, until he is warm through and can't feel the burn anymore. It's a relief when the bottle is empty. Around midnight, Mary smashes a wine glass and cuts her finger open on one of the pieces. Blood drips onto the floor and she sits there, crying and cradling her torn finger. While Kyle scowls in the corner, Ricky stumbles around looking for a medical kit. He thinks about calling Dad; he's out of his depth and wants someone there who can act like an adult. Eventually, they find a bandage, though, and Mary sobs her way to bed. It must be one in the morning. Kyle says that Ricky should stay over, but they're both too drunk to blow up the air mat, even though they try. Ricky finds a cushion and a blanket, and curls up on the sofa, which isn't long enough for him to lie flat. The room spins as he falls asleep.

The next morning they're back on the beach. 'Do you think we should check on your mum?' Ricky asks, glancing at his friend. It's 11am and the sun's still lingering behind a wall of winter cloud.

Kyle shifts on the sand. 'He's gone off with another woman. Mum's known about it for months, apparently.'

Ricky realises now just how drunk his friend was the night before. Kyle must not remember the conversations. The cursing, the raised voices, the All Blacks egg cup that got thrown across the room. He knows the whole story.

'What happens now?' Ricky asks. He finds a pebble nearby and picks it up, rolling it between his fingers, not sure what to say or where to look.

A shrug. 'Nothing.'

'Maybe breakfast?' Ricky says, trying to keep his voice light. He gives Kyle a gentle nudge. 'You'll feel better after you've eaten.'

Kyle nods. 'It was cool to see that whale yesterday, wasn't it?'

Ricky puts his arm around him. It was so cool.

Chapter Three

Margaret

Margaret has had fifteen years to adapt to the rainy season, but every year she still sweats through the humidity the way she did that very first day in Kuala Lumpur, when she was not long into married life.

'Did you pick up the coconuts?' she shouts. She stands on the upstairs landing, directly beneath a ceiling fan.

She hears Roger shut the front door, kick his brogues under a nearby rack, then climb the stairs.

'I haven't had time, honey, sorry. Didn't you go, Marge?'

She toys with the waistband of her short linen pants. 'I don't want to go back there.'

Roger takes both her hands in his own. He is a gentle man, fat with years of desk-life. 'Gosh, I'm pretty sure they've forgotten all about it by now,' he says.

'I just feel so damned stupid. Why am I the only person that can't seem to get used to all these changes?' She lets go of his hands – too hot for body contact – and steps away.

'Go get your coconuts,' he says. 'You have to. It's the only way you'll stop feeling embarrassed about this.'

She shrugs, half-nodding. She walks away from him and, as she goes, the air grows thicker – in the bedroom, she feels like she's swimming. It's Roger's one miserly streak: to have the air conditioning units on only when both of them are home. If they go out, they come home to a furnace. When Margaret's home alone, she puts the AC on full and doesn't tell him. Anyway, since they got solar panels, it's basically free.

'You're right.' She stares at herself in the mirror, hands on hips. 'I need to just get on with it. Pretend it never happened.' She brushes a stray piece of frizz from her forehead. Impossible, in eighty-six per cent humidity, to keep her hair straight.

Roger sinks down on the edge of the bed and the mattress creaks. He pulls the orange tie from around his neck in one fluid movement.

'I'm going, then. I need the coconuts for our meeting tomorrow,' she says. 'Wish me luck?'

The edges of his mouth twitch. 'No need. Come on, you're made of meaner stuff than you think.'

She strides out of the room and down the stairs. Slipping her feet into blue rubber sandals, she retrieves a purse from a hook near the front door. She pauses and looks down, then decides to leave the purse, pulling money out of it to stuff in her pocket instead. She turns the door handle and marches out.

Things have changed since they first moved to KL. It wasn't semi-coastal back then – no ocean breeze, no harbour. But the polar ice melt had its effect. She didn't look out from her bedroom window, in days past, and see a dark, distant mass of mangroves. It takes the trees five years to become established – she read it in a copy of National Geographic she was flicking through one day at the dentist's – so they are fully independent now, and full of life. Roger loves it. He stands at the bedroom window with a gigantic pair of binoculars and searches for fish eagles. No more trips into the mountains to see the hornbills – now he has all the wildlife he needs right on the edges of the city. And the government seems to have it under control; they seem confident the water won't rise anymore. They've started taking the environment very seriously over the last few years. She thinks back over her life and wonders how many tons of plastic she used to get through, before it was all banned.

The Fish

It seemed like the ocean encroached slowly, but within a few years, islands were swallowed, and a harbour was built on the edge of KL. It was a disaster, or course, for so many, but they were careful about it not damaging the city. The rivers had swollen and the asphalt had started to crack, so the highway into downtown was rerouted and lined along its whole edge with a living wall of plants. Now, when Margaret goes into town, she soars above the houses on a bridge. It's very pretty, for a road.

The coconut stand is a few kilometres from the house, and in the evening it sits in the shadow of the highway. Margaret pulls herself into their electric car and reaches to the dashboard to click the remote that controls their front gate. The barrier is metal, solid, and taller than a man. When they moved in, she wanted the gate taken out – it felt like living in a prison. But Roger convinced her to let it stay. 'It's just the norm in this neighbourhood to have a gate at the edge of your compound, honey,' he'd said, pointing at their neighbours' properties. 'Just the way they do it here. We'd look kinda crazy if we were the only house on the street without it, wouldn't we?'

She turns on the car and waits a minute for the AC to get going. Roger drives with the windows open because he thinks it makes him look like a local, but it's too sticky for that today – her forehead is slick with sweat. She puts the car in reverse and backs slowly into the street.

There are five blocks of suburbia to cross before she makes it to the highway. She likes to think about what sort of little paradise each family has inside, behind their gates. Papaya trees for some, orchids for others. Widescreen TVs for most. During Eid all the gates spring wide open, and families and neighbours come together to break their long fast. It's Margaret's favourite day of the year: the food is amazing, the conversations quiet and loving, the houses open to all. It's a time of giving. Every year she waddles home stuffed, saying a silent prayer of thanks for the feasts she's devoured. Every year she aims to meet a new neighbour, extending her waddles to the next street and further. It makes no difference that she and Roger are Christians. That's not what it's about.

As she drives slowly along, she notes the gates she has seen behind and smiles. The air-conditioning fan rattles: a welcome buzz in her ears.

Up on the highway the sky is orange and she can smell something like jasmine. It must be growing on the wall. It will be dark in an hour; she can hear the bedtime cries of birds from the trees lining the streets below. She hangs in the left lane – only one exit to pass before hers – and with her free hand twists at a wiry knot in her hair. She tries not to think about the last time she went to the coconut stand, but an anxious squirm starts to rummage around her stomach and she begins talking to herself. *Maybe they're shut for the evening or gone away on holiday and there'll be no one there.* She wouldn't even have to get out of the car. Yes, it's far too late for them to still be there.

Pulling off the highway, she spirals down the exit ramp and lands at street level, turning left and ignoring her disappointment at the first sign of a fully stocked and serviced coconut stand. She can see the couple who run it: they are standing behind the counter, with stacks of green spheres before them. And the monkeys are there, just like last time. Her hand shakes as she puts the car in park.

The rising sea levels drove them in, off the swamped coastlines and into the city, and the macaques now parade with confidence through the suburbs. Their appearance in her neighbourhood, though, is recent. For a long time they were waylaid in the fringes of town. Margaret scowls. Their eyes are set close, the colour of amber. They look devious. Their fingers grip like vices. She knows this because she had several of their hands wrapped around her arms, last time she came here. She had made the mistake – so stupid – of walking to the stand with a shopping bag filled with groceries. Nothing short of an invitation. The coconut-stand couple had warned her, waving at the bag and calling out to her. But she didn't understand. It was only afterwards, hysterical and sweating, that she realised what they had been saying: *Leave the bag in the car.* They were shouting in English, too, so she couldn't even blame her poor Malay language skills. It was so embarrassing.

The troop had waited until Margaret's arms were full of coconuts, of course; six vessels of sweet milk balancing in the space between her hands and her chin, and the groceries dangling from her arm like treasure. Then they made their move. Margaret didn't see it coming and when the first paws hurtled, fast and strong, up her back, she screamed with all the strength her lungs would give her. Shouts went out from the coconut stand, arms went in the air, coconuts rained to the floor, monkeys leapt, groceries spun and she kept on screaming. She whipped around, both hands on the hessian shopping bag, and threw herself into a tug of war. But she was outnumbered. As the husband from the coconut stand appeared next to her, broom in hand, and took aim at the nearest beast, a small one – a particularly mischievous one – scurried up Margaret's body and began to prise her hands from the bag. She could see its teeth, bared at her in a snarl. With a final shriek, she abandoned all and ran back to the car. On the way out, reversing frantically after the onslaught, she nearly hit a cat. Absolutely bad luck in Malaysia – they love cats.

But Margaret tries not to think of this as she turns the car off. She smooths her pants over her thighs, watching the wrinkles in the yellow fabric disappear, and takes a deep breath. She has a handful of cash in her pocket, that's all. No bags. Through the car window she looks over at the nearest group of monkeys, gauging their mood. Two of them lazily groom a third, and a fourth and fifth slouch nearby. She knows it's an act. Macaques are masters of feigned serenity.

The sweat is thick on her brow as she pushes the car door open and slowly plants her feet on the ground. She says a prayer under her breath – a quick plea for peaceful deliverance – and takes her eyes off the monkeys to look towards the coconuts. The couple are both smiling, and they chat to one another as they watch her. Taking them in, she sees that the husband has the handle of a broom in his hand; he gestures it towards her, eyes twinkling. Then, a few steps later, Margaret realises that the coconuts in the woman's arms are not what she thought. They seem to have fur – she is holding the cat.

Forgotten all about it, oh, sure.

Margaret's walk is self-conscious and jaunty, but she forces herself to keep a steady pace. She pulls a big smile onto her face and makes eye contact with the couple, then points to the monkeys and feigns a laugh. *How ridiculous it was, that incident. What a hoot.*

What actually happened, after that last visit to the coconut stand, was not that Margaret went home and laughed. She stumbled into the house, stripped naked in the front room and told Roger to examine her for signs of broken skin. 'Not a mark on you,' he said, after a good look. He took a step back and admired her, then glanced to the wide front window. The curtains were open. 'See, honey? I told you the gate was a good idea.'

She searched online for the symptoms of rabies, just in case. *Fever, headache, nausea, hyperactivity, anxiety.* She spent three days feeling anxious about feeling anxious, and then on the fourth day, in a whirl of hyperactivity, walked headfirst into an open cupboard door. She added headache to her list of symptoms and drove herself to hospital, where they took her temperature and told her to go home.

But she tries not to think of any of this as she draws closer to the coconuts. When she is only five feet, she reminds herself that God is on her side. But then, on her periphery, there is a sudden movement. A creature, sleek and grey, runs across a patch of open ground, and she instantly sidesteps and turns, raising her hands to her chest in combat stance. But the monkey is gone. Not interested in her at all: it has seen something else to pursue. It disappears into the dusty shadows behind one of the highway pillars. She drops her hands, feeling stupid.

'*Monyet*,' smiles the coconut husband, teaching her Malay. '*Monyet* is OK.'

Margaret nods. She smiles, relieved to have made it. 'Hello, hello.'

The wife now shifts the cat in her arms, lifting it slightly towards Margaret. '*Kucing* is happy.'

Margaret nods at the *kucing*. 'I'm so pleased,' she says, reaching over the stand to run her fingers through the cat's brown fur. 'Could I have six coconuts, please?'

'Six?'

'Yes, six please,' she says, pulling a note from her pocket.

The couple smile and exchange fast words with each other, which Margaret doesn't follow. In her first couple of years in KL she made a real effort to learn the basics of the three most spoken languages: Malay, Mandarin and Tamil. Malay was hard and the other two seemed nearly impossible. She did her best, or maybe not quite her best, but she did try, and she did learn a bit. She's picked up some slang over the years, too, but always feels self-conscious when she tries to use it herself. And so many people speak English – or they do with her.

She pockets her change and leans forwards to have coconuts stacked into her arms. The husband stops at three and then scoops up another three himself, smiling. He walks around the end of the stand to join her.

'Goodbye,' says the wife.

'Thank you, goodbye,' replies Margaret.

As the husband walks next to her, she feels a deep sense of gratitude to him. Yes, they remember the incident and, yes, they laughed a bit. So did Roger. So did everyone who heard the story. That drives Margaret mad; she bets they'd all feel differently if they'd been attacked by monkeys. Rabies is no joke. But anyway, here is this man by her side, helping her out. This feeling is familiar to her – even since her first day in KL, she has felt cared for. It's one of the many reasons it only took two weeks for her to start calling the city *home*.

As they draw closer to the car, the husband pauses. He looks away to the right, into the long shadows of the highway bridge, and squints. Margaret stops, too, one pace ahead, and shifts her load. Her companion mutters something, his brow creasing. Three monkeys stand in a close group, staring at a long, silver cylinder that lies in the dirt by their feet.

Margaret squints, too, to bring the cylinder into focus among the gloom, and as she does so, it twitches, lifting one of its ends into the air before flopping back to the ground, sending the monkeys backwards a step.

'*Ikan?*' says the man to himself. His frown deepens and his lips purse in confusion.

Now the monkeys draw closer to the cylinder again, the largest of the group extending a hand, and again the thing moves. This time it flips over entirely, end to end, and lands in a new patch of dirt half a foot away from where it started.

'Well, it sort of looks like a fish…' Margaret says. She looks back to her car then and sees that it sits in deep shadows. It's getting late. Roger will be wondering where she's got to. 'Um, shall we?'

The man pulls his eyes from the monkeys and shakes his head. He gives Margaret a shrug and smiles, and together they walk to the tailgate of her car.

'I did it!' Margaret says ten minutes later, rattling the front door shut behind her.

Roger looks up from the TV and raises his eyebrows.

'No cat issues, no monkey attacks. Nothing!' Her smile is so wide that her eyes are almost closed. 'Now, honey, would you be amazing and go get the goods out of the car for me? I'm pooped.'

She flops onto the sofa next to him and pulls the remote from his hand, ignoring how his eyes roll.

He sighs. 'You are something, Marge.'

Chapter Four

Ricky

In a salt-stained wooden house three kilometres out of Claremouth, Ricky stirs in his bed. He's been snoring and there's a wet patch on the pillow next to his mouth. As he turns over, he cradles his head, palm pressed across his ear, as though to block out the outside world. His bedroom window rattles in its frame. Along its bottom length, small pools of water are forming. One has stretched across the sill and started to drip, drip, drip onto a pair of underpants that lie on the floor beneath. The windowpane is frosted out with raindrops. Above his head, under the edges of the roof sheets, the wind howls.

Ricky opens one eye. *It's still night*, he thinks. Still dark. But his phone says 11.30am. He frowns, rubbing his eyes. He sees a message from Kyle. It's a picture of a tree on its side, roots in the air. *Random.*

He rolls from his bed, pushes his feet into his slippers and goes to the window. The air in his room smells cool and fresh – none of the usual stale sea salt. His nose touches the glass, fingers grasping the wet frame. He has to squint; the windowpane is so covered in raindrops. He makes out a scene of heavy grey. It's raining so hard it seems as though the sky itself must be breaking up and plummeting to the ground.

He doesn't bother getting dressed. His long basketball shirt balloons out behind him as he hurtles into the living room. His floppy hair bounces against his forehead.

'Oh no, you made it, mate,' Dad says, looking round from the patio doors where he and Janie are standing, watching the storm.

'Yes! Told you,' Janie says Dad. She has Checkers in her arms. His black-and-white fur is ruffled and on end.

'All right, I guess you win,' Dad says to her. He puts a hand in his pocket, pulls out a crumpled note, flattens it on his palm and then holds it out to Janie.

She looks smug as she shifts the cat, takes the money off him and shoves it in the back pocket of her jeans.

'I thought you'd sleep through the whole thing,' Dad says, turning to Ricky again. 'We had a bet on.'

'I told you,' Janie pipes in. 'Even he can't sleep through this.'

Ricky frowns and joins them at the patio doors. 'She's nine – she's not old enough to gamble. What's going on out there?'

'Yeah, it's really bad,' Dad replies. 'Much worse than they predicted. We were watching it on the TV before the power went out. Christchurch, bloody hell. They suffer it, don't they? Whole place is under water. Again.'

'Ricky, you should've seen it,' Janie says. 'These aren't like the normal floods. The rain started in the night and it hasn't stopped yet. Me and Dad have been watching it since six. That's when the thunder and lightning started.'

Ricky wrinkles his nose. 'You've been up since six?'

She nods and drops the cat on the floor. 'Yeah. I'm not old enough to go out late like you do, remember? So I don't sleep through the biggest thunderstorm ever. Anyway—'

Ricky interrupts. 'I wasn't out that late.'

Dad snorts. 'Mate, we all heard the 2am shower solo. And the toaster popping up about five times.'

'Anyway, Ricky,' Janie continues. 'That old cathedral, the half-fallen-down one in Christchurch? It's gone. The wind just...' She mimes picking something up and tossing it into the air. 'It's gone.

Then the floods washed it away. Oh, and the roofs! People's roofs have been blowing off. It's crazy as.'

Ricky looks around, panicked. 'Roofs blowing off? Well, should we, I don't know, get out of the house?' He stares up at the ceiling.

'No, mate, I fixed this place up when we moved in, remember? Gotta trust your old man. Safer inside. If the sea doesn't wash us away, that is.'

'What about the rabbits?' Ricky presses his nose to the glass, searching in the direction of their hutch.

'They're fine. In the garage. Your mum brought them in before she went on her morning shift.'

As Dad finishes speaking, a huge gust of wind batters into the house and every window shakes in its frame. Ricky thinks he can hear the walls creaking. Janie takes a step closer to him, and he lifts an arm and puts it around her shoulders.

'Look,' Ricky says, using his free hand to open the photo that Kyle sent him. It makes more sense now he's seen the storm. Janie takes the phone from him and makes a little *woah* sound under her breath, then hands it to Dad.

He takes his eyes off the window to look at the picture. 'Kyle sent you this?' he asks, using finger and thumb to zoom into the image. 'It's a beech. Mountain, maybe. Nice tree – shame it's come down. Not too big, would have had a load of years in her yet. Healthy roots.'

Ricky rolls his eyes at Janie. They're used to this kind of analysis. Dad is a trained tree surgeon. He is in love with trees. Once the storm blows itself out, Ricky knows he'll be round to the McGills' to have a look at the fallen beast. He'll offer his services to remove it; Mary McGill will say no – she doesn't care for domestic things since her husband walked out – and Dad will saw it up and take it away anyway, because he likes trees too much to leave it alone. Mum will try to convince him to log it and stack it up for the fire, and Dad will avoid that, saying it's too beautiful to burn.

He hands the phone back to Ricky, who leans down to Janie again. 'See the way it's crushed the picnic bench?' he says to her.

She looks at him, anxious. 'Could a tree crush our house, you reckon?'

Dad scowls. 'Could if we had any trees on this god-forsaken plot.'

Ricky gives Janie another squeeze. Dad has been trying to plant trees since they moved to the house six years before. Every time he tries, he fails. He always rages that there's sand everywhere. They're only 200 metres from the beach.

The rain lashes against the windowpanes and the wind makes the house shiver. With every gust, it feels as though it rocks on its foundations. Ricky wonders what's being said about this storm and whether Janie's stories are true. He opens the news app on his phone and scrolls through the round-up that he ignores most mornings. It shows a headline from the *Claremouth Post Online*: *Beast From The East – No Ordinary Storm*. This isn't a typical storm, he reads; it didn't come off the Tasman Sea to the west, like most of them do. This thing filtered down from the north, whipping across the North Island before scattering east across the South Island. It licked around Blenheim and then hit Christchurch in the early hours of this morning. Then it sent a tentacle across to the West Coast, throwing itself against the Southern Alps. It's the tail end of a huge tropical typhoon that has spiralled its way from the Malaysian and Indonesian peninsula. The forecasters knew it was going to bring some wet. But nothing like this.

He moves on, to an article from Christchurch. Janie is right. Floods have taken out whole buildings; two of the bridges crossing the Avon River have collapsed and Highway One, heading north towards Kaikoura, is impassable. The Waimakariri River takes no prisoners – it's swallowed half the suburbs in northern Christchurch, and the airport, too. The pictures are insane. It's like the apocalypse.

Ricky closes the app and sends a message to Kyle: *Got any electricity?*

Kyle's reply is quick – he's clearly got his phone in hand. Probably using the storm as an excuse to talk to Charlie, his ex. They might have broken up months ago, and she might be seeing someone else, but Kyle's still obsessed with her. It doesn't help that she leads him on.

No electricity, Kyle says. He sends through a selfie. He's outside, hood up, rain all over the lens, eyes squinting and a looming black sky. Ricky recognises the beach behind Kyle – he can see the path that leads up to the McGills' backyard.

You idiot, Ricky types back.

Janie leans up to have a look. 'What's he doing?' she asks, voice high-pitched.

'Being a dick.' Ricky shakes his head, smirking.

Their dad takes a glance, too, then narrows his eyes at him. 'Don't get any ideas, mate. You're staying right here.'

Kyle's house is nearly as close to the ocean as Ricky's. At high tide the beach is just pebbles. At low tide, like it will be now – unless the storm has disrupted it – there's half a kilometre or so of sand before the waves start rolling in. It's dark sand, more brown than yellow, sometimes even grey, but it's soft. Janie's too young to remember them moving out here, from an estate in town. Ricky was excited, though. Closer to Kyle, and the ocean. They got the cats after they moved, too, and the house is way bigger.

Another message comes in from Kyle: *Shit!*

Then another: *There's a boat.*

It's practically on its side. It looks like it's being washed into shore. Can you see it from there?

Ricky peers out of the window. 'Kyle says he can see a boat from the beach. Like, a wrecked boat.'

He walks quickly away from the patio windows.

'Where are you going?' Dad calls.

Ricky answers over his shoulder. 'To get the binoculars.'

'Quick, then.'

Ricky goes to his room to pull a pair of jeans on, then grabs the binoculars from the kitchen and heads back to the patio doors. He sends Kyle a photo of Dad standing next to the window with the binoculars in hand. Sleek black hair tied in a ponytail at the back of his neck, bushy eyebrows tickling the rims of the eyepieces. He adds a message: *Dad's gonna call it in, but he can't see anyone on board. Crew must have bailed. Might come out to meet you?*

Kyle replies: *Yes! Start walking. Will land somewhere near I reckon.*

'Looks like a little trawler from what I can see,' Ricky's dad says. 'It's got a rakish lean on.'

Despite Dad's earlier warning, Ricky isn't worried about convincing him to let him out to meet Kyle. Theirs is a trusting relationship – his dad treats him like an adult, as much as he can. Ricky knows that Dad knows that him and Kyle cause no trouble and suspects he's almost disappointed with that.

'You know I've gotta go watch this thing come in?' Ricky says, pointing a finger outside, towards the boat. The rain is still hitting the windows like pebbles on water, heavy and solid. He has to talk loudly to be heard.

Janie lifts a hand and tugs on his arm. 'No, Ricky,' she says.

He looks down at her. 'Hey, don't you wanna come, too?'

She shakes her head, frowning, and transfers her hand from Ricky's arm to Dad's.

Ricky looks at him. 'Someone should probably be there when it comes in. There could be crew. We might need to help. I could call you, eh?'

Dad's eyes light up a little, excited to be involved.

'Fine,' he says. 'But don't mess about or try anything heroic.'

Ricky shows him the photo that Kyle sent through of himself on the beach. 'Look, it's fine. No danger. Just some big waves that I won't go anywhere near.'

He turns from the window and sees his red hoodie on the back of the nearby armchair. 'I'll text you,' he says, heading for the door and grabbing the sweater as he goes.

'I'm serious, mate. Watch yourself,' Dad says, voice as earnest as it gets. 'You're no use to us drowned.'

Ricky winks and strides out of the room. He's at the back door, putting on a waterproof, when Dad thrusts the binoculars into his hands.

'I'll try the police, but I don't reckon I'll get through,' Dad says. 'Phone lines are dead, aren't they?'

Ricky frowns. 'Come on, they must be backed up by a mobile network. Anyway, surely you've got one of them in your contacts?' Everyone in Claremouth knows everyone in Claremouth.

Dad smiles and gives his son a quick shove on the shoulder. 'Nice. Of course. I'll text Nigel.'

Ricky looks at his sneakers and then back to Dad. 'Shoes?'

Dad thinks for a minute then shakes his head. 'No shoes. Off you go.'

Ricky walks along the beach, head down. His jacket isn't very waterproof; he can already feel the wet creeping in. He's wondering whether the police will send anyone. Not in this weather. Not to this fight.

The boat is off to his right. It's too far away, and the sky is too black, to get a decent picture. He pulls his hood tighter around his face and slips his phone back in his pocket. The binoculars hang heavy round his neck. The rain comes at him sideways. His feet are submerged, and his jeans are soaked through and heavy. The beach has become a long pool that ripples in the wind. Gusts thump into him, making him stagger, and he wonders whether he should go back. Janie said the lightning stopped hours ago, though.

The boat looks small, with some raised pieces like masts. Are there people on board? He gets his phone out again and does a quick internet search for 'fishing trawler', trying to figure out what he's looking at. He guesses at a crew of four people, max. But where are they?

With every step he gets a little closer to the boat and the boat gets a little closer to him – it's rocking so wildly, anyone on it must have been thrown out long ago, or battered to pieces in the cabin. Not a nice thought. Maybe they abandoned the vessel much further out at sea, before the storm hit. They would have seen the clouds looming, and signalled a larger boat to come and pick them up.

He strains his eyes up the beach, looking for Kyle, but sees nothing. Just slanting grey. He looks back to his feet – it's not an easy walk; the sand is so soft. It squelches, trying to suck him in. The churning surf laps the bottoms of his jeans with every wave. He stops to turn them up, hitching the wet denim nearly to his knees. Barefoot was the right decision.

He should reach Kyle about the time the boat makes it to shore. They'll watch it come in together and see how it beaches itself. Maybe look for signs of life, if it holds fast.

Where are you man? he messages Kyle. *Can't see you.*

The wind intensifies, making him stagger. It's not like a gale that you try to float against as a kid, jacket sides held out like wings. He's never felt wind like this before. It pulls, then it pushes. It's two hands and a sharp shove.

Ricky lets out a yell. He can see a figure through the sheets of rain. Kyle walks with hands in pockets, head down. A lone traveller against the rain, the wind, the battering ocean. The boat is still to Ricky's right, close now; through the binoculars he can read the name on the side of the hull: *Ikatere*. A Māori god or legend, but he can't remember the story. There are letters and numbers, too – WLGT2035 precedes the name. It splashes in and out of the waves, red writing on white. How far up the beach will the boat come?

'What took you so long?' Kyle shouts.

Ricky shrugs. 'I'm fat,' he cries back.

He sees his friend's shoulders rise and fall a little – a laugh. 'This is crazy,' Ricky yells.

They come together across a few metres of turgid sand and stare at each other. Kyle has a distracted look, anxious.

'Talking to Charlie, huh?' Ricky asks.

Kyle shrugs. 'She asked me to go over there. Her dad's stuck in Christchurch.'

'Woah.' Ricky takes a step back, puts a hand on Kyle's shoulder, pretends to stagger with shock. It doesn't really work; the wind makes him stagger anyway. 'She booty-called you. And you're still here?'

Kyle looks embarrassed, narrows his eyes and fixes them on the boat that's now less than 100 metres from them. 'Well. Shipwreck. Don't see that every day, eh.'

Ricky grins. 'Nice one, mate. Long time since you've chosen me over her. Always knew you loved me more.'

Kyle shoves him, shaking his head, smiling. He gestures backwards, away from the sea, suggesting they move in the opposite direction from the boat that's about to hit.

'Do you think they're on there?' Ricky asks, taking a few steps back.

Kyle shakes his head. 'I've been watching it for a while. Surely someone would have come out, tried to signal, sent a flare or something? By now?'

Ricky nods, convinced.

'Hey, look.' He points to the horizon. In the distance the first storm clouds have started to break. The grey sky is morphing, slowly, into a moody blue and somewhere, at the back of all that, is a hint of sunlight.

'Storm's easing,' Kyle says. 'About time.'

The boat's close enough now for them to see that the winch on its deck holds a taut silver cable which disappears into the waves. Ricky wrinkles his nose. 'Net's still in?'

Before Kyle can reply, they hear the first scrape of the hull against land – the boat shifts, pitching further onto its side, and both boys instinctively take another step backwards.

'Did it hit a rock?' Ricky shouts.

The boat doesn't stop – the waves toss it onwards, pushing it against the sand. With each thrust, it creaks, groaning under the weight of the water.

Kyle tugs his hood down and Ricky does the same. The rain has slowed.

They watch the boat pitch against the wash. It grinds its way into the sand, tilting at a crazy angle. Each wave beaches it further, pushing it onwards until it sits in the surf, a great gouge in the sand beneath it. Waves smash into it from behind, rocking it wildly back and forth until, finally, it is steadfast, held tight by the wet grip of the sand. It lies abandoned. Wounded. They see no signs of life aboard.

'What the…?' Ricky takes a few steps forwards, eyes narrowed at the nearside of the boat. Kyle follows, warily. The thing looks like it could move at any moment.

There is a wriggling mass in the surf – it flickers and writhes, pressing against the slanted hull.

'Wow. Net's definitely still in,' Kyle says.

The fish are there, held tight among the fibres. How far have they been dragged? They're like a swarm. Half-land, half-sea. They squirm about. Their silver edges flicker in the grey. Their mouths, open wide, are stuck in the net, heads pushed through the holes, bodies wriggling for freedom.

'Cool,' says Kyle, taking the binoculars from his friend to get a closer look.

Ricky nods. 'So cool.'

'How many fish, you reckon?'

Ricky shakes his head. 'Maybe a thousand?'

Kyle raises his eyebrows. 'Maybe five thousand. You know. Like Jesus?' He lifts his arms to the sky.

Ricky frowns. 'No, mate. Jesus had two fish. And five thousand people. Right?'

'Oh yeah. And some bread? There was bread involved.'

Ricky looks at the wet sand all around them. 'Can't see any bread.'

As they watch, a wave forms out to sea, even bigger than the ones that came before it. It is pushed on by the rage of the dying storm, gathering strength as it roars ashore. It scrapes stones off the seabed. It sounds like a six-lane highway. It charges to land.

It hits the body of the boat with a noise of thunder, and the white-and-red hull lurches and shifts in protest. Kyle and Ricky take several steps backwards as the wave boards the boat. The writing at the helm is pushed beneath the waves, nose in the sand. The small crane on the deck, winched to the net, groans with the weight of its heavy catch. The wave spreads the fish, net wide, further up the beach. They writhe like snakes in a bag, thrashing in the breaker.

As the huge wave recedes, the boat shudders upwards, pulls its head from the sand and shakes its heavy skirt of fish. Ricky sees the net begin to split. It seems to shiver, breaking apart and opening its meshed web. The bodies slither out, silver. They flip, flop, and rest. They scatter across the shallow pools that cover the beach. They dart off, into the whitecaps. Fish everywhere.

'Oh my God,' Kyle says. 'They stink.'

'Hey,' Ricky replies, nudging him. 'Oh my *cod*.'

Chapter Five

Cathy

We follow the Pennine Way, Ephie's parents leading. The steep hills are nothing to them – they walk them every day. I breathe heavily and feel my cheeks turn crimson. Sheep lie in the shade of drystone walls, not yet sheared, their lambs fat and boisterous. Horseflies come for me when I stop to catch my breath. Einstein, June and Nicolas's ancient Westie, tumbles through the cotton grass to the left of the path. Nicolas talks about the *spanakorizo* he's planning to make for tea, and Ephie jokes that the longer he goes on, the more Greek he becomes. June groans and says they've eaten nothing but spinach all summer.

'I have to hold on to my heritage,' Nicolas says. 'I am the only Greek around here, after all.'

'There's a family from Thessaloniki in the next village – don't listen to him,' June says.

'These villages are so far apart, though, it hardly counts,' he replies.

'Do you feel isolated? Are you getting on with your neighbours?' Ephie asks. It has only been eighteen months since they moved from Sheffield. In that time Nicolas has tanned to a deep brown, his skin weathered from hours of walking and gardening. June is still pale, but now her cheeks are red and her curly hair a little wilder.

'We're getting on fine – they're all very nice people,' June says. 'One of the ladies over the road even tried to convince me to join them at the WI, but then I remembered the trouble you two had with that woman where you are, and I thought I'd give it a miss.'

'I don't think you should judge the entire Women's Institute by her,' I say. 'Some of them must be nice.'

'Nah, they're probably all bitches,' Ephie says.

Her mum gives her a worried look, not catching the sarcasm, and I decide I'd better explain a bit more.

The woman in question, who we found out later to be a quiet member of the Barvusi WI, was behind us at the Co-op checkout one day when her granddaughter, who must have seen us holding hands, said something like, 'Granny, are they married?'

'No,' the woman said quickly. 'Not properly.'

I'd barely had time to blink before Ephie turned around.

'Same-sex marriage has been legal in the UK since 2014. And your granddaughter, thank God, is growing up in a generation that sees it as nothing other than completely normal,' she said.

The woman took a little step backwards. Her granddaughter took her hand. 'God certainly doesn't have anything to do with it,' the woman said.

I could feel Ephie coiled like a spring then, ready to release. She would obliterate the grey-haired woman in front of her, and the enmity would stretch on for evermore. It could creep into places we didn't want it to, like the pub or the milk round. I stepped forward to intervene.

'We don't want to cause an argument,' I said, trying to sound placatory. 'But we are married, and we love each other, and we're very happy. If you don't feel that's OK, please could you keep it to yourself?'

The woman sort of clicked her tongue and tugged her granddaughter's hand, and they went to another till. The little girl watched us through round eyes, so I smiled at her, and she smiled back.

'We were in the pub the night that we'd had the run-in with her, and we spoke to a few people about it,' I tell June, watching the path as I walk.

'And they were fucking outraged,' Ephie interjects.

'Watch your language, Ephyra,' June says.

I try not to laugh. 'There were a few of us in there: Bill the barman, one of the younger couples, David Evans – our crazy fisherman – and a teenager or two. We all ended up having this big discussion, and they were all saying that they were really proud of their resident lesbians.'

Ephie shrugs. 'Which still makes us feel like a bit of a spectacle, but at least they're supportive.'

I carry on. 'I think someone – I don't know who, perhaps Bill – had a word with her after that, because the next time I bumped into her in the Co-op, she made a point of saying good morning and smiling.'

'No apology, like?' June asks.

Ephie jumps in. 'Come on, Mum, no southerner would be that plain about something. She probably thinks she apologised with the smile.'

'I'm just glad it didn't blow up into anything else,' I say. 'She may not feel any differently about us, but at least she's keeping it to herself now.'

Just ahead, with Einstein beside him, Nicolas pauses and looks at us. '*Agapi mou*, I'm so pleased to hear this,' he says solemnly. 'Because I was planning to come down and have a stern word with her.'

Ephie grins, catches her father up and puts her arm around him.

June gives me a nudge. 'If he's got a stern word in him, I'm the Queen of England.'

'I won't have people treat my daughters that way,' I hear Nicolas say, as him and Ephie walk on, and I want to cry a little bit because he loves me.

In the garden that evening we have a barbeque – salmon steaks and halloumi, roasted peppers dripping in oil, *spanakorizo*. I grab a thick cotton throw from the back of the car and spread it across the grass. It's Malaysian batik, all swirling flowers and reds on blacks – the remains of a roll bought years ago from a haberdashery in Camden – and Ephie stretches her legs out, a plate of food beside her. The flowers of the fabric crinkle beneath her. She is a cheetah, long-limbed and exotic. She runs her feline eyes over me first thing every morning to make sure I'm still there. She has claws, too.

I've been thinking for five minutes or so of stealing the half scone that rests on her plate, thick with cream. Einstein is next to me on the rug, and I know he's been thinking the same. When she brought the scones out, June said they were to make us feel at home – a bit of West Country in the Derbyshire hills – but Ephie says that's just her mum's excuse for buying clotted cream.

'Just you fucking try it,' she jokes as I reach for the scone.

No one can curtail her swearing – she enjoys it too much. Ephie spent her formative years at a comprehensive school in Sheffield, taking shit from nobody.

I pause, hand hovering over the plate, and look at my wife. I see the way her eyes are narrowed, ready for a fight, and try not to laugh.

'I'll divorce you,' she says.

I pull my hand away, pretending to be shocked. 'Over a scone?'

'Stranger things have happened,' Ephie says, raising her eyebrows. She picks up the scone. 'Could you pass me the cream, please? I think I need a bit more.'

I don't know how she does it but, God, she even looks beautiful when she's smug.

'Greedy,' I say.

'It's mine.' She reaches for the knife.

I leave her to the scone, lying back, and Einstein does, too. The evening sun filters through a silver birch at the end of the garden and bees buzz over foxgloves that poke up through the pebbles at the edges of the lawn. I have a warmth in me that is total content-ment. The village air smells of grass cuttings.

'It's going to rain,' Ephie says, mouth half-full, eyes on the sky. Far out over the hills to the south, clouds are forming into thick blooms of grey.

'Wasn't forecast,' I frown.

She picks up the nearby bottle of Assyrtiko – her dad always buys Greek wine. 'It might come to nothing. Do you want more, my love?' She pours me another glass without waiting for a reply, then tops up her own.

We stay outside until the air is cool and the sun is low on the western horizon, just a slice of orange against the gathering night. Her parents take their leave of us, peeling out of wooden patio furniture and wishing us goodnight. Ephie curls up next to me, the bones of her spine showing through her jumper, and rests her head on my lap.

When the two of us first started seeing each other, I said her name as often as I could. Ephyra Calathes. It sounded so exotic to me. Like a sunset against pillars of stone. Nicolas, a soft-spoken intellectual with a good head for numbers, moved from Greece aged seventeen, eventually got a job as a maths teacher in a school, and fell in love with a paediatric nurse from Huddersfield. They raised their daughter in Sheffield, then moved out to the Peak District when retirement came. Ephie thinks they live a life of perfection: of nature, home-grown vegetables, rolling hillsides, a long marriage still blessed with love. But I know better. One thing is missing for them; they look at her with longing. Their only daughter, and she chose to live at the opposite end of the country. She chose me. When they moved out of Sheffield, we tried to convince them to consider Cornwall, but it was never going to happen. June Calathes has too much north in her for the south.

Ephie and I met in Bristol, both students. She'd done two years of a medical degree, before deciding she hated it. When I met her, she'd transferred to the second year of molecular biology, a course I couldn't comprehend. I was studying textiles at art college. She was an anxious student who feigned confidence and was sometimes obnoxious. She chewed her nails to the quick and wore thick eyeliner. Her hair, the colour of black coffee, was always bleached at the tips, always messy and frayed, so that she looked like she should audition for a punk band. I was so intimidated by her. Bristol fitted her like a glove, and I felt like a Cornish milkmaid, provincial and always losing my way round the city. Sometimes, even now, I catch myself in the mirror and wonder why she chose me.

We dated for the rest of her university course and I got a job at the student's union. Her friends got to know me. My friends weren't convinced by her. We called it quits when I went home, back to Cornwall, to look after Mum. A bit more than a year later, when she'd recovered from the chemo and the cancer and the endless hospital trips, I went back out into the world to find Ephie and she was waiting. It was remarkable. She told me she'd had a couple of girls in her bed, and even a boy – I remember her describing him as low-hanging fruit – but had spent the year dreaming of me. I told her I'd walked along the beach every day and cried, because I was so worried Mum would die.

Mum had practically kicked me out the moment she was well enough, to carry on with my life. 'You're so mopey without that Greek girl,' she said. Ephie and I moved in together. She chopped the blonde out of her hair, so that all that was left was coffee, and it was the best drink I ever had.

We moved to Cornwall for many reasons, but it helped that it was cheap. During the year that Mum was ill, I'd seen the Grim Reaper hovering over her, and I couldn't be far away if he ever swooped again. Add to that the fact that I yearned for the sea, and that Ephie had never lived near the coast and wanted to try it. Plymouth University had opened a campus near Falmouth, specialising in environmental marine research – enough lab space for Ephie to pipette to her heart's content. As soon as she got a job, we packed the car. It was the same year we got married.

For a while I had work in a gallery in St Ives, which was enough to get the mortgage. When they made me redundant two years after we moved, Ephie convinced me to make something more of the sewing I'd been subsidising my income with. Brides and brides-maids always needed dresses altering, and that had kept me busy at the weekends. Suddenly unemployed, with a severance package that would last two weeks, I built a website with Ephie's help and set up Clever Cockatoo, mostly selling baby clothes, hand-stitched in my studio. I learnt to buy fabric online, knowing from the tech-nical description just what it would feel like. African wax prints make the best baby rompers: easy to stitch, and they sell like hot cakes. I also upgraded the wedding-dress alterations for full-dress commissions and found a shop in Plymouth that could service my sewing machine. We've been in Cornwall seven years now and Ephie runs her own small lab group. She is a doctor, and even though it's not the medical type she set out to be when she was eighteen, I hope she's proud of herself all the same.

When the sun is finally gone from the garden, we gather our-selves up and fold away the batik. I stretch my arm around Ephie's waist, and she wraps hers across my shoulders. We walk from the garden like two pieces of a puzzle, nestled against one another, and climb into bed that way not long after. Sometimes it almost makes me sick how beautiful we are together.

On Sunday afternoon we head home. The car is loaded with goods from June and Nicolas, who wouldn't let us leave without two cakes, a basket of soily new potatoes, two punnets of green-house tomatoes and three bottles of wine, which they always have in stock in shockingly vast quantities. After three hours on the motorway, Bristol is nearly in our sights.

The sky is dark above us and heavy with intent. Ephie sings at the top of her lungs to a Bristol punk band like the one she used to look like she should join. Now that I know she can't sing at all, the idea of her in a band is a joke. I gaze out at the gathering storm.

A mile or so later, with the line of the Cotswolds obscured by oncoming cloud, heavy raindrops begin to fall. They hit the windscreen like grain scattered on dry earth. They get heavier. They bounce. They reach a crescendo of silver, and I look over and see Ephie frowning. The rain intensifies and she reaches to click up the volume on the radio, determined not to let it interrupt her solo. It feels like we are in a tin can, in an endless ricochet of white noise.

'This is insane,' I shout, peering out of the windscreen. 'It's so heavy!'

She glances sideways at me and grins. She raises a fist to the roof of the car.

'Oh, come on! Is this all you've got?' she shouts at the sky. In front, brake lights show through the incessant back and forth of our windscreen wipers. I raise a hand to my mouth, searching for a nail to chew, and then shudder a little as the rain strengthens to something biblical.

Ephie's eyes widen. 'You're kidding me.' I barely catch what she says over the din of the storm.

'Slow down,' I bark.

She puts her foot on the brake. The world beyond the windscreen slips out of focus, drowned out and lost. Red brake lights show up as round, diffuse blobs, wavering in the grey light. The windscreen starts to steam up and we slow to a crawl, wipers thrashing. The rain keeps coming. I tell myself it's just a storm, no big deal, and check Ephie's expression. She is gripping the steering wheel tight, leaning forwards in her seat.

'Bit scary,' she says, squinting. 'Find something to wipe the windscreen with, will you?'

I twist in my seat, looking round, unsure how to help. 'What do you want?'

'I don't know, anything. I can't see a thing.' She reaches forwards to press the flat of her palm against the top of the windscreen, and moves it back and forth, clearing a little space in the steam. I turn the car fans up, adding to the barrage of noise.

The back end of the car in front of us comes up quickly. I squeal. Ephie presses the brake hard and we stop, too.

She turns her eyes on me, irritated. 'Not helping, Cathy.' Her voice is sharp.

'Sorry.'

'Well, did you find something to wipe the windscreen with?' She shouts to make herself heard over the rain and the fan. The music has been almost completely drowned out, but she swats the off switch anyway. The air in the car is cold now. It smells like wet earth and it's full of tension.

'There isn't anything, Ephie. I've looked. Everything's in the boot. What do you want me to do?' I snap.

She lets out an angry sigh and mutters something about *doing everything herself*. The car starts to beep a warning as she unclips her seat belt. She reaches to the bottom of her T-shirt and pulls it upwards over her head. It's grey, with an outline of a bear on the front, and she whips it off, and then pushes her seat belt back into place. She reaches forwards to mop the windscreen while I sit, feeling useless. I try not to stare at the lace of her bra. I'm surprised she's even wearing one – she hardly ever bothers.

I have an idea and pull my right trainer off, then tug off my sock and use it to clear my side of the screen.

'Here,' I say, thrusting the damp sock towards her. 'Put your T-shirt back on.'

She takes the sock and almost smiles, but it's all lips and no eyes. 'Thanks, love.'

Her attention goes back to the windscreen. The rain hasn't let off, not for a moment since we stopped moving, but its direction has changed. The wind's picked up and now the deluge comes down at a relentless slant. I lean forwards to look outside. All around us, puddles are forming on the tarmac. They stretch out like hot springs, bubbling with the onslaught of landing rain. To our right a stream gushes alongside the central reservation, like nothing I've ever seen before. Ephie clicks the headlights on. It's 3pm, mid-July. It's practically dark. I seriously start to wonder whether we'll make it home. Maybe we'll have to spend the night on the motorway.

Ephie keeps her hands on the wheel, though we no longer move. Her T-shirt is still off and the thin brown hairs on the backs of her arms stand upright, pulling her soft skin into rows of goosebumps.

'It'll pass,' she says.

The car shudders, buffeted by the wind, and outside the rain changes path again. It is like a flock of starlings, murmuring with the rhythm of the wind. It falls straight, pitches right, then makes a sharp turn towards the car in front. A huge fork of lightning flashes across the sky off to our right and I gasp. The thunder that rolls in afterwards is loud and menacing.

'Bad idea,' Ephie mumbles, frowning and leaning towards her driver-side window.

'What?' I follow her eyes, see a head appear over the top of a car in front.

'Some guy's getting out,' she says. 'Why would you do that?'

Our car rocks again and I press my palms flat against the dashboard. Another bolt of lightning shows, thunder booming after it. The rain continues, rapid-fire, and over the noise of it I hear the wind. It doesn't howl. People always say the wind howls. This is more like an amplified vacuum cleaner, a noise that could suck us into the sky.

'What's happening?' I say, keeping my voice loud over the storm.

Ephie doesn't say anything; she's got a crease between her brows and she uses my sock to clear the windscreen again, to get a better look at whatever is going on.

I can see a man's head moving around above the top of the car in front.

'What's he doing?' I ask. 'Are we moving?'

'Will you stop?' she snaps, throwing me a frustrated glance.

'I just don't understand what's going on.'

She takes a deep breath in and points at the car in front of us. 'I think the car one ahead of this one has broken down. The driver got out and started trying to get the bonnet up. That seems pretty stupid, even to me. Anyway, then he came to the window of the car in front.' She shrugs. 'I assume they told him to bugger off. As if anyone's going to get out and help in this weather.'

She pauses, watching the scene.

'We'll have to go around him,' she says, crunching the gearbox into first.

'Ephie,' I say. 'I'm kinda scared. Should we really drive in this? What if we break down, too? Is this the tail end of that typhoon that we saw on the news or something?'

'I don't know any more than you do.'

Frustration rolls off her – I can feel it in the air between us. I try for a joke, smiling my way into it. 'Come on, you always know more than me.'

'For fuck's sake, Cathy. No, I don't always know more than you. You're just useless at thinking for yourself. I'm not your mother.'

The car in front starts to move, pulling out around the broken-down vehicle. Ephie puts on her indicator and turns her body, looking out of the window behind me to search for space to pull into. We inch forwards through the puddles.

'I can't see a thing,' she says. 'Will you open your window? Look behind?'

I don't want to show any more signs of uselessness – I want to help. After all, it's not me trying to drive through a monsoon. I flick the window down as quickly as possible and the noise of the storm instantly grows. It comes in at us like a hurricane, cold and fierce.

'Is it clear?' she shouts.

I stick my head into the storm and look back at the endless queue of cars, rain hammering into my eyes. 'Um... no. You'll have to edge out.'

Together we find a space in the traffic and Ephie nudges the car out. We crawl along in the middle lane, barely breaking 10 mph. The orange hazard lights of the broken-down car glare at us as we pass, scattered into prisms by the rain on every surface.

'Poor bastards,' Ephie says with a shrug. 'What a time and place to get stuck.'

I twist in my seat to look. 'I think it's a group of men. Not a family or anything. They'll be fine.'

'Oh, is it?' she asks, eyes still narrowed with concentration. 'Ha, maybe it's a stag do.'

I glance out of the window and wrap my hands around the top of my seat belt, trying not to talk, to give Ephie space to get us out of the storm. I know it's stressful, to drive in difficult conditions, but my brain keeps going back to her comment. *I'm not your mother.* Is that how she sees me, as a dependent? She is the quick thinker, the adventurous solutions-finder of our relationship. I make a few dresses and cook most of the meals. But it's not fair of her to call me useless. I'm not useless.

'What's the matter?' she says through the silence.

For a second I consider bluffing serenity, but I'm not really in the mood to fake it.

'Are we kind of... patriarchal?' I ask after a long pause.

She's not expecting a question of that depth and her head whips round to look at me. 'We?'

'Me and you,' I reply, looking away. 'Us.'

'Patriarchal?' She's incredulous. She starts to laugh. 'Cathy, we're lesbians.'

'I just... Well, you just said it, didn't you? I'm useless. You feel like you have to mother me.'

She purses her lips, thinking. It only ever takes Ephie seconds to figure me out – or to think she has.

'So, I'm the man? That's what you're saying, isn't it? If we were a straight couple, I'd be the man – I guess I am the tomboy – and you'd be the woman. And because I earn more than you, and probably do more driving, it's a patriarchy?'

I sigh. She's rounded it down to less than the sum of its parts – simplified it so elegantly that it's hard to refute. 'I'm not just talking about money and driving.'

'No, you're talking about dependence, I think,' she replies after a moment. She reaches to turn the windscreen fan down a notch – now we're moving, the steam is starting to clear.

I sigh again. 'It's hard to have this conversation with you.'

'Maybe at this moment in time it is, Cathy,' she says, rounding on me. 'I've been quite busy here. This journey isn't a breeze. Now you're trying to get me into some marriage counselling session. Isn't there a time and a place?'

I hate her. 'I'm not trying to counsel you. You're being ridiculous. I'm trying to point out that you said I was useless, and that upsets me. I know you're driving – well done, you. But only one of us can drive at a time. It's not like I can do the pedals while you turn the wheel. So what do you expect me to be in this scenario, other than useless?'

'Cathy, what are we even arguing about?' she shouts.

I shake my head, frustrated and angry. 'I don't know.'

There's a pause. When she speaks again, her voice is a little softer. 'Maybe there are things that are uneven about this relationship, but isn't that the point? We complement each other. It does frustrate me sometimes that you're not more decisive. I feel like I have to take charge of every stressful situation—'

'It's not like you give me any chance to,' I interrupt.

'Fine,' she says. 'You're right: it's all my fault.'

I look at her, and her lips are pursed, brows low.

'Hey, maybe the rain is easing off a little?' I try.

'Maybe.' She pauses. 'Cathy, please don't call me a patriarch. I don't hold the power here. I'm not controlling you or making decisions for you. Am I? I hate the idea that you think that.'

'Look, it came out wrong. That's not really what I meant. It was about dependence – you said that. I just feel sometimes that if something happened and we weren't together, you'd handle it better than me.'

Now she smiles. 'I'd be existing off nothing but fish and chips, and frozen pizzas. But, yeah, I'd be totally fine. Not upset at all.'

Reaching over the gearstick, she puts her hand on my thigh and gives it a squeeze. She drops the snarky tone. 'Please don't let there be a situation where we aren't together. I'd be a fucking mess.'

I weave my fingers through hers. 'OK.'

So she does need me around.

I am so relieved when we finally push our way through the back door. We have been in the car for eight hours, and the words *useless* and *patriarchy* have hung in the air between us for the last five of them. I thought we'd never get home. The storm tailed us the whole way, throwing bucketfuls of rain until it seemed normal to drive through puddles the length of two cars. We stopped again at the end of the motorway, to get some food and buoy ourselves up for the last, long part of the journey through Devon and Cornwall. Every corner we took, it was like the apocalypse had been through just before us – mud strewn across the roads, trees down, floods.

At a corner somewhere near Bodmin, two deer lay dead in the centre of the road.

But we are back, and I let out a long sigh of relief as I fill the kettle.

'No electricity,' Ephie says, coming into the kitchen.

I look down and see that the digital clock on the front of the oven is blank. All I want is tea. I slam the kettle down.

'I'll get the camping stove,' I mutter. I know where it is, in the cupboard under the stairs, with a gas canister nearby.

'Oh my God,' Ephie says.

I pause at the tone of her voice and look back. The sky outside is still dark and moody, and she is silhouetted against the kitchen window.

'What?' I ask, suddenly worried.

'Come and look.' She stretches a hand back in my direction, fingers imploring me to join her.

When I make it to her side and look out, I see a stormy sea and an orange beach. I squint, wondering how the sand has changed colour.

'Starfish,' she says dreamily.

I squint and see that she is right. Our beach is covered in orange starfish.

'The storm must have washed them up,' she says.

I don't reply, just keep staring, picking out star shapes among the piles of orange. It looks like all the starfish in the world must be there. They are layered thick. Not an inch of light-yellow sand.

'Weird,' Ephie says. 'Shall we go down?'

I look at her – see excitement in her eyes. I don't want to go down there, to this alien beach at the end of this horrible, long day.

'I'm tired,' I say. 'Go ahead without me.'

She gives me an imploring look and I smile, to reassure her. 'I'll make us some tea and relax a bit. You go explore.'

With that, she's gone. I retrieve the camping stove and set a pan of water to boil. *Not useless*, I tell myself. *Quite capable.*

Chapter Six

Margaret

Margaret finds the car too high for an easy step down, so she half-jumps, half-slides from the driver's seat, purse on shoulder. The church stands across the road from her, with a flat roof and a big red cross on the front that almost makes it look like a drugstore. The walls are painted creamy yellow. In the back of her car are six coconuts, stacked into a crate in the footwell, each one sporting a round hole in the top – she drilled them herself – with straws sticking out. She leaves them where they are, nestled close to one another.

Crossing the road to the church, she is buffeted by a strong wind that pushes her forwards. She lifts a hand to pull a tress of hair from her mouth, but it whips back against her cheek the minute she lets go of it. There must be a storm coming.

It's still light out – it's only 6pm – but she knows that in an hour, once prayer has finished, there will be a hot darkness. She misses the extra hour of summer daylight she'd have in Northern California at this time of year – it's been a very long time since she ate dinner without night pressing in at the door. And the drop of the sun is so complete in the tropics. No twilight.

She reaches the church entrance all fluffed up, like she's been through the tumble dryer. She flicks the hair out of her face again and pulls on the metal handle. It's a simple church – no spire, no shine – but it doesn't matter. God doesn't need to aesthetically please; He can show Himself anywhere. It fits in OK among the brothels, too, sitting unloved on the other side of the street. Besides, her Sunday church is better than this one – it's plain old beautiful.

In the meeting room at the end of a beige corridor, her friend Jane calls out, 'Marge, come and meet these girls from the Kingdom Trail. They're on month four and they're a little homesick. They're from Arizona.'

Jane is a skinny German redhead in her early forties, with skin the colour of white rice. She puts her arms behind two girls and gives them a gentle push towards Margaret, then drifts off to talk to a different group. The young women look about eighteen and their eyes dart around the room. Margaret smiles. They look like they're not sure how they've ended up in this unremarkable church on a sticky KL backstreet.

'How are you?' Margaret asks.

One of them mumbles something and the other talks over her. She tells Margaret they've just come from Thailand, and that this is their fourth country on the Mission; they were in Guatemala and Nicaragua before that. 'It's very different here, in Asia,' the girl says. 'The showers get hot, but the food is worse. Too much sodium—' Margaret feels herself frowning. Malaysian food is the best in the world.

'Well, it's great to have you two,' she interrupts. 'Why don't you take a seat? We do a prayer session before we go out.' She gestures towards two empty chairs on the other side of the room and the girls walk away. Margaret likes them, these young missionaries. They remind her of herself at eighteen – full of faith and ready to see the world. But too much sodium? She just can't understand closed-mindedness.

She heads towards three women who stand at the front of the room. 'Hey, gals,' she says, putting her arms around two of them and slotting herself into their little group. 'How are we?'

They greet her with squeezes and smiles. One of the three is Jane, the German redhead. She winks at Margaret and then quickly looks at her watch.

'We should get started,' she says, turning to the room. 'Hi everyone. Thanks so much for coming. These meetings are really important.' She smiles at the American girls. 'We usually start things off with some prayers. Everyone, please take a seat. Lyrics are on the screen. And let's quickly go round the room and introduce ourselves, as we've got some new faces with us tonight.'

Margaret whispers final greetings to her friends and then takes a seat near the front of the horseshoe of chairs. Jane checks the laptop that's plugged into a projector at the front of the room. Once all is quiet, she starts the introductions. 'I'm Jane,' she says, 'I started this outreach Mission twenty years ago, when I first moved to KL. Our aim is to connect with working women in the red-light district. A lot of the brothels are just over the road, and that's where we'll be going once we've said our prayers. This work has been a big challenge, but we're given strength by God, and we have achieved amazing things. Some of the connections we've made stretch back years now. That's because of the hard work and support of all of you.' She turns her eyes briefly to the ceiling. 'So, thank you, Jesus, for sending me this wonderful group of women.'

The introductions go round the room. They are mostly white expats from a range of countries, with a couple of locals thrown in. Margaret is the last to speak. 'I live out in the burbs,' she says, 'and have done for nearly fifteen years now. Before that, Tahoe, California.' She smiles towards the centre of the table. 'And thanks to Jane, our organiser. She sure works hard on this.' The group breaks into scattered applause.

Jane takes a seat and Allison, a quiet Canadian, starts to strum the tune that fits with the lyrics on the projector screen. Margaret knows it always takes a bit of coaxing to get everyone into song, so she sings as loudly as she can to start with. Jane, Allison and Chitra do the same – they're the four oldest members. The most practised. The rest of the table quickly throw their voices into the mix until the room is full of song.

Margaret loves this part of church. She loves to sing. She knows the songs so well, she doesn't even think; she just lets her mind drift off to the top of the room and then out, into the gathering darkness and the world beyond. It gives her a sense of physicality and strength in her body that she doesn't get from anything else. Her muscles relax. The cells inside her line up somehow. When everyone joins in beautiful harmony, a shiver goes up her back. God is listening. Their voices in unison bring an energy to the room that skims across her skin and makes the hairs on her arms stand on end.

When the third song is complete, Allison keeps the rhythm going with her guitar, strumming a little louder to fill the room, and Jane starts the prayers. It's all impromptu – all feeling and no scripture, just honesty bouncing from wall to wall.

'Jesus, we thank You. We thank You for supporting us, for loving us, and for showing us the way. We ask You to guide us this evening as we go out into the world. We ask You to support us as we make connections. We ask You to give us strength, and we thank You, Jesus, for being here with us. Enter into us, Jesus. Show us the way.'

Margaret's first meeting with the Mission was nearly ten years before, and when she turned up, everything about it was new. She'd spent her life in church, but her parents weren't born-again. She'd only ever been to more traditional church sermons – never been to a prayer session where people rocked back and forth in time to the rhythm of a guitar and a chant. She found it difficult, the first few times. She was self-conscious. She didn't know what to say when the chant came round to her – didn't know how to let her mind leap right over the cosmos and into the arms of God.

She'd always called her upbringing progressive. Her parents were good Christians, but not conservative: they didn't want her abstaining and marrying the wrong man at eighteen because of an old-fashioned interpretation of the Bible. They were insistent on her going to college, to get an education and meet people from outside of their small town. When she was eighteen, Margaret went off to San Diego with one large suitcase and a potted succulent, and she spent three years in a library filled with sunlight, majoring in English Literature. She went to church twice a week – Sundays for worship, Tuesdays for fundraisers – and that was when the first Mission caught her eye; it called to her from among the feathery fronds of the jungles of Madagascar. She wasn't brave enough to sign up, but the idea of it led her to the 'Travel and Nature' section of the library stacks. There, she crossed continents in the sticky carriages of railway cars and boarded banana boats to mosquito-swamped shores. At night, she dreamed. It was her marriage some years later to Roger, a successful financial consultant at a large international firm, that started her journey to KL. She never looked back. She loved the heat of the city, and the women at this prayer table. It wasn't just that they came together in a common cause; there was more to it than that. Some of them were outsiders, too: expats thrown into the tropical heat, mostly following husbands, and left there to carve out a new life. They were sisters.

Nearly ten years on, she slips into the meetings without a second thought. As the prayer bubbles around the table, each woman finds a rhythm of her own, words of her own, silence of her own, and the energy in the room intensifies. It darts towards something feverish – something full of action. Jane's voice is resolute among the three guitar chords, her eyes trance-like, slipping around the room without seeing. The tingle at the back of Margaret's neck extends all the way down the length of her spine. She's forgotten completely that she's in a hot antechamber in a little backstreet church. She is part of something. When it comes to her, she picks up the prayer and feels its rhythm. She slots her voice into the beat. She lives for this connection: with God, with her friends, with a purpose.

The prayers end as quickly as they begin. No winding down – Jane wants to keep momentum. Margaret never sees the signal, but something makes Allison stop strumming and the room jolts quickly into quiet. The women sit there like pigeons, their ruffled feathers sinking back to flat. But they're jittery – they could break into flight at any moment.

Jane explains that they will split into groups – a four and two threes – to visit the brothels. Margaret will be in the group of four, with Chitra and the two young Americans. Allison and Winsie will head the second group, and Jane the third.

'Coconuts!' Margaret says once everyone's on their feet. 'I'm parched from the singing. Come on, girls, nutrients and energy.'

They fan out around the back passenger door of Margaret's car. The wind is still raging, slapping them with hot palms, and now the air has taken on a sweet zing. Above the stink of city life there's a saccharine taste to the street. Margaret hands the coconuts out, shouting above the gale. It's a funny tradition, evolved from suggestions from past members that their meetings involve refreshment. For a long while Chitra tried bringing durians to each meeting. Margaret hates the stuff ('Like cheese and onion,' she tells Roger) and the other expats mostly agreed. Chitra took it well and the durians didn't last. They settled on coconuts.

Margaret stacks the empty husks back in the car and Jane takes a bunch of flyers from her purse, dividing them up between the three groups. 'You'll need these,' she says. Then there's the tiniest bit of loitering. The movement from church to the illegality of the brothels never loses its edge of stress. The doormen might not let them in. The women inside might not speak to them. The customers could get aggressive. And the conversations – they could often be painful. Outside the church, the little group kick their heels a bit, discuss tactics briefly. Jane rounds the performance off with a final statement: 'Ladies. Let's remember, as we go, that

Jesus is at the heart of all the connections we make tonight.' With that, they head into the night, shoulders against the wind. By the time they've walked half a block, it has started to rain.

'OK, girls, quick,' Margaret says to her little group, hustling them left along the pavement. 'Let's try and get inside before this rain hits.'

'There's our door, up ahead,' Chitra says, pointing. 'They should recognise us OK. Shall I do the talking, Marge?' Margaret nods.

They approach an open door. The walls around it are painted baby pink – a faded, street-dirty baby pink – and the corridor that stretches from the entrance is lit with a red light. There are no women in sight, just a man sitting by a table outside. He's wearing flip-flops and a navy polo-shirt, the cotton neck stretched wide and slack, and the bottom edges of his jeans scrape the floor at his heels. He's looking up at the sky, assessing the rain. His thick black hair flops out from a central parting.

'Who's that guy?' asks the young American that speaks more. Her voice is thin and wispy against the wind, and her forehead is pattered with raindrops.

'Just the doorman,' Margaret replies. She sees the girl frown and says, 'I know – no radio earpiece, gold chains or tattoos. Not what you expected, huh?'

The girl looks away, embarrassed, and Margaret reaches out and puts a hand on her arm. 'I thought the same, first time I came,' she placates.

The door is one of several along the street. Red light, pink walls, ordinary-looking gatekeeper. The Mission hasn't managed to form contacts with all of them; the ones they're going to tonight are well known to Jane and the others. Margaret recognises the man – he recognises her, too. He stands up, nods his head slightly to the four women, flashes two rows of white teeth and crosses himself. They say hello. With Chitra, he speaks Malaysian English

– fast, and full of words and phrases taken from several languages. But when he speaks to the whole group, he drops the slang and his accent changes. They rattle through a couple of pleasantries as the rain really starts to come on, drops hitting the ground all around them and soaking into their clothes. The man beckons them inside, squinting up at the sky, and the women rush in. They're half-soaked.

Inside, the pink walls stretch on, sad and gloomy in the low light. A single corridor slinks into the depths of the building. The ceiling is a carpet of cobwebs, each thread hanging heavy with dust. The four women press into the space like hares stumbling into a rabbit warren. They're out of place and nervous. They're shaking rainwater from their heads and brushing wet hair out of their eyes. Margaret's sandals squelch with every step, like a rubber duck has followed her in.

The man speaks Mandarin to a woman who stands in a nearby doorway, a line of mistrust between her brows. To Margaret's ears, the language always sounds abrupt, full of rising and falling notes, as well as the occasional one held longer than her English tells her is necessary. The woman replies, glances at the newcomers, and nods slowly. She is wearing a tight red dress, and with her six-inch heels, she nearly reaches Margaret's height. The man talks back and crosses himself once more, grinning. He's making jokes – Margaret knows that. The men don't take them seriously. The woman in the tight red dress smirks back at him, reaches out an arm and pats him gently on the stomach. Then she lifts her eyes back to the strangers and the laughter in them is replaced with wariness.

'Hello,' she says, in English. She bows her head slightly. 'Pleased to meet you.'

'Hi there, my name is Margaret. We are visiting from the church over the road.' She waves her arm back towards the street, as if that will help.

'Christians, yes. We good Christians,' says the man. His smile reveals a gold tooth – it flashes somewhere on the right of his mouth.

'Oh. Good,' Margaret replies, doubtful.

'Yes, yes. Christians OK. Come in,' he says. He turns away from them, an arm gesturing for them to follow. As he goes, he speaks loudly into the corridor and other women begin to appear from doorways. Faces press into the pink haze. There are five, maybe six women, each wearing a mask of cautious curiosity.

'Hello,' Margaret says ahead of her. 'Hello, everyone.'

She glances behind her as she walks and sees hardly masked horror in the faces of the two young Americans. The corridor stinks of bottled jasmine. Margaret starts to sweat. The cool relief of the rain that lashes the streets outside will not penetrate this place. She shifts the collar of her linen shirt and rearranges the chain of a gold pendant that hangs against her chest. As she does this, the man disappears into the depths of the labyrinth. The women, insiders and out, are left alone.

'Nice to meet you,' Margaret says, first in English, then Mandarin, then Malay. She looks to the closest woman and tries to make eye contact. The woman's breasts push out against the edges of a tight black vest and her hair falls straight to her shoulders, sleek and touchable. Her face is painted on, rosy cheeks and red lips over light skin. All the women in the corridor are beautiful. Their clothes are tight and sexy, the kind of thing young Americans would wear to a nightclub.

The black-vested woman nods demurely, a small smile beginning to show around her eyes. Margaret takes a careful step towards her and reaches to grasp her hands.

'Hello. My name is Margaret.'

A little nod again, a frown, and then a tiny voice. As she speaks, the woman presses a hand to her chest.

Margaret listens carefully. '*Sung?*' she asks.

'Suong.'

'*Suong*,' Margaret repeats, trying it out. 'Hello, Suong. Nice to meet you. My name is Margaret. I came from the church.'

Suong's eyes crinkle in confusion. One of the other women from the corridor comes to her side. This second woman points to Suong and says something in Malay – it's not a word Margaret understands and she glances back at Chitra for help.

Chitra nods. 'Suong is Vietnamese.'

Margaret resists the urge to throw her hands over her head, not that this is an unusual occurrence. Lots of the women they meet are not Malaysian – some are Chinese, Thai, Cambodian. Flesh is traded across borders. Margaret is used to feeling useless when it comes to language. A bumbling westerner with no communication skills.

'Do you think anyone in here can speak to her?' Margaret asks Chitra, who shrugs.

'Someone will be able to, but I doubt they're going to stand and interpret for us.' Chitra pauses, then nods down the corridor. 'Marge, I'm going to go and chat with the lady in the sari. I think I recognise her from somewhere, but I can't place the connection. Is that OK?' When she sees Margaret hesitate, Chitra puts a hand on her arm. 'Have faith. Keep smiling. Come on, you two.' She beckons to the American girls and they follow her along the pink corridor, each one looking around, eyes like dinner plates.

Margaret turns back to the second sex worker – the one who explained in Malay that Suong is Vietnamese – and again introduces herself in English. When the woman nods, Margaret continues. 'I want to talk to you about Jesus, and the peace and love that I find through my relationship with Him.' She pulls the small crucifix that hangs round her neck forwards while she speaks, hoping it will help explain who she is. She's role-played these conversations with the other women in the Mission. As she speaks, she searches for eye contact, first with the Malaysian woman and then the Vietnamese, then back again. Non-verbal cues count for a lot, too – that's what she hopes.

She reaches into her purse and pulls a couple of flyers out. Splashed across the top of them in large letters is the title: *Foods of the World*. It's written again beneath, in Chinese characters. The Mission has been planning their world-foods festival for six weeks now. It's going to be a cultural affair, a welcoming event, and only for those invited, because they don't want to risk the church's over-eager congregation scaring these women off. Margaret plans to make tacos. Jane will cook sausage and sauerkraut. They're hoping for a good turnout.

'I'd like to give you this,' Margaret says, handing a flyer to each of the two women. 'Come to the church, meet everybody... There will be a lot of food. Cuisines from lots of different countries. And a chance to ask us questions. You can find out a bit more about Jesus. It will be fun.'

As she delivers this explanation, Margaret can't help her attention drifting mostly to the Malaysian woman, who's at least partly following her. She smiles widely and looks down at the flyer, then back to her. When Margaret finishes speaking, the woman lifts the flyer to her chest and presses it against her, as though she's been given a gift. She turns to Suong and points at the flyer, chattering rapidly in Malay and then gesturing towards Margaret. Suong doesn't understand, and her friend shrugs and puts an arm around her shoulders. She turns back to Margaret.

'Thank you, *la*,' she says. 'My name is Christina.'

She looks back down at the flyer. Along the bottom is a row of flags, to show that they are representing lots of different countries at the festival. She points to them, then looks at Margaret. 'You?' she asks.

'Oh, well, let's have a look,' Margaret says, leaning in to look at the flyer in the woman's hands. The USA flag is fourth in the row, flying proudly. Margaret points. 'Maybe you recognise it?'

'USA?' Christina says without hesitation.

Margaret nods.

Christina points to herself. 'Malaysia,' she says. Then she looks at Suong and frowns.

'Vietnam,' Margaret jumps in, pleased to help.

When the flyers have been handed out and Margaret has introduced herself to nearly all the women in the corridor, she makes her way to Chitra, who is speaking to someone in an orange sari. Margaret always finds her eyes drawn to the details of the place. The metal-framed beds with worn-out sheets, the squat toilets in the corner of each of the girls' rooms, the mirrors on the walls, tubes of lipstick on the bed. Part of her feels it's her duty to take it all in and understand as much as she can about these women she hopes to connect with. She can't expect to come here and not notice anything of the world they live in – would it be a disservice to them, to pretend it was different? Her eyes are not drawn to any one room in particular – there is little personality or privacy. Each space is no more individual than the last. It's the women who stand in the doorways that are the distinguishing features. Each of them is a bright light among a backdrop of grey.

The young Americans are incongruous at the end of the corridor. They see Margaret coming towards them and look at her with hope. They can't converse with anyone but her and Chitra, and they're not practised at trying. They probably feel useless. 'I only speak Spanish,' the quiet one whispers, as Margaret draws close.

'I wish I could speak Spanish,' Margaret says. 'Are you both OK?' Before they can answer, she continues: 'We should get going. I'll let Chitra know.'

Margaret pauses when she sees the doorman reappear, this time talking loudly to another man. The reaction from the women working the corridor is instant. They take paces forwards, lift chins and smile. The two men make their way slowly along the corridor. Margaret watches from a distance as the doorman extends a hand towards them. She sees the client's eyes roam over the young American girls' faces and their white, white skin. A laugh passes between the two men and the pimp shakes his head. *Not those, they're not ours*, Margaret imagines him saying. They turn their attention back to the other women. They're both full of mirth. Camaraderie seems to be involved in surveying the goods. Margaret's skin crawls.

As the client walks down the corridor, the sex workers make passes at him. Playful caresses, a squeeze on the arm, a pat on the stomach. Smiles and laughs. Margaret doesn't bother to try to understand what the women say – it's obvious from their body language that they're cajoling. *Choose me*, they're saying. *Don't let me down, lover – you know I'm worth it.*

Margaret catches Chitra's eye. She agrees with a small nod that it's time to go. As they look at each other, the red bulbs above their heads flicker. There is a moment of darkness, over before it begins. Margaret glances to the ceiling.

The bulbs waver again, then go out. They are plunged into darkness. No more pink. No more anything. Around them, people begin to shriek.

'Everyone, stay calm. It's just a blackout,' Margaret hears herself saying. She's not sure who she's talking to. The darkness around them is complete. Her eyes feel robbed, brain unable to understand. She reaches out, hoping to make contact with someone. 'Where are you all?'

There is too much noise. The women in the corridor have all broken into worried speech, with Malay and Mandarin and more bouncing off the walls like ping-pongs. There's probably some Vietnamese in there, and English is working its way into Margaret's left ear. An American accent. 'What's going on? I can't see anything. I hate this,' she hears one of the girls say. Then a man's voice sounds through darkness. Margaret recognises the voice of the doorman, speaking loudly in Malaysian English – she tries to find words she understands among his rapid sentences, but he's talking too fast.

'Chitra? Are you there?' she calls.

She feels a hand against hers through the darkness. 'I'm here, yes, I'm here,' Chitra says. 'He's telling the women not to worry. And... it sounds like he's lost the client. Girls? Come closer, where are you?'

One American voice says, 'I'm here.' The other asks, 'Lost the client? What do you mean? Lost him where?'

Through the darkness both girls start speaking at once, drowning each other out among the ongoing echoes of everyone else in the corridor.

'Let's not worry about that,' Chitra cuts in. 'Now, I've got my hands out. Girls, can you take hold of them?'

Margaret senses bodies pushing closer. She reaches her hands out, too, and as she does, a light flares up further down the corridor. Shadows fly across the walls and they see the silhouette of a man holding a phone aloft, flashlight beaming. He is speaking orders to the women around him. Margaret hears them respond, and then his voice softens. Laughter scatters into the darkness.

'OK, ladies,' Margaret says. 'We've got to abandon this mission. Take hold of each other's hands.'

A second light bursts into her vision. One of the American girls has found her phone, too. In the darkness the flash is harsh. Margaret squints and glances away.

'Well done,' she hears Chitra say. 'Now, let's use your light to make our way back to the street. Once we're there, we can go to the church and wait for the power to come back on.'

'What about all the other women?' Margaret mutters, tugging a little at Chitra's arm. 'Should we take them with us?'

They hear a bark from the doorman then. They look up the corridor just in time to see the shadow of a second man racing towards them, his hands braced against the walls for guidance. There is no time to move before he crashes into them.

'Watch out!' Margaret cries, flattening herself against the wall.

'Be careful,' Chitra reprimands. 'You're going the wrong way. The exit is back where you came from.'

The client replies, in clipped Chinese, and turns swiftly on the spot. As he goes, the torch in the young girl's hand illuminates his face. Margaret has a moment to stare into the whites of his eyes, and then he is gone, off stumbling towards the street.

'Gosh, there's no need to panic, is there?' Margaret says, mostly to herself, as the four of them regroup. 'OK, let's get going. Oh no, wait! This lot?' She flaps a hand down the corridor, towards the other women and the pimp.

'We'll check as we go by. Can you lead the way, please?' Chitra asks their torchbearer. 'I'm right behind you. We're all right behind you. Marge isn't afraid of the dark, so she can bring up the rear.'

The four women form a chain, each with a hand on the shoulder in front, and begin the short walk back to the street. When they reach the doorman, his light held aloft, Chitra speaks quickly with him and relays to Margaret that they have candles and will stay put until the power is back on.

'Let's get back to base, then,' Margaret says, selfishly relieved to be able to think only of themselves.

When they're nearly at the door, the quieter of the two Americans speaks. 'What's God's purpose in this?' she says.

Margaret's too surprised by the depth of the question – she's been worrying about lightning – to even reply. She shakes her head and pretends no one said anything.

When they get to the street, there is a little light. The sky is a deep, dense blue, and it shows a road filled with water. Wind howls through the shadows and the rain falls sideways, in bucketloads. Margaret knows that if there were trees on the street, they would be tugging at their roots, branches lashing against the storm. She thinks of the little papaya tree in her back garden and grinds her teeth. On the sidewalk in front of them the water is half a foot deep. They have been inside for less than an hour. She's never seen a storm like this before.

'Looks like we're swimming to the church, then,' she says, trying to sound cheerful.

'We can't!' says one of the girls. 'It's too deep.'

'It's OK,' the other replies, her quiet voice whipped away almost instantly by the wind. 'We've hiked through the Colorado River, remember? This is easy. Look, that's the church right over there.'

A flash of lightning strikes above them. It screeches as it zigzags out, long legs forking down to earth, making a pink gash across the rain-filled sky, and for a moment the whole world is luminous. Margaret glances sideways, shying from the electric glare, and sees each woman in profile against the night. The American girls stand hand in hand, ready to wade into the delta. Margaret has a second to wonder at how young they are. How flawless. Beside them, Chitra stands with furrowed brow, hair pushed back from her forehead. Her mouth is slightly ajar, as though in silent wonder. Before the lightning has even faded, the thunder follows – a rage-filled rumble. It drums down onto them like the roar of a beast and each woman falters, steps backwards a little or moves her hands to her head, protecting herself from the harmless boom.

Without another word, they step forwards and wade into the street, two by two. The water feels cold as it rushes against their shins. Before long, Chitra has lost both flip-flops. In the middle of the road the water reaches Margaret's thighs. She tries not to think what could be in there, floating about, as she hitches her purse well out of harm's way, as though holding it aloft in a monsoon will keep it dry. Good job her phone is waterproof. It must be drifting around in a puddle at the bottom of her bag. She thinks of Roger, then. She pictures him at an upstairs window, watching the world's theatre unfold before him. She hopes he isn't worried – isn't wasting time feeling anxious over her. Perhaps he stayed at work, where his colleagues could keep him company.

When they make it to the other sidewalk, they turn right down the street. The church is not far away, and the flood is lighter here. The flashlight is gone now and the four women have found their night vision. They dart right and left, dodging obstacles. A sandwich-board sign, wounded and flat on its side. A streetlight. A mailbox. A wicker basket.

At the church doors, they find dry ground. No flood in the ark. Margaret reaches for the door handle – she's so happy to see that simple church – and as another bolt of lightning rifts the sky in two, the little group rush over the threshold. The door closes behind them with a blissful, sturdy bang, and the howl of the storm recedes.

'Listen,' one of the girls pants.

From somewhere in the building, they hear the slow, peaceful strum of a guitar.

Chapter Seven

Cathy

At night, now, it is not just the sky that shows us stars. Two weeks since the storm and still some of the starfish that were washed up in their hundreds wriggle up the harbour wall. We thought they would sneak back down to the surf. A lot of them did. But some resisted the pull of the ocean; some are land-lovers. They spread their orange arms across the solid ground, no tickling waves to caress them. They pile up in the gaps between rocks, like satsumas, soft and fleshy. The gulls do not eat them. The air does not dry them.

'You know those purple ones in the States?' Ephie says, her eyes shining in the light of her laptop. 'They're called *Pisaster ochraceus*, the purple sea star. They're very important in their local environment.'

She leans forwards, eyes on the screen, and I watch her, waiting for my lesson.

'They live near the shoreline, and they are an indicator of how healthy the area is,' she continues. 'When their numbers either plummet or boom, it's basically a sign that something's wrong.'

She frowns, muttering something to herself, and types a little.

'Something's wrong?' I ask, but she doesn't respond.

'They reckon they're producing this sort of... slime?' I continue, speaking a little louder. 'They were talking about it on the radio the other day. It keeps them hydrated and it's foul-tasting, so it keeps the birds off.'

Ephie pulls her eyes away from the laptop. 'Yes, we're about to start analysing it. The question is, have they always been able to produce it? It can't be an adaptation, surely—'

'You've never tested it before? In the lab.'

Her nose wrinkles. 'Tasted it?'

'*Tested*, you fool.' I shake my head. Dismiss the image of my wife, in a white lab coat, licking a starfish.

It isn't the first time we've discussed them – how could we not have, with Ephie working in a lab predominantly focused on marine analysis? With them crawling up the sea wall right under the house?

The storm, a worldwide tempest, emptied five-pointed fish onto shorelines across the globe. The news had come in slowly at first. Each local newspaper assumed the phenomenon was just that – local. But social media spread the pictures more quickly; then the international outlets like *Cabled* and *ViralFeed* caught on. *Ten Things You Didn't Know About Starfish*, or *Eighteen Dogs That Are Totally Freaked Out By Starfish*. Ephie saw the best one: an online advert squashed into a box next to the article she was reading: *Ten Things Jesus Said About Fish*. We're both ignorant about that – not a well-read parable between us – so she called me over and clicked, curious. Jesus said a lot of things about fish, it turns out. Don't think he mentioned starfish, though.

But those were all laymen stories and Ephie's too well-trained for postulation. Her news alerts come through from *European Scientist*, and her colleagues are some of the experts. They're asking the questions that the mainstream press isn't bothering with. Namely: why?

A couple of the stars have made their way onto the kitchen windows now. They take their time over movement. It's fascinating to watch. They don't slither or wriggle at all – they glide. One of the satsumas from the beach separates itself from the group, flattens, stretches its peel out into five limbs, and then takes on angel qualities. It hovers infinitesimally above all surfaces and drifts smoothly along. The limbs do not move. It is as though the starfish sits on a clear plastic sheet which is being very slowly pulled by an invisible hand.

Now that they're on the glass pane, I see how they do this. Their secrets are invisible from above, but the two creatures on our kitchen window have their undersides facing me. They are bare and on display, unabashed, and I study them. I try to do the washing-up, but they are too alien to ignore – my hands don't stay in the sink for long. I press my nose to the glass.

They are millipedes. The underside of each star arm is covered in tiny legs. They remind me of the little eyestalks at the front of a snail, except these don't have eyes. Each tiny leg is a tube and each tube, no longer than the nail on my littlest finger, ends in a little white disc. This is the point where adhesive is secreted, allowing the star to stick to our window, or a rock, or a tasty-looking mussel. These legs – a squirming, curious mass of tentacles – search surfaces for food and then funnel their prey into the middle of the muddle, to the very centre of the starfish, where the mouth and stomach are found. Starfish digest their prey externally. They push out a section of their stomach, slip it into the tiny gap which their hundreds of legs have prised open in the shell of their chosen mussel, and surround the mollusc in digestive enzymes. Then they suck the whole lot back in. Like a spider: liquidise first, eat second. Ephie's not the only one who can use the internet.

I'm not sure what they're eating when they're stuck to our kitchen window. Slugs and snails, I guess. We would both like that; Ephie because of the precious rice paddy, and me because I get bored of hearing about the precious rice paddy. Slugs can swim. That's another thing we've discovered. Snails, too; they crawl to the top of the rice stems and rest there with their yellow shells standing out among the green.

Today I avoid the window – I've procrastinated enough on sea stars – and instead focus on tidying my workshop. Stray material has gathered on every surface; the floor is scattered with patterns; white threads of cotton blossom across the arms and back of my chair. I pick at them, considering getting the vacuum cleaner. Why are there starfish on the kitchen window? Ephie as good as said that there must be something wrong in the ocean.

Yesterday I watched a cat padding along the wall that separates us from the sea. It stopped to pause at every orange star, to sniff anxiously and hiss. Not to lick or touch. Watching it, I felt the hairs go up on the back of my neck. That cat knows something we don't. I wanted to invite it in, to ask it: *Why are you scared of them?* Cats are only semi-domesticated. They have plenty of wild instinct left in them.

I shake my head to break the thought, looking down again at the white threads. I go downstairs to search for sticky tape in the drawers of Ephie's desk.

'What do you want?' she asks, smiling as I come near.

Her office is one corner of our dining room, a single step down from the kitchen, with a view of the Atlantic. If more starfish come, she will see them first. Her desk is tidy, always, and free of dust. A corkboard covers the wall above her laptop and onto it our life is pinned. A photograph of our wedding, nearly seven years old and dog-eared; a letter confirming a hospital appointment; a wall thermometer, tacked into place the year our gas boiler was replaced with the hydrogen one; a red sticker that reads, *It's my first blood donation!* Next to all these are Ephie's own papers. To-do lists, reminders, notes coated in her scrawling hand, detailing results, ideas for experiments, who knows what. Every bit of the board is ordered – no chaos; that's not Ephie's style. If we had more than two starfish on the window, she'd go outside and line them up.

'I need sticky tape,' I say, gathering her thick velvet ponytail in my palms.

She opens a drawer in the left of the desk. Her hair slips from my grip.

'Wrapping presents, are you?' she asks.

She pulls the tape loose and hands it over, eyebrows raised. I tilt my head slightly, run a finger up the back of her neck.

'No. For me to buy you a present, you'd have to be really nice to me.'

I turn and leave. Sway my hips slightly as I walk away. Wish I could glide, like a starfish. Except, I don't want to be a starfish.

It's no use – the hem just isn't straight. I throw the dress on the floor in a moment of recklessness, then quickly pick it up again and hang it over the back of my chair, smoothing out the creases.

Some days it feels as though my pins are conspiring against me. I cut my fabrics one millimetre too many off-pattern and I snag threads. I stare at my products and they look like school-play costumes, stitched by a devoted mum. I can see wonky overlocking and gaping necklines. The worst part is, I only have myself to answer to. No co-workers to step in with encouraging words. No one else to blame.

Ephie works two days in the lab and two at home. The fifth day she teaches undergraduates. I think all the students fancy her, but she says the idea is ridiculous, that she's a grown woman to them, not a prospect. It's on the lab days that things seem to go wrong for her, if they do. I've come to understand that *results* are an evasive and temperamental thing among scientists. Experiments can be weeks in the set-up, and months in the happening. I don't really know the details of what she does, but I've been in there and seen the benches and fume hoods and those spinny things that the test tubes go into. She says they have tanks of starfish all over the place now, but not in her lab, where everything is *far more molecular* than that.

I do get jealous of her, with the job contract and the colleagues to conspire with when things aren't working out. Running a small business can be lonely. If she weren't in the house two days a week, I'd have developed an imaginary boss by now. As it is, I talk to myself in the mirror. Or I talk to the clothes themselves. Today I've been swearing at the final bridesmaid dress. Two of them are finished, bar the final adjustments, and hanging from the back of the bedroom door like a pair of flat, shadowy women. The third has been on my dummy, then on the sewing machine, then back on the dummy, then on the floor and now on the back of the chair. Nothing about it is working. I pick the empty mug off my desk. It hangs from my fingers as I stomp downstairs, and the last bit of cold tea slips out of it and splashes on the runner. I don't care.

Ephie doesn't look up when I enter the kitchen. When she's absorbed in something, it's hard to pull her out of it. Even when I crash my mug down next to the sink, she keeps her eyes on her computer screen, fingers typing away.

I don't have to deliver the dresses until next week, and even then there are still two weeks for fittings and adjustments. There's no need to stress. But the bride could hate them. *They look a bit home-made*, she might say. Or she could just keep quiet and fake-smile, then send me an email later that details all the reasons she hates them. That's happened before.

'I'm going to have a break and go for a little walk,' I say to the back of Ephie's head.

I eat a biscuit from the jar on the kitchen windowsill and peer at the starfish while I wait for her to respond. We've named them Devon and Cornwall, because they're always right up next to each other, competing. Devon (or maybe Cornwall – they look the same) is moving slowly, slowly, towards a snail that's slimed onto the window ledge. I grimace, but sort of want to stick around for the destruction. It's like watching a disaster movie in slow motion, seeing the starfish eat. An unhurried death via liquidation.

'What are they doing?' Ephie asks.

She looks at me with a little smirk. 'That face,' she says. 'It's like you're watching surgery.'

I roll my shoulders and stretch my arms above my head, moving away from the window. 'This last dress is driving me insane. I'm going to go for a walk. Do you fancy a break?'

She shakes her head. 'I've got too much to do, my love. Bring me back something.'

Outside, the sun is struggling through patchy grey clouds, left over from this morning's rainstorm. Since the end of July, the rain has been lighter – only short, sharp showers that show up just as you've put the washing on the line. The kind Mum calls April showers.

I have the beach to myself. I slip my flip-flops off. The sand is cold and firm beneath me. On days like today, when I feel unproductive, I can never shake the sense that I'm wasting time. If I'm not going to achieve much work I may as well do something useful, like go to the supermarket, or clean the house. That's usually when I walk to the beach. Some days when it's warm enough, we put our swimming costumes on in the house and then run straight down here. It's the privilege of being local, taking nothing with us. What's the need for shoes or shirts or towels? We don't even lock the back door – there's no crime in Barvusi. It's not warm enough for that today, though; there's a cool edge to the air. The wind is strong and it makes my eyes water.

I take a seat on a rock to the right of the harbour. It's still damp from the storm – I feel it through my jeans. I look out to sea, watching each wave drift rhythmically home, and try not to think about the hem, or the gentle anxiety that sits alongside it. I glance back, towards the house. It's not far away, perched above the high wall that rises from the sand behind me.

'Cathy!'

The shout makes me turn. David Evans is striding towards me, a hand waving urgently. 'He's not Welsh,' the barman told us in the pub the first time we met David, years ago. 'Don't let the name fool you. He's Cornish through and through. Mad as a hatter.'

I feel myself frowning, wondering what's got him so animated. I often see him on the beach, but he doesn't usually seek me out. We save our chats for the pub.

'Cathy. 'Ere, come look!' he shouts. 'Someone 'as to see this.'

Fresh from his boat, he's wearing his huge yellow overcoat. I can hear it flapping in the wind as he marches towards me.

When he reaches me, he's out of breath and his face is pale. There's dread in his eyes.

'I ain't never seen nothin' like it,' he gasps. 'Cathy, you gotta…'

He gestures again, across the beach and towards the cliffs that rise on the west of the harbour. 'There, you can nearly see 'im. Over there.'

'David – what?'

I stand, driven by his frantic energy, but see nothing in the direction he points.

David can't be still. His sou'wester is scrunched up in his right hand and he slaps it against his thigh. He paces on the spot, feet scuffing lines through the sand. Reaching forwards, he takes my hand. 'Over 'ere. Come on.'

Before I can resist, he starts tugging me across the beach. His hand is warm and dry, but I feel it fidgeting in mine. What is he taking me to?

We are halfway across the beach when he stops, scans the sand ahead and then points. 'There! Oh my good lord, Cathy. You see it?'

Before I can answer, he tugs me on in the direction he's been pointing. After a couple more paces I catch something coming into view across the sand. It's not a body – not a corpse that's floated ashore or anything like that – it's too small. I breathe a sigh of relief and squint towards it.

'What is it, David?'

He shakes his head and stuffs his hat into the front pocket of his overalls, then tugs at his wiry beard. 'Bugger's walking about,' he says. 'I ain't never...'

Stopping, he turns to me and takes my other hand so that he's holding both. He squeezes them tight and looks at me with a crazed expression. 'I don't know what this means, Cathy. I don't know how he's doing it.'

'Come on, then,' I say, frowning. 'We'd better go and look.'

I feel nervous as we walk onwards. Fear rises from David like a smell.

The thing we head towards is about the size of a cormorant, and a similar shape – tall and slender. From the way David's been calling it 'he', I assume it's an animal of some kind. Perhaps it's wounded and acting strangely because of that. Perhaps it's dangerous.

'You see?' David says after a few more paces, pointing again.

I see something my eyes can't comprehend. I stop walking and blink, confused. There is a fish on the sand; I see it clearly. But it is not on its side, lying still. It is partly upright. It moves. I can see its gills, off the ground and wide open. It looks as though it's standing up.

'What on earth?' I put a hand to my mouth, trying to understand. 'How did it get there? What's it doing?' I almost shout – David's hysteria is infectious.

'Fins are long, see,' David says, pointing, shuffling a little closer. 'Cathy, should I catch 'im?'

'No!' I put a hand out to stop him.

I don't want anyone near that fish. I don't know why – it's only a fish – but there is something horrible and inconceivable about it. It shuffles, a controlled and purposeful movement across the sand. Fear rises in my chest, but at the same time I walk closer. I feel drawn on by an irresistible curiosity.

When we are only five metres or so away from it, I stop. David stops, too, muttering and wringing his hands.

It is a cod; I see that. It has that long, rubbery-looking whisker protruding from its bottom lip. That is how I always recognise them when we go to the fishmonger's. It's average size, about thirty centimetres in length, and its skin is wet and slippery, a muddy brown colour that blends well with the sand. Looking at its eyes, I can't help but shiver – they are like jelly, glazed and unblinking. The gills are splayed open, as though it's drowning in air, desperate to breathe, and its side-fins, usually short and stubby, are long enough to prop it up in the sand. Like a seal with its head raised.

It sees us. It turns, lumbering awkwardly, and moves away, leaving behind a slick of disturbed sand.

I put my hand out, taking hold of David's arm.

'Ah, 'tis fine, look,' David says, shaking his head as though to rouse himself from a dream. 'Back to the sea 'e goes.'

The cod slouches on towards the shoreline, where the waves drift in. It moves slowly, but with an awkward grace. I can't peel my eyes away. The first waves begin to reach it, frothing around its curved tail and its strangely long fins. With the third wave, it flops flat onto its belly, like a picture frame toppling over. I gasp at the sudden movement and grip David's arm tighter. With that, it is gone, swallowed by the surf.

'Well, I've seen it all now,' David pants, eyes wide.

I turn to him. I want to shake him, shout at him. 'What the hell was that, David?'

He wobbles his head, a sort of shiver that moves through his whole body. 'Dunno,' he says. 'Strange thing, that be. Very strange. I got to go.'

Without another word, he loosens himself from my grip and begins to walk away, pulling a packet of chocolate digestives from his jacket pocket as he goes and stuffing one nervously into his mouth. I can hear him talking to himself as he crunches, and then he's out of earshot and gone, back to the main part of the harbour. I look around me, shocked to suddenly be alone.

I am ankle-deep in water. It has seeped out of the sand and my feet have sunk without my noticing – I can feel the beach sucking against my toes. I feel trapped, buried, and let out a desperate cry as I pull my legs free.

What have I just seen?

Only a fish. The sea is full of them. But this wasn't like any other fish.

I begin the walk home, desperate to get back. As I go, I think through the image, ready to tell Ephie. It was like this; it moved like that. I don't know what words to use but I have an urgent, uncontrollable need to share this with her.

When I pull open the back door, I shake my head a little, trying to clear my thoughts. My breath is shallow.

'Nice walk?' I hear her call.

Without answering, I cross the tiles that line the hall and make my way to her. She has her back to me, eyes on her laptop. 'There are some very strange stories on the internet today, Cath,' she says, clicking the mouse.

When I don't reply, she turns to me. She is smiling, but she frowns when she sees me. 'Love, where are your shoes?' she says, looking down at my sandy toes. 'Are you OK? You look a bit... crazy.'

Chapter Eight

Ricky

When it happens, it's an anticlimax. They've been lying in the sand dunes for over an hour and Kyle's fallen asleep, mouth open and head lolled to the side. He misses the whole thing.

Ricky's watched every video about fish walking that he could find, most of them more than once, so there's no surprise left in it really. There are only ten or so clips, but the numbers are increasing each day. The first one, the one that went viral, was from Cornwall, England. He's heard the behind-camera screams of the videographers, and the wild, shouting explanations of what they're looking at. *It's a fish. Oh my God. A fish. It's walking.*

He's desperate to see it. He feels left out. He wants to be a part of this hysteria that's beginning to show. So, of course, his first land-fish sighting can never live up to expectations. It isn't like a great white shark comes shuffling out of the surf with five rows of teeth. It's a blue cod. Fifteen centimetres long. Brown. It looks awkward. It isn't worth waking Kyle for. Ricky feels disappointed, and that's disappointing.

Chapter Nine

Margaret

Roger's flicking buttons on the TV remote when Margaret comes home from church. She's had a long day – seven hours of summer school followed by two hours of church politics – and she's tired. The sky outside is dark, and Roger sits behind an empty lager bottle.

'How was your day?' he mumbles, eyes still on the TV.

'It was OK,' she says, stifling a yawn. July and August are her busiest months. She's never really needed to work in KL; Roger earns more than enough for both of them. But when a friend of hers at church suggested some years ago that she'd be perfect for summer-school tutoring at one of the international schools, she decided to give it a try, and found she liked it. It gave her purpose, and it meant she was occupied during the peak of the tourist season, when it was too busy in the city to do anything fun anyway. So she's been doing that for maybe six years now, and she thinks she's gotten quite good at it. She takes full classes, not just small groups, and teaches English Language and Literature. The days can be long, but they go by fast.

'You want another, honey?' she asks, dropping her key card on the table and breezing past. They don't drink all that much, but there's usually a beer or two in the back of the refrigerator. She deserves a drink. School feels kind of crazy at the moment and going to church hasn't provided her with the serenity she normally expects of it. Everyone is caught up on the same one topic: fish.

She walks into the dark kitchen and opens the refrigerator wide. She stands there for a long moment, hands on hips, and basks in the cool that seeps out from the open door. In the light of the refrigerator her body casts a shadow, wide and untidy, onto the floor behind her. It never used to be this sticky in August, not when they first moved to KL. The wet months were always from fall to early spring, but now it seems like the humidity is relentless all-year round. She grabs two beers, not using the tips of her fingers but wrapping her entire palms around them, maximising contact and savouring the cool against her hands. Then she gets the bottle opener from the top drawer. By the time she's walked back to the couch, both beers are dripping with condensation.

'Good day?' Roger asks, watching her open one bottle and then the other.

Margaret frowns. 'Field trip next week. They just decided. To the mangroves.'

Roger nods, taking his beer from her. 'Mangroves? Why are you going out there?'

'To look for fish.'

Roger frowns, shakes his head a little. 'Nonsense,' he says.

Margaret tilts the drink to her lips, letting the cool beer rush down her throat. At home in the US they make really nice beer, full of hops and flavour – she drank quite a lot of it last time she made it home, over two years ago now, when she visited a microbrewery with some old friends. There's nothing like that in Asia. They still mostly get Yantai, China's premier lager, or Elephant, from Thailand. They do the job. Elephant's better – it has a sharper taste – but it's still not great. For a while she and Roger imported Californian wine, but the customs charges got so high that it stopped being worth it. She takes another sip of her beer. Tonight, she'd love something a little stronger. Bourbon on the rocks – that would do it.

The Fish

'It's going to be scorching,' she says. 'But you know all these strange news stories? Well, that's why we're going. The students are excited – they keep asking questions about the fish. I don't know... I feel kind of weird about it.'

'You'll be fine. Everyone needs to relax a little, stop making such a big deal about it,' he says, continuing to flick through the TV channels.

She looks at him quizzically. 'Yeah, but nobody knows what's causing them to come on land. Some people are talking about radioactivity. A toxic waste spillage or something.'

'Everyone always has a conspiracy theory.' He looks at his wife. 'Come on, honey. Don't get all worked up about this.'

'I can just imagine one of those kids' parents suing the school or something. They're rich enough. Who else would send their kids to summer school?' she says. But Roger's already gone back to the TV. He purses his lips a bit, as if to say: *Who knows*, and then has another sip of beer.

Margaret sighs, frustrated that he won't discuss it. She gets off the couch. 'Gonna lie down a bit,' she says, taking her beer with her.

She climbs the stairs, one sweaty step after the other, and then slumps into their bedroom. She's way too hot. Reaching for the wall, she flicks on the socket into which a free-standing fan is plugged. The thing whizzes to life on her dressing table, shoving a drift of sticky air at her. She puts the beer bottle down and leans towards the fan, hands on the table, watching its plastic blades spin round. 'Ahhhhhhhhhhhhh. Ooooohhhhhhhhhhh.' She meditates into the draught, always fascinated by the way her voice thrums. She thinks this is the hottest KL has ever been. Either that or she's hit it, finally, at age forty-seven. She thinks back to Roger, sitting next to her on the couch just now. His forehead was shiny – he was sweating. Boiling up. It's not just her; it's the weather. She doesn't know if that comforts her or not. Forty-seven, but maybe not yet.

She flops into the chair where she sits to do her hair each morning, pulls the front of her shirt down and then leans over the fan, letting the cool air flow across her chest. She almost longs to go back to school, where the air-con runs non-stop. They offered her a term-time post once – part-time, teaching literature – but she turned it down. After two months of summer school, she's always exhausted and ready for a break. She couldn't imagine how hard it would be to teach all through the year. The kids would have been different, too – another type of teenager to learn. The summer-school kids are mostly the sons and daughters of well-off Malaysians. The rest of the year the prestigious school is the territory of the children of expat diplomats and bankers. The kind of children she and Roger would probably have raised, if they could. Their smiling pictures are framed all over the school, holding trophies and diplomas and awards. The kids all graduate and go to good universities in big cities: New York, Hong Kong, London, Singapore, Oxford. She can't teach those kids; it would be too tiring. Her Malaysian students are just as smart, but they somehow don't have the same entitlement.

These last couple of weeks the classrooms have been full of fish chatter. Margaret takes the older kids, and their questions have been endless: *What are the fish eating? Why are they on land? How do they breathe? Are they dangerous? Will they take over the world?* It freaks Margaret out that she doesn't have the answers. Kids are so switched on, more than anyone realises. They use the internet to figure everything out. They watch everything they can get their hands on, then chat about it non-stop. Right now they're watching the newest batch of storytellers: the self-proclaimed experts stirring everything up and claiming to have explanations for what's happening. Not true, of course. How can some internet-famous twenty-one-year-olds know what's going on, when no one else does? It's working wonders for their fame, though – every time

Margaret turns her back on her classroom, the kids start watching another viral video. There's a British girl whose latest upload was doing the rounds today. 'Oh my God! I'm, like, out on the beach looking for these fish... Isn't it mental? Oh my God, oh my God,' the girl says. She wears bright red lipstick and talks very fast. Margaret lived in blissful ignorance of her until she confiscated three phones streaming that same video today.

So the Head of Science, Dr Brown, who always sticks around for summer school, has insisted on this field trip. 'There are many hypotheses,' he told everyone in the teachers' lounge. 'But no black-and-white answers. I suggest we let the kids look for some themselves.' *Investigative*, he's calling it. *Observational*, the other teachers corrected. There have been all sorts of wild rumours. Radioactivity. GMOs. Oil spills. Margaret thinks it's completely reckless, to take kids out there. But Dr Brown is the most senior staff member, and the strongest willed, so no one disagreed.

Cooled a little, she moves away from the fan and sets her beer on the bedside cabinet. She fluffs a pillow and pulls a well-thumbed copy of the New Testament from her top drawer. She lies down, head on the pillow, and opens the book.

Roger is mid-sentence before she's even aware that he's speaking. She frowns, glances around the room. An open copy of the New Testament is on her stomach.

'Fast asleep,' he says.

She mumbles agreement and rubs her eyes. 'Time is it?'

'Just after ten. You should get undressed, honey, and go back to sleep.'

He's in his pyjamas. That's never changed about Roger: mid-Californian summer, mid-tropical thunderstorm, he's always worn – always will wear – full-length cotton PJs. She sleeps naked, except for underpants.

'I'm putting the AC on, Roger. It's a furnace in here, you know it is.'

'It'll cool down overnight,' he replies.

'No, it won't,' she says.

'You know I can't sleep with that thing on,' he complains.

'Just for an hour or two – I'll set the timer.' She reaches to grab the remote, turns to the unit above the bed and pushes an upwards arrow until the little digital read-out says 70 next to a tiny clock face. When she's done that, she looks up at him. 'Come on, sweetie. I had a long day. It was non-stop with the fish conversations and I feel stressed, OK?'

He rolls his eyes. 'Not that again.'

Her voice is stern. 'I need a good night's sleep.'

Of the two of them, she has always been the one that does the thinking, and the worrying. He is a phlegmatic man, solutions-focused and certainly not interested in philosophical discussion. Sometimes Margaret imagines there's a wall inside her husband's brain, stacked up to keep questions out and emotion in. Behind the wall is a little man, sitting on a chair, whistling, with a finger in each ear. In front of the wall are a few business meetings, a football game, a barbeque with friends and maybe a new set of golf clubs. They've had fights, in the past, about his ability not to worry. When the US had refused to sign the Venice Agreement six or seven years ago – the agreement that would deliver the single largest piece of environmental legislature ever written, finally – she fumed about it for days. She still blames her homeland for the sticky KL heat she lives in; they were the only western country not already converted to renewables. But Roger had just frowned and changed the subject to something he found more agreeable. She was furious with him. 'Thank God you're not raising my children, with that sort of resolve,' she shouted. It was the worst thing she's ever said to him, because he's the reason they never had children, whether they wanted to or not.

'What's the problem?' her mother had asked, about a year after the wedding. 'His swimmers no good?'

Margaret shushed her, quick as lightning, and gave her a stern look. 'Never say that again, Ma. Poor Roger.'

'Poor Roger? What about you, Marge? You should've had him tested before you said your vows.'

Her mother – dead now, God bless her – was a no-nonsense woman. No mincing her words. No keeping her thoughts to herself. Margaret said that maybe she didn't want kids anyway.

Her mother looked at her, blue eyes steely, and for once in her life held her tongue. Margaret knew she did, because the effort was visible. It was like she formed the sentence, rounded it off and then swallowed it back. Once this was done, she put a hand on Margaret's arm, rested it there for just a moment and then got up to leave.

'You could adopt,' she said just before she walked away. Her voice was kind. 'Or not.'

Margaret gets off the bed, pulls her clothes off and stands for a moment in the breeze of the air conditioning. How does she feel about this hotness that sits all over her, bubbling away? It could be the beginning of the end of something, for her. But she pushed the thoughts of that something away from her years ago. No use for it. She was happy. Is happy.

Let it just be the weather, she feels herself praying. Jesus hears all her hopes and thoughts. *Don't let me grow old.*

When the day of the field trip arrives, she's nervous. She snaps at Roger over breakfast.

She doesn't know what they'll find at the coast. Since the storm, that night in the brothel, tourist boats have been coming back from the coastline with photos. The fish are breathing air. Is that something fish can do? She shivers, imagining their slimy bodies.

'How many will we see, sir?' one of the students shouts from the back of the bus.

Dr Brown turns in his seat, puts an arm over the headrest. 'We may not see any,' he replies. 'That's the way nature is – it does what it wants. Maybe the fish won't show.'

There's a chorus of disappointed comments and cries from the students.

'What about the starfish?' one of the others calls.

Dr Brown raises his eyebrows. 'Oh yes, the starfish are still around. We'll see those, I hope. They've started researching them in the USA now, to determine just how they've survived on land this long.' He pauses, scans the back of the bus. The students have stopped listening.

'It's really interesting,' he says, lowering his voice and speaking directly to Margaret, the only person who hasn't looked away. 'The mucus they're excreting to keep themselves moist in air is also making their skins oxygen-porous. Like frogs and toads. It's called cutaneous gas exchange.'

'I see,' Margaret says.

'But as for why they've started breathing air, nobody can tell,' he continues. 'A team in South Korea has theorised that strand-lines are no longer hospitable for large populations; that acidification is driving the starfish out of the ocean. The same could be true for the fish, of course. I personally think that the storm we experienced two weeks ago simply washed the fish up and a few of them have discovered land to be quite liveable – this is also a popular philosophy. But nothing's proven yet, of course.'

There's something about Dr Brown's science theories that makes the fish situation seem less insane. Margaret wonders whether he sees an end to it.

'What about predators?' she says hopefully. 'There must be something eating the fish once they come onto land. Fish eagles?'

Dr Brown nods his head vigorously. 'Well, that's a very good question, Mrs Dixon. A very sensible question.' He runs a hand through his straight black hair. His jaw is slightly too big for his face, so that his teeth stick out when he speaks. It reminds Margaret of a horse. 'The fish *may not* be evading predation, not like the starfish seem to have done. You mention fish eagles – there are three species in Southeast Asia, though the grey-headed fish eagle is most widespread, so we may see one today; they look a bit vulture-like, in my opinion. Well, sightings of them *have* increased in recent days. I saw a little report from the KL Ornithological Society. But then the problem with this data, you see, is that sightings may simply have increased because people have been going to the coast to look for fish, and in doing so, have seen eagles. Cause and effect. It's a quandary.'

Margaret finds her attention lessening. Dr Brown talks, once you let him, as though he's the keynote speaker at an international conference. She sets him off, some days when she's tired and feeling mean, and sees how long he'll run for. One lazy afternoon in the teachers' lounge he talked for forty minutes about the potential of artificial technology in mimicking biological systems and viral epidemics. She barely said a word. He's an OK teacher, though. Enthusiastic.

'Well, we'll see, won't we?' she says, and then looks out of the window.

A shriek goes up when they see the first one. Then a rush to one side of the boat, and students pressed up against one another, each trying to get a look at it. The chatter intensifies, everyone exhilarated, swapping notes on where it is, which tree, how far down: *To the left a bit, no, the right.* Margaret feels curiosity tingling up her spine.

'Mrs Dixon, can you see? You must see it,' shouts Dr Brown, beckoning her towards the trees in question. He has a look of pure incredulity, as though he stands on the edge of human exploration.

Slowly, gripping the seats of the boat as she goes, Margaret pulls herself to standing and walks towards the commotion. There are so many of them piled onto one side now that the vessel has tipped a little, and the floor slopes. She feels unsteady. The students shout, some crying out in disgust, some pointing. Ten or twelve cell phones hang out over the sides of the boat, desperate to capture the scene. Margaret tries not to look at the phones, nervous that they're about to drop into the water below, that someone will then lean down to retrieve one and capsize the boat.

It takes her a moment to spot the fish. The mangrove roots twist and turn out of the water like tentacles, brown and densely packed. Between them there is little light, mostly shadows. The fish is not there near the roots, though. It is halfway up the tree, sitting in the crook of an upper branch. Margaret squints as she looks at it. There is something very weird about the way it rests there, propped up on two sturdy front fins. It is a fish in a tree.

As the boat drifts closer, the noise of the group seems to startle it – it starts moving, using long fins like legs, pulling itself further into the grove. The students make a chorus of *ooh* and *aaah*. The fish's eyes are grey and its scaly body shines with some kind of wetness. As it moves, Margaret's sense of reality is lost – she feels as if she's watching a nature documentary, floating in front of a screen, not here in a boat. The air around her head thrums. She watches the fish as it moves forwards with a slow, unstoppable drive. It seems to be aware of them. The hairs on her arms stand on end. She looks around her, eyes darting, worried suddenly that every tree near them is filled with fish. That she is being watched from every direction. Moving back to the empty part of the small boat, she peers into the mangroves on that side, to reassure herself. When she sees no other fish, she lets out a relieved sigh. She is pleased to be floating. Separated from it – from *them*. God knows how many there are.

'Disgusting,' she hears one of the students saying.

Another replies, 'Amazing, *la*. Look at it.'

More of them join the discussion, some desperate to see more, others horrified by the idea. As the boat drifts close to the grove, the long spindly tree branches cast shadows over the tour group and the skipper gives a burst of the engine. They are propelled forwards with a rumble, into more open water. As they move into the shimmering green ocean that sits between the mangroves, the fish is barely visible – it has shuffled off, further into the depths of its dry habitat. Margaret looks down, keeping her eyes focused on her hands.

On the way home, Margaret wants something normal to do, something domestic, so she stops to pick up *lemang*. She and Roger discovered the coconut rice during *Hari Raya* several years ago. It's been well over a month since the end of Ramadan, but the vendors are still there in a lay-by between the school and home. The air smells of ash and sweetness as she gets out of the car.

A fire pit is shielded by a line of leaning bamboo sticks. Each one is hollowed out and filled with glutinous rice, cooked slowly over the open flames with salt and coconut milk. Banana leaves poke out of the tops, to stop the rice from sticking to the bamboo. Unwrapping *lemang* is like undressing a person in wet clothes – you must peel off the leaves to expose the moist flesh inside.

Margaret says hello. Two brothers and their wives run the venture, and Margaret watches the women carefully turning the bamboo sticks to make sure the rice inside is evenly cooked. They don't wear gloves; they are too tough for that. One wears a yellow headscarf, the other orange, as though each has begun to mimic the flames next to which they work.

Margaret asks the brothers how they are. They look very similar, except for their heights. The taller one has a sliver of belly showing at the bottom of his shirt; the shorter wears a green baseball cap with an NY logo on the peak.

They tell her they have lots of customers and are doing good business. 'You're a teacher?' one of them asks. They speak good English, only throwing in Malay words when they get stuck.

She tells them that she only teaches at summer school. She shrugs as she says it. It's a meaningless term, really – no summer in Malaysia.

The brothers nod. One of them says, 'Teaching today?'

She tells them about the field trip. 'To the mangroves,' she says, and they look at her, unsure. 'Ocean trees,' she explains.

'*Bakau*,' says the brother with the green cap. With his hands he fashions a many-trunked tree in the air, makes a long whoosh sound though his teeth and then draws waves with his fingers beneath the boughs.

'Yes,' Margaret says, smiling. 'The mangroves.'

'*Bakau*,' the brothers agree, both nodding.

From behind them, the orange-scarfed wife speaks, a long sentence that ends with a frown. The taller brother replies, then turns back to Margaret.

He says: '*Ikan*? Did you see them?'

She nods. 'We saw the fish,' she says, folding her arms. 'Six or seven.'

The taller brother cuffs the other on the shoulder and makes an astonished noise in the back of his throat.

Before either can speak again, Margaret sees their eyes refocus over her shoulder. She glances behind her and sees other customers: three women getting out of a car. The brothers say a quick goodbye and move off, smiling. The yellow-scarfed wife brings her two bamboo sticks. They have been split lengthways, perhaps with a machete, and tied back together with string to stop the rice spilling out.

'*Terima kasih*,' she says to the woman. She takes the bamboo bundles and walks back to the car.

Everyone knows about the fish, then. The brothers didn't look scared. They had an excited look, as though they were discussing magic. But the fish aren't magic. They're real, living and breathing air. They're weird. Margaret doesn't know what will happen. Maybe their numbers will increase. Maybe they will be a new wave of evolution – they'll lead to some new world species that will be dominant in 500 years' time. A huge ecological shift. An image from a documentary pops into her head: a beaver. They were reintroduced to a river in Northern Montana and once they were there and settled, everything started working again, somehow. The other animals, the plants, even the shape of the river all went back to how they should have been before the poachers came. Everything balanced. It's not going to be like that with the fish, though. They shouldn't be on land. What will they do to the balance?

She clicks her seatbelt into place and turns on the car, shaking her head a little. She's planning to make one more stop before home, to pick up fried chicken to go with the rice. It's a treat they rarely have, in a vague hope to save their waistlines, but today she can't resist the thought. She wants the comfort of lemongrass and chilli, of greasy chicken skin and an evening in front of the TV.

Roger has the table laid when she gets in. 'How was your day, honey?' he asks, taking the shopping from her and setting it down on the dining table.

She looks at him, busy peeling open the rice and pulling chicken from containers. When she doesn't reply immediately, he doesn't press the question. She shrugs. 'I don't want to talk about it.'

Chapter Ten

Cathy

There's something about the contrast of every view in Cornwall. That sounds pretentious, of course; a kind of arty – *Isn't the light down here enchanting?* – thing to say. That's what all the grandiose St Ivers say, over on the north coast. It's what Mum says – she's a printmaker, and she lives in Hayle, not St Ives. And I'm biased, of course. I grew up here; couldn't live without it.

But what I mean is there's a simple sea-cliffs-rolling-hills charm to the place. A blue-green contrast. There's always a slant to the landscape as it leans out towards infinite ocean. Storm-battered rocks break the waves. It can be the Caribbean, too, on a good day. That's whimsical, but the sands really are quite white.

Ephie grew up among the northern peaks. She loves getting onto the moors. She feels at home among the yellow grasses and granite tors, where you can imagine feeling the stone radiating up through your soles. We go to Bodmin every summer, when the heather adds purple to the landscape. She makes me climb Brown Willy and we laugh all the way up at the thought that someone named it that. From there you can see Rough Tor and what feels like the whole of the county, opening out down to the sea. 'There must be some online smut about this place,' Ephie said the first time we went up there. 'You know, "someone likes it rough next to Brown Willy".' She laughed, a dirty little chortle from behind closed lips, and wrapped her arm around my neck, pulling me close.

We haven't been up there yet this year. There's too much going on by the coast right now for us to have made time for the drive inland. The fish numbers are still small, but it feels like a big change is upon us. I feel as though the world is tilting a little, into a space it wasn't in before. It's evolving. Ephie frowned when I said that out loud. A thoughtful sort of frown, not an angry one. 'Evolution takes generations,' she said. 'We *think* all this fish stuff is happening so quickly, but what's been going on under the surface and for how long? It's not like lightning zapped the sea and induced overnight genetic changes.' She snapped her fingers. 'This isn't a comic book.' She won't have supposition or wild overreactions. She wants sense and curiosity.

Around town there's been a lot of chatter. Nobody minds the starfish – that's the interesting thing. They look beautiful; maybe that's it. They move very slowly, too. All of us who live along the harbour have a set of stars on our windows; a lot of the houses further up the hill have them, too. They're creating a fish-tank effect, as though we've all gone out and bought exotic marine pets to admire while we load the dishwasher. The cod are another matter, though, and I understand why people are nervous of them. I'm suspicious, too. We all adopt the same stance when we discuss them: arms crossed, brows knitted. The cod are ugly. They're quite big, too, when you see them out and about on land, and they have that unsettling way of moving. Every time I see one, I'm transported back, somehow, to a little pool of sinking sand and my first meeting with one. A shiver goes up my spine. I've seen plenty more of them now, but still there's something intangible about the way they move, as though you see them doing it and then afterwards wonder how it happened. They use strangely elongated fins to prop themselves up. They have none of the angelic glide of the sea stars. Their tails flap against the ground, giving them a momentum that propels them along. And they don't open and close their mouths, as they do in water, but just leave them open. Each fish walks behind this gaping hole, up out of the Atlantic.

We can see them from the house – we're close enough – with binoculars. Often they seem to choose the concrete slope of the boat launch to make their exit from the sea – perhaps that is easier for them to move against. Once on land, they don't stray far. They mostly stick to the beach, between the low and high tide lines. We have seen them sucking at the seaweed, but I don't know why. I looked it up: cod eat crustaceans and other fish, not bladderwrack. Further up the beach they nudge the starfish in a way that looks competitive. As though the stars are the infantrymen, sent ahead to clear the path, and the cod are the commanders, now ready to take their place in the comfort of the warm sun. They're not threatening, though, the fish or the stars, so I don't know why I think of war.

On the local news – we watch it most nights before bed – they're talking about the fish more and more. The science and environment editor is getting a lot of airtime, conducting interviews with people in white lab coats who are sometimes from the same department as Ephie. They stand on the fringes of arbitrary beaches – Barvusi hasn't featured yet – and ask difficult questions. *The African lungfish*, they say, *have been recorded migrating onto land for the last five to six years.* Then they switch frame to a tank in a lab, with a long eel-like creature curled peaceably in the bottom. They have little legs, these guys, and a rudimentary set of lungs. And they're ugly, too. I swear they choose the unattractive fish for the broadcasts, to rally us against them. They don't show us a beautiful manta ray; they give us this eel-like thing. Something to stir up our Biblical repulsion. But anyway, *The cod don't have these lungs*, they go on to say (so why show us the lungfish?) – they seem to be using some kind of skin-based oxygen transfer. 'Bring out the toads,' Ephie comments. 'They do the same.' She's a real know-it-all, despite claiming to understand only one bit of science that's *mostly genetics stuff.*

When they've finished with the scientists, the news team usually interview a member of the south-west branch of GreenUnity who uses phrases like *plastic pollution*, *environmental disaster* and *ocean acidification*. They've coined themselves a term that they're using a lot at the moment: *neo-evolution.*

'What the fuck is that supposed to mean?' Ephie asks, the first time we hear it. She is not a fan of GreenUnity. 'They're not nearly as informed by science as they like to pretend,' she says. 'They campaign to make our world greener,' I counter. She scoffs. I like them; I send them money once a month.

I will concede, though, that they don't seem to have a clue what they're talking about when it comes to the fish, which would be fine for them to admit – it seems nobody knows much at this point. The oxygen skin-transfer thing was discovered in Monterey Bay, California, and hasn't even been proved to be the case for fish outside of that region.

'I guess giving something a name makes you sound more knowledgeable? More in control of the situation,' I suggest, when the GreenUnity report finishes.

Ephie shrugs. 'The research is happening, so it won't be long before we know more. In the meantime, the people who write these press releases just make up whatever they want.'

She is reading something on her phone, barely looking up at the TV. I pull my knees to my chest, curling up to her with my head against her shoulder. 'This fish thing isn't going to be a problem, is it?'

She shakes her head.

'It does feel like something's brewing, though, doesn't it?'

She doesn't reply, just carries on scrolling through her phone.

*

So we haven't made it to the moors yet this year. But I hope we do once the fish situation settles down. There are only so many news reports that people will watch before they grow tired of a topic. Then we'll pretend it never happened. Ephie and I also have another tradition to keep: it is our seventh wedding anniversary. The wool year. I tried taking up knitting, some months ago, to make something for her. I was hopeless. Too many fingers involved and no sewing machine. I gave up. But I had all the wool by that point, so I stitched indigo onto a backdrop of sea-green cotton, picked clouds out with white merino, looped an acrylic into rolling green fields. I'll never be an artist like Mum, of that much I'm certain. But we can hang it in the downstairs loo – a Cornwall landscape – and have a laugh at it every time we go for a wee. I should add a woollen fish or two, maybe, to the lower ground. I'll save the artwork until after dinner.

'Seven years, Cathy,' Ephie calls later, when she hears me coming down the stairs. She watches me. 'God, you're beautiful.'

I skim a hand through the front of my hair, pleased – I have made a little effort – and roam my eyes down the length of her as I approach. She's wearing her favourite jeans, the ones that hug the underside of her bum. Above that, her slender brown arms extend from the soft edges of a grey silk shirt. She has two empty champagne flutes in her right hand. An emerald hangs around her neck, a drop of the ocean, and her brown hair is pulled back, parted in the middle. She must have got ready while I was in the shower and sneaked from the bedroom before I could see her.

'Do you know what I found?' she says, watching me approach.

Her smile is encompassing. She is a wildcat, enticing me in. I shake my head, look at the glasses in her hand and assume it has something to do with bubbles.

'Come,' she says, taking my hand. Together we walk from the living room to the kitchen. She lets go of my hand at the dining table. I take a seat.

'Remember all that port we drank in Lisbon?' she says, putting the glasses down in front of me. I think back to our wedding day: the small group of family and friends, the Mediterranean sun. I watch her pull a bottle from the kitchen shelf. It is one I don't recognise – how long has this thing been there, wedged among the rum and brandy? When did she smuggle it in?

'I thought,' she says, placing the bottle in front of me, 'that it would be lovely to relive a bit of Lisbon. So I got some port. It's seven years old.'

She smiles, reaches for my champagne flute, pulls the glass into her hand and walks away from the table with it.

'But port's an after-dinner drink, so let's save that for later,' she says, putting the champagne glass next to the kitchen sink. She opens the fridge and leans in. I watch the way the splash of light from inside sharpens her cheekbones. 'We need something light now,' she says, turning back to me with another bottle in hand. 'The finest *vinho verde*, straight from Northern Portugal. It took forever to arrive. It finally came this morning, while you were out.'

'So that's why you convinced me to take Rosie up on her coffee offer this morning.'

She almost rolls her eyes, but she's pleased with herself. 'That's why Rosie *had* a coffee offer this morning.'

I smile. Ephie is cunning. Not quite cunning enough to realise that I knew she was up to something, but crafty nonetheless. I won't let on.

She pops the bottle open, pours two glasses and passes one to me.

'So here's to seven years married, and seven years in this lovely little ship of ours,' she says, lifting her glass to the kitchen ceiling and then leaning towards me to toast. She sits down, takes a sip of her drink, then another, and then uses her free hand to take mine. She grins, looks around a little. 'I think this place is the reason I love you so much.'

I brought her to Cornwall early on in our relationship, when we'd been seeing each other for about seven months and I was still wondering every day whether she liked me. Ephie was a tough orange to peel. She could be detached and sometimes churlish. She gave me personal facts aplenty – she doesn't like horses and she's not a confident swimmer; she lives to feel fresh air against her skin and only listens to music that's loud enough for her not to get bored – but never with much emotion attached. Cornwall helped me to figure her out a bit, though. We were students; we booked a B&B for two nights, the most we could afford, and had fish and chips on the beach. I got her drunk one night in a wine bar in St Ives, and she blurted out three irretrievable words: *You're the best*. We went from there. We came here, with a stop in Lisbon.

When we've drained our glasses, twice, we walk along the coast path to a restaurant two bays over, where the smoke of a pizza oven rises above the rocky cliff and the waves beat below. On the walk, I look out for seals. Ephie talks about work.

After dinner we walk a bit further still along the coast, until we're west-facing and can watch the sun go down. My stomach is full of calzone, brain soft with the comfort of a big meal. We find a grassy nook and sit down, Ephie sighing contentedly.

'I love life,' she says. 'This is perfect.'

We're both drunk on the company and the view and the wine. She leans towards me and licks my cheek. A long, wet stroke of her tongue. 'You're delicious,' she says.

I snort and push her away. She nudges me in the ribs, looking smug, and then links her fingers through mine. The sun is low, nearly touching the horizon, and the air is chilly. She leans closer again and puts her head on my shoulder, nose nuzzling against my neck. 'I think my bum's getting wet,' she whispers. Mine is, too. I pull her closer.

'We used to debate everything, remember? Politics, our favourite movies, gender,' she says.

'The way you pronounce things wrong,' I reply.

'I do not!' she says, shoving me in the thigh.

'You say debate, but it was mostly you trying to get me to take positions on things,' I say.

'It's good to have a strong opinion.' From the way her face moves against my neck, I can tell she's smiling. 'Remember that time, over breakfast, talking about whether human lives are worth more than animal lives, or something like that. I was winding you up and you were raging about the orangutans. You got so angry with me, but you're so goddamn nice that the worst thing you could think to do was turn the toaster up while I wasn't looking.'

I start laughing. 'Your toast was so burnt.'

'Heaven forbid,' she says, laughing, too.

I push her backwards so that's she lying on the grass, then lean after her. 'Don't fuck with me, Ephyra,' I say, nose close to hers, my gaze falling into the pools of her brown eyes. 'I know how to use a toaster.'

When we begin the walk home, the horizon is a hard line against a sky of grey, the sun long vanished. The night smells cool and the path winds before us, black between charcoal hedges. I hold Ephie's hand and lead the way. The stars will flicker on soon, lighting our journey. Beneath us, waves rush in and out from an unseen beach.

The wine in my blood has warmed me, made me soft, and I want my bed. We walk in silence. By the time we make it back to Barvusi cove, with its electric lights and humans, my brain is drifting into a place where dreams are the past and the past is the future.

'The ethics of procreation,' I mumble.

'Huh?' Ephie says, surprised from her hush.

'That was one of our debates. Whether it's ethical to have babies,' I reply.

'Yep, and I always said we could take more flights if we didn't reproduce. We were so young when we used to talk about that,' she says, her voice distracted.

The far end of the beach is beside us and some stars are overhead. The distant streetlamps of town cast just enough light for me to glance back and see her eyes on the sea.

'I was never sure either way,' I reply.

'Hey, a little you would be cute,' she says, squeezing my hand.

I go back to watching the path and try to sound nonchalant. 'We still could.'

'There!' she shouts, almost before I've finished speaking.

I feel her hand break away from mine. Her jeans rustle as she changes direction, forks off the path and walks quickly onto the beach. As she hits the pebbles, her footsteps start to crunch. She is a noisy shadow. She stops not far away and bends forwards, towards the ground.

'Look at this,' she shouts.

As I approach, sliding among the pebbles, she turns her phone to the torch setting. It splashes white light onto the beach and illuminates her face against the night.

'Oh wow,' I hear her say, and I move a little quicker, wanting to see what it is she's impressed by. As I draw level, I notice that she has stopped near a shallow rock pool. The water shows up black and smooth against the jagged shadows of the rocks.

'Cathy, it's a cuckoo wrasse,' she says, pointing a little to her left, in the direction of the sea. 'Someone at work was telling me about them the other day. He said they live among rocks, and eat shellfish and crustaceans, and he saw one washed up after the storm.'

I flinch a little as I see what it is she's looking at. A fish is perched surreptitiously on the rocks at the edge of the pool. It's like nothing I've seen before. It's blue and orange and yellow, patterned like a tropical beauty and nearly thirty centimetres in length. It leans over the edge of the rock pool, its wet head just above the surface, as though searching for something.

'Where has that come from?' I ask, taking a little step backwards.

'They're native,' she says. 'They're a really interesting fish: all born female, and then some of them turn into males during adolescence.'

'Turn into males?' I ask.

'Yeah, isn't that weird? They're hermaphrodites, basically. But that's not the weird part anymore – it's that this one is moving around on land. Look at it! That's stranger, isn't it?' She pauses and fiddles with her phone, maybe taking a picture. 'Only the males have this blue colouring. So this must be one of the change-lings. Isn't he a beauty?'

She presses the screen of her phone again, and then begins to describe the fish and our location, commenting for the video she must be recording.

The fish is undoubtedly beautiful. Its body fades from grey at the front to orange at the back and its fins are yellow. Electric blue stripes pattern its sides. This fish would do well at a Pride celebration. I could almost reach out and touch it, except its eyes are hollow and wet and dead-looking, and it's slouched on land like a lazy beach reveller.

Ephie continues to narrate, and the more I watch the fish, the more certain I am that it's aware of us, too. I expect it to glance up at me. I feel nervous, waiting for it to move.

'What's it doing?' I ask.

'Excellent question, Cathy,' Ephie says to the phone. From the reflection of her torch beam on the rock pool, I see her face scrunched in thought. 'Hunting?' she ventures.

Her phone makes an electronic shutter sound when she takes a photo. She takes two more, one click after another. Just as the third click goes off, the fish thrusts the whole front half of its body into the rock pool. I gasp at the sudden movement and clutch Ephie's shoulder. Beneath the water there seems to be a struggle. The back half of the fish, still on land, thrashes about against the rocks. Ephie shuffles closer, the camera recording.

When it emerges from the black water, the fish has something in its mouth. Its fat blue lips are wrapped around the edges of a mussel.

'Wow, look at that,' Ephie says. 'This land-living cuckoo wrasse has just hunted and caught a common mussel.' She drops the commentary voice and looks at me. 'I bet no one's observed this kind of hunting behaviour before, Cathy. This is so crazy. *Why* would it be out here and not in the water?'

I take a step away, wondering what the fish will do next, perturbed by its switch from languid to aggressive. The wrasse starts to move, too, wriggling around and shuffling off, with the mussel clamped firmly in its jaws. It travels with the same awkward fin-instructed wiggle as the cod. The colours of it fade as it gets further away, until finally it blends into the darkness and the oncoming surf. I take a quick look around me, to see if there are any more, but we're alone.

Ephie sighs and pushes her phone into her back pocket. 'I'm so pleased we saw that,' she says.

'Let's get home,' I reply, taking her arm and pulling her back towards the path.

'It's not just the cod, then,' she says. 'I wonder what other species will make it onto land.'

I shiver, the wind picking up as night lengthens. Electric-blue flashes are on my mind. Soon we might have a beach patrolled by glamorous air-dwelling cuckoos on midnight hunts for mussels. No space left for humans. The dominion of fish.

'Something's happened in the ocean,' Ephie says. 'To drive them out. Like, something bad has reached critical mass.'

'Yeah, but if that was the case, wouldn't it be affecting every-thing? Wouldn't there be whales and sharks and all sorts out here?'

'Well, I guess not all of them have these adaptations that let them survive outside the water,' she replies. 'The fish we've seen, and the ones they've got in the lab, have all got these elongated fins. Whales and sharks would be too big for that sort of thing... I don't know. Also, the life cycle of fish isn't long. Three to five years, maybe? So, over ten years, they could have developed an adaptation or two...' She trails off. 'Maybe these are juveniles that we're seeing. The offspring of the original adaptors.'

'Yeah,' I say. 'Maybe.'

Offspring brings me back to where we were. To the conversation I was prodding at before we saw the cuckoo wrasse. I was warm then, and now I'm cold and sober. It's too late; the moment has gone. It's slithered into the sea, along with today's roaming cod and that cuckoo wrasse. I shrug to myself. It could be back tomorrow, though. It could have legs. Stranger things are happening.

Chapter Eleven

Ricky

'I wasn't even halfway through my drink. Can't they have some humanity?' Ricky sighs.

Kyle drops their empty pizza slice wrappers into a bin and rubs his hands on his jeans. 'No one from our year was there anyway.'

'But everyone was just starting to talk about the fish.'

'Yeah, I'm kinda glad we got kicked out,' Kyle replies.

'What? I'd love to hear what some of those dickheads from Year Thirteen have to say about it.'

Kyle raises a hand. 'Do we have to talk about it every second? Anyway, one of those dickheads bought our drinks.'

Ricky rolls his eyes. 'The drinks we never finished. What now, then?'

It isn't the first time they've been kicked out of The Swan, but they still go in sometimes to try, on a Friday night when other people from school are out. Tonight, one of the girls from the year above was in there with half her class, celebrating turning eighteen. Ricky has a crush on one of her friends. Being asked to leave for being underage right in front of her probably hasn't improved his chances. He has eaten two slices from Stars Pizza and tried to forget about it.

As they walk, there's a whiff of sea salt in the air, a normal smell for Claremouth. The grey town has a single main road that slices right through to the ocean. Grids of suburbia branch off on either side – a retail park with a Countdown at one end and the Tasman Sea, blue and boisterous, at the other.

'Well, what now?' Ricky asks. He rearranges his cap. A soft rain falls from the sky.

Kyle pulls his phone out of his pocket. 'It's only nine.'

Ricky thinks the group from the year above will end up at someone's house, once The Swan shuts, so he'd like to hang around and see if they can be a part of that.

'Don't you want to go home and look for fish?' Kyle asks. He thinks it looks pathetic to hang around.

'Yeah, nah, they go back to the sea at night, don't they?' Ricky replies, knowing his friend isn't interested in fish but just wants to go home. 'I suppose we could go back with torches and check that, though. Maybe they're doing something even weirder at night?'

Kyle shakes his head. 'Let's go on the beach and see if there's anyone we know. If not, we'll head home.'

They walk down Main Street. Ricky wonders whether they'll see fish walking on the beach. He's been reading a lot about their appearance. He enjoys the conspiracy theories the most.

'Four possibilities, from what I can tell,' Ricky says. 'One: oestrogen. Its concentrations have been increasing in water since women started taking the pill in... when was that? The sixties? Anyway, it changes the fish's genes. Fucks them up, stops them hunting so well.'

He looks at Kyle, waiting for a nod or some other sign that he's been listening. He gets nothing.

'OK, number two,' he continues. 'Plastic. Several possibilities here: there's no food left in the ocean because there's so much plastic everywhere, so the fish are coming on land to look for something to eat. I know they banned the single-use bags and loads of other stuff, but they haven't cleaned the ocean up yet, have they? Have you seen it, mate? Those whales that wash up dead, and then they slice them open and find them stuffed with plastic bags. It's like, you know, when you go to your gran's house and open up the cupboard under the sink and there's, like, a bazillion plastic bags stuffed in there, all screwed up and twisted? That's what the whales' insides look like.'

'My gran's dead,' Kyle says.

'Not relevant. Anyway, so the other thing that could be happening with the plastic is some genetic thing, like with the oestrogen. Microplastic getting into their DNA, or something like that. Or maybe both those things are happening together. Genetics and the plastic-bag-inside-the-whale thing.'

'Right,' Kyle says. He thinks a moment. 'So in both these scenarios you've got mutant fish?'

Ricky nods, happy that his friend's engaged. 'Yeah. Like, not zombie fish or anything. That's stupid. But yeah, GM fish.'

Kyle lifts an eyebrow. 'Go on, then,' he says.

Ricky frowns. 'What?'

'You said four possibilities. You've only covered two.'

'Oh, right. Three: aliens have been living in the oceans for hundreds of years, colonising and waiting for the right moment to begin to take over the world. And right now, well, they can sense we're weak, right? Overpopulation, climate change, loss of biodiversity. It's all pointing towards a mass extinction. It's the perfect moment for alien invasion.'

'So that marlin we saw wasn't a marlin? It was an alien?' Kyle asks.

'No, it was a marlin. Don't be crazy. But it was being controlled by alien telepathy.'

When this gets no response, Ricky continues. 'It's great, isn't it? That's my favourite theory.'

Kyle sighs. 'And the fourth?'

Ricky shakes his head. 'Can't remember. Three, then. Alien being the most likely.'

Another sigh. 'I sort of miss your chat about conservation of endemic species, you know. Haven't heard about a Kākāpō breeding programme in ages.'

'Don't think the fish will affect the Kākāpō. They won't make it into the bush, will they?' Ricky replies. 'But hey, Mum's started buying this possum-merino wool for her knitting. Good use of the possums they're trapping, maybe. She thinks she's doing a good thing for nature each time she makes a hat. It's real soft.'

'Amazing,' Kyle says, rolling his eyes.

At the end of the road they hit soft sand. A group of driftwood sculptures crowds the entrance to the beach, standing spookily in the low glow of streetlights from the road behind the dunes.

'They're as crap as last year,' Kyle remarks.

'I like the one of the blue penguin,' Ricky says, pointing to a small statue at the end. 'It's way too big, though – they're only calf height.'

'I don't think biological accuracy is one of the competition rules, eh?' Kyle mutters.

The boys look around in the half-light. Ricky shivers. A cool wind comes off the sea, and the rain's finally soaking into his sweater. Kyle's only wearing a T-shirt, but it doesn't seem to bother him. 'There's no one here – let's go home.' Kyle says.

Ricky agrees. They move further from the dunes, until their footprints have sharp edges in the hard, wet sand. The tide's out and the sky is nearly black. The sound of waves rolling home echoes against the soft rain. Further up the beach, where there's a concrete promenade and a row of houses, orange light spills onto the sand from windows and lamps. Nearby, nearly in the surf, four men play football. Their limbs are silhouetted against the night sky.

As they draw closer to the men, Ricky stares in disbelief.

'What the fuck?' he shouts. 'Stop it!'

He marches across the sand to the group, leaving Kyle trailing behind. He can see now that they're not playing football. There's no ball. They're aiming their kicks at fish – he can make them out, silvery and limp against the half-light. The men's legs swing back and forth above the sand. One of the fish rises into the air, floppy, then skids to a halt further along the beach.

Ricky can see the men now, too. They don't look much older than him and their faces are angry. They are worked up from their violence. Each one of them is wearing white sneakers, and they've all got the same long hair. Ricky recognises them from school – they're in the year above. The tallest one, the one doing the most kicking, is called Donovan. He's the leader of the group. He's a bully. Ricky doesn't know the names of the others.

'Oi, guys. Come on, don't be dickheads,' Ricky says, frowning. He tries not to look at the half-dead things lying around between them. In the orange light he can see smears of blood across the sand.

'Nobody asked you,' Donovan slurs. 'Fuck off.'

'Yeah, go back to the pie shop,' another of them joins in. They all laugh. There's something slovenly about their voices – something uncontrolled. They're drunk, or high.

Ricky clenches his fists, but he keeps his gaze low and tries not to make eye contact. The fish lying on the ground are blue cod – he recognises them as the same type he and Kyle have seen come ashore. In this light, with sand smeared across them, they're brown, not blue. There's a dead one near his feet – he can see its lips puckering up to him. He sidesteps, careful not to tread on it. When the fish walk, slinking onto land in a way his eyes somehow can't understand, they almost don't look real. They look scary but beautiful somehow. This dead one looks different, though. Ordinary. Like a fish on ice in a shop window, but messed up. He prefers them alive.

It had taken Ricky around thirty minutes to catch on to the news about the fish walking on land. He saw it on someone's social first, then searched every forum and chat group he could find, trying to figure out what was going on. He called Kyle at 7am the morning he spotted a trumpeter on the beach behind their house. That was way better than a blue cod. That made him feel like a kid on Christmas morning. Since then, the rows in his spreadsheets have been stacking up. Blue cod, trumpeter, grouper. He watches them from his bedroom window, or the dunes next to the house. The numbers have increased slowly as the days passed. Kyle was with him when he saw the marlin – a great beast of a thing, with a dorsal fin like a sail. It lumbered onto the beach just north of Ricky's house, scanned its long-spiked face around the sand, as though looking for something, and then settled near the tide line. Ricky watched it for two hours, binoculars pressed to his eye sockets. Kyle got bored and put a movie on.

The ground is scattered with fish scales. 'Seriously. This is sick,' Ricky says, looking up at Donovan. 'You wouldn't do that to a dog, would you?'

Donovan stares back. Beneath his bushy eyebrows his face is full of disgust, like he's just found shit on the bottom of his shoe.

'These aren't dogs, are they?' he says slowly. He takes aim again and sends another kick into the head of the nearest fish. It slides across the sand, leaving blood behind. 'They shouldn't be here.' He kicks again.

His friends laugh. The fish should be dead. Its brains are half-spread across the beach. But it still writhes. Its mouth opens and closes, somehow. Next to it, only a handspan away, one of its kind lies broken, body torn in half.

Donovan moves forwards again, ready to kick, and Ricky throws himself at him, shouting, 'Stop it!'

He grabs hold of Donovan by the arm and tries to pull him off balance but he responds quickly, turning to put both hands on

Ricky's shoulders. He shoves hard, pushing him down, and Ricky lands on the sand with a thud. The air goes out of him.

'Hey!' Kyle shouts. 'Come on, guys.' Ricky lifts his head and sees his friend spreading his hands in front of him, placatory.

'Gonna stick up for your boyfriend, are you?' one of the nameless boys says.

Donovan holds up a hand to his friend. 'Come on, we're not homophobic.' He turns back to Kyle. 'But I don't tolerate people getting in my way.'

Ricky takes deep breaths as the air returns to his lungs. He shakes his head a bit. Blood pounds in his ears.

'If you and this idiot are an item, it makes no difference to me,' Donovan continues, pointing back at Ricky.

'We're not. Look, we don't want any trouble,' Kyle says. 'Ricky just gets a bit worked up sometimes. Ignore him. He didn't mean anything.' As he speaks, he walks quickly over to his friend, head low, and reaches a hand down. 'We're sorry. We're just gonna go.'

Ricky's heart is beating fast and, in his head, he's screaming at these idiots. Kyle looks at him. 'Don't,' he mutters, pulling him up. 'Just don't.'

'These fucking things are disgusting,' Donavan says, his voice loud over the waves. Ricky and Kyle both turn to him – he's gesturing, with fingers pointing and arms stretched, like he's ready to deliver a sermon, and they feel compelled to stay and hear him out.

'It smells like shit,' Donavan says, poking an angry finger towards the fish. 'It's ugly, and it smells like shit.'

He lifts a foot up, hovers it high over the head of the fish he kicked moments before. The fish's mouth gapes open, then closes.

'Go back to the ocean,' he says, eyes wild. 'You stupid, ugly fish.'

He brings his foot down: a fast, hard stamp. Beneath the white edges of his sneakers, blood and scales ooze into the sand.

He stamps again. 'You've – fucking – ruined – my – shoes!' he shouts, stamping with every word. His friends cheer him on.

Ricky breathes fast, still feeling rage coursing through his veins.

'Come on,' Kyle says, giving him a soft shove on the shoulder. 'Let's get out of here.'

They turn away just as Donovan starts speaking again. His voice is softer now, taunting. 'Aww, you boys didn't enjoy that, did you? Are you sad for the poor little fishy?'

His friends snigger. Ricky tries to keep his shoulders up as they walk away. He wants to look like he means business. He's terrified of an attack from behind, though. He snatches a glance back, but they've gone back to the fish, laughing and kicking.

'Glad you stayed down,' Kyle says.

'Absolute cunts,' Ricky spits once he's sure they're out of earshot. 'He's, like, mentally unstable.'

'Yeah, he's a psycho,' Kyle agrees.

Ricky's jaw is tight. 'Maybe he'll drown.'

Chapter Twelve
Cathy

Mum's terrace house in Hayle – the home I grew up in – has an orange door and a Cornish palm tree right outside. The windows at the back look onto the long, narrow garden, where the bird feeders are always full, and she claims she once saw a chough eating peanuts. It was long after I moved out, so of course no one could verify it but her.

We sit at the kitchen table, drinking tea and eating ginger biscuits. It has been too long since I've visited and her tomcat, Tina, eyes me suspiciously from the doorway. 'He wants feeding,' Mum says. 'He's greedy and eats every meal as though he's never been fed before.' Predictably, Tina is considered by all the neighbours to be a female cat. Mum is contrary and enjoys this deception.

She wears a tunic I made her years ago, which she's patched on the shoulder and stained with printing ink across the front. Her hair, short and curly and always a mess, is tamed beneath a green bandana.

'You look skinny,' she says.

'I'm fine – stop nagging.'

'And Ephie?'

I tell her Ephie's fine, too. Better than fine – she's working harder than ever and enjoying it. Mum makes a little hmm noise and I know she's keeping some thought to herself.

'Have you been working?' I ask, glancing at the walls, which are covered in prints and sketches, mostly her own.

'Nothing any good,' she sighs. 'I don't feel very creative right now. There's always stuff to write up, too.'

More and more she spends her time *not doing art*, as she says. She has a regular column in the *West Country Gazette*, where she interviews local artists and argues with the Editor over what counts as the West Country. She always talks about the time he tried to make her cover a sculptor from Bristol and she refused. Dorchester she allowed, though, because the artist took inspiration from Thomas Hardy, and *Tess of the d'Urbervilles* is one of Mum's all-time favourites.

'It's just another thing, isn't it?' Mum says.

'What?'

A sliver of late afternoon sun illuminates the teapot, and she picks up another biscuit. 'This fish lot. I know that everyone's losing their minds about it, but it's one more thing in a long list.' She sighs. 'Volcanoes erupt more, the polar bears are gone, half the coasts are gone – God, is there any time of the year now that we don't get floods? And have you seen the price of wine?'

I can't help but laugh at the last one. She continues.

'There'll be no trees left soon, you'll see. All this conservation and reforesting, but wait till it gets just a little bit worse. People will be out getting every last bit of wood they can find to keep warm.'

'And they'll eat their dogs, yeah, I know.'

Tess, good as it may be, is thoroughly depressing from start to end, which says something. This dystopian foretelling Mum's so good at, mixed in with a drive to exorcise a twelve-month battle with breast cancer, is what led to her last big collection – the one that got her shortlisted for the Turner Prize.

'Maybe it will be good, if this fish thing can wake people up a bit,' she says.

'Wake them up so they do what?' I ask.

'So they just stop ruining everything!'

She doesn't have the answers any more than I do, of course. And the practicalities of looking for everyday solutions – of understanding the world, piece by tiny piece, like Ephie does – are beyond us both. So it's like a weight, one that I hope the people with power and resources will do a little more to relieve. And things do change: they built the GPower hydro-plant at Falmouth, since Ephie and I moved to Cornwall.

We bought the cottage in Barvusi when the housing market crashed. It was the second year that half of central London flooded, and suddenly the big bad environmental change was here, in England. The rest of the country had been flooded long before, of course – the north-west coast seemed to be permanently under-water. But London. The foreign investors pulled out and headed for higher ground. Houses worth millions dropped to affordable homes overnight.

Ephie and I knew it was the only way we'd ever afford to buy, by jumping in just then, and so we did. And it wasn't just in London that people were finally scared. That same year the salvage efforts in Venice failed, and the Italian government announced that the city was beyond repair after years of tidal surges. Half of it was in the sea, for good, and they'd leave the rest to follow.

Houses were cheap then, especially coastal ones. We were lucky, I suppose. It didn't feel like luck, though – it felt like an investment in an unsettled future. The country was in turmoil, politically and socially, and nature – that great beast of a woman – was out to get us all. Ephie and I were still in Bristol. I was working at the university, still in the SU, and every day I and the rest of the team got more and more obsessed with the daily news, until it became all we ever discussed. We watched and debated as the euro slid down the currency ratings, and the pound soon after that. The dollar went, too, and the Americans did not like that, not when the yuan was climbing. We talked a lot back then about how bad things were looking. It was as though we hadn't even noticed anything going wrong for the ten years before. Suddenly, everything was against us. Ephie and I ran to Barvusi with our tails between our legs. We've had sea salt in our hair ever since.

'A lot has changed since we moved home,' I say to Mum, trying to sound hopeful.

She's at the sink, refilling the kettle, and it's like she doesn't hear me. 'The only thing I can seem to draw right now is fish,' she says. 'And what's the point in that – it's the last thing people want to look at. It's the last thing *I* want to look at.'

My phone goes off, vibrating against the wooden table and making us both jump. A picture of Ephie flashes on the screen.

'Hey, love,' I answer.

'Where are you? Put the telly on,' she says in a loud, fast whisper.

'I'm at Mum's. What's going on?'

'We're on the news, Cathy. Channel One. Quick, I'm on the news!'

I keep the call live and head to the living room, Mum behind me asking what's happening. There's a brief search for the remote. 'Can you see me? Can you see me?' Ephie keeps asking.

When I get the TV on, I see the front of Ephie's campus and a woman in a sky-blue blouse being interviewed. The news banner at the bottom of the screen says, *BREAKING: Cornish lab confirms bacterial infection in walking fish.*

'There she is,' Mum says, pointing. Ephie's still whispering in my ear: 'Have you got it on yet?'

Behind the woman in the blue blouse, the other staff are lined up, some in lab coats. Ephie's to the right, off-centre, holding her phone to her ear.

'I see you!'

I watch her look straight at the camera and wave. Over the phone, she giggles. 'Better go,' she says, and I watch her hang up.

'Who's that woman, then?' Mum asks, nodding at the screen.

'Must be the director – I know it's a woman. Shush, we'd better listen.'

The shot changes then, to one of the reporter walking down a corridor inside the building – through glass windows you can see people working at lab benches.

'This is where the team, led by Dr Ephyra Calathes, has been working long hours to solve some of the mysteries surrounding the appearance of fish on the land around our coasts. Using cutting-edge genetic testing techniques…'

I send a message to Ephie: *They just said your name!!*

'…Monterey Bay Aquarium Research Institute has used samples from across the entire US West Coast. These have been combined with samples from our own coastlines, collected in South Wales, Dorset, Devon and, of course, right here in Falmouth, Cornwall. The team have made an extraordinary discovery.'

'What are they saying, then?' Mum asks, frowning at the TV.

'Shhhh – how will we know unless we listen?'

They go back to the live segment at the front of the building and there's Ephie again, smiling. She has her arm around the person next to her, a small Chinese man called Jianyu. He's her right-hand man. They've worked together for years.

'What does this discovery mean for us?' asks the reporter.

The director in the blue blouse takes a moment to think. 'This is a good first step,' she says. 'Now that we know what's causing this strange new behaviour, we can begin to answer the next questions: how and why. By continuing to collaborate with research institutes in Monterey, and even further afield, we can corroborate our findings and work together towards a solution. Our sequencing so far suggests that this bacterium is a mutation of one commonly found in marine species across the globe, which explains how this phenomenon can be so widespread.'

'But what does it all mean?' Mum asks the TV.

'What next, then?' says the reporter.

'We carry on. We have a good idea, based on the wild type, that this bacterium is non-infectious to mammalian species. But that's something to clarify. As for the molecular mechanisms by which the physiological changes occur in these fish – that's the next big question. We've already started to work on that. The team behind me are exceptional, and they're working incredibly hard, along with every other department in this building. It's been a real institute-wide effort. We want to thank everyone here.' She glances back. 'And thanks to our collaborators at home and abroad, and our funders.'

'She's good,' Mum says, nodding with admiration. 'Didn't understand much of it, but I liked it.'

The segment moves on to a piece in Monterey, with the US reporter standing next to the aquarium. I text Ephie to tell her she's famous, and she sends me six smiley faces back. We turn the TV off.

'What *does* it all mean, then?' Mum turns to me.

'I don't know, but I'm sure I'll hear a lot more about it later.'

She looks disappointed. 'You're not staying for tea, then?'

Chapter Thirteen

Margaret

Summer school is over and Margaret finally has some time to spend on herself. She wants to do something completely normal, something American, so she drives into Bukit Bintang to look round the malls. The bright, regular indoor lights, the shiny clean floor tiles, the bustle of shoppers – it will all help to soothe the unsettled feeling that lies over her like a mist. She wants to get herself a watermelon smoothie, and drift about looking at cocktail dresses and swimsuits.

It's been three weeks since the fish started showing up in the suburbs. They move with an awkward slither. The first time Margaret saw one in the street, outside the house, she blinked to clear her eyes. She could see it, bunched up somehow on its tail, head up above the ground. But like the time she first saw that fish in the mangrove tree, her brain told her, with a deep animal certainty, that it was impossible. Fish don't walk.

The local news says they are mostly types of bream. They're about half a foot long, with yellow stripes and pink scales. There's a ghostly, sickly look to them, like they've been caught in the sun too long. Their large eyes have hollow black centres. They don't move very fast, but they seem to have no problem with dry land. Finally, Margaret has a reason to be thankful of the gate outside their front yard. It keeps them out.

On the sky highway she tries to keep her mind off all this as she cruises in the middle lane. She flicks up the volume on her Joni

Mitchell record until it drowns out the sound of her tyres on the asphalt. When she hits downtown, there's a rush-hour jam; she queues patiently, humming, then parks up in the big underground lot beneath the Rotunda. The escalators take her up to street level. Stepping over the threshold into the mall, the air conditioning hits her and all the hairs on her arms stand on end. She breathes a sigh of relief.

She doesn't often go to the Rotunda – it's too upmarket for her – but sometimes it's nice to look. Two women walk past her with their sunglasses on, both slender and superbly tidy, wearing clothes that are either too tight or far too elaborately poufy. One talks on the phone, while the other rearranges the large designer shopping bags weighing over each of her shoulders. They look rich; there's no other way to describe it. Margaret stares as they go past, and though she can't see their eyes behind the dark lenses of their glasses, she's sure one of them turns up her nose. Margaret looks down at herself. Cotton slacks and flat, functional shoes. The floor is so glittery she can see her reflection: a doughy white face and frizzy hair. She is nearly fifty, and she looks it.

She sighs, feeling uneasy with herself. There's a stationery store nearby called Bamboo Malone, where a poster on the outside window promises: *Luxurious, 100% recycled artisan stationery products.* Crossing the threshold, she picks up a pen from a lacquered holder. It is beautiful: made from a single thin bamboo stick, with patterns engraved across it. She turns it over and reads the tag on the end: 'Hand-carved by local artists and produced from carefully managed bamboo coppices. In support of biodiversity.' That explains the price tag. She looks a little closer, running a finger along the intricate patterns, and realises they are tiny waves. Around the top of the pen, so small, are pictures creating a narrative. First, a fish swimming. Second, a tilted fish, moving towards upright. Third, a fish tilted a little more, and so on. The final tiny image around the circumference of the pen shows an upright fish, tail parted like legs beneath it. It looks jaunty and comical.

Margaret puts the pen down and leaves the shop. They follow her everywhere. Even in the mall, she can't get away from them. And these businesses will jump on anything – it's disgusting.

There has been talk recently of some kind of bacteria that's infecting the fish. Margaret doesn't get what this has to do with them living on land, though. She just knows that people, in the US particularly, have started using the word 'zombie'. That makes her feel a whole lot worse about the whole thing. One news reporter from New York said they were 'basically rabid fish'. Margaret nearly had a heart attack, hearing that.

The Malaysian government doesn't want people to panic, so they're calling the fish a temporary disruption, and asking people to stay home. They brought the PM in for the propaganda campaign. Now his face is everywhere, looking down on them from billboards or staring up from newspapers. He warns people to stay away from the fish – definitely don't eat or catch them. There has been some illness, but it doesn't stop people. Margaret's seen it herself; they just gather the fish up into open arms. She'd never be able to do that.

Still feeling like a frump, she decides to leave the Rotunda and go to Soul, one of the cheaper malls over the road. She can get some lunch there, too. Making her way along the dazzling corridors towards the exit, she reminds herself she doesn't need any of these fancy overpriced clothes anyway.

Reaching the plaza outside, she feels the heat of the city hit her, and is confronted by a crowd of people. They are all gathered around the huge fountain that sits in the middle of the plaza, where water gushes down into a pool beneath. She stops short, scanning the crowd and wondering why there are so many people there. The luxurious quiet of the Rotunda usually extends some of the way into the street, but this morning there is a sense of excitement in the air. Above the noise of the road there's the rumble of many people talking at once. Margaret's stomach bubbles. Everyone in the crowd is facing the fountain, and she focuses her attention there, too.

She sees an enormous shrimp. She wipes her hand across her eyes, confused and blinking, and the shrimp is swallowed up by the crowd.

She must have seen it wrong, whatever it was. Margaret pushes some way into the throng, feeling the heat of other bodies close to her, keeping her purse tight in the crook of her arm.

It comes into view again – a giant shrimp, human-sized, with two great bulging black eyes. She puts a hand to her mouth, horrified. She realises that it is a human shrimp.

Then she sees a fish, then a second fish, then a starfish. They are humans wearing costumes. She looks away, closing her eyes for a moment, then glances at the crowd, wondering what on earth she's looking at. Some people are grinning; some have mouths open wide in shock. Others look angry. Many are holding cell phones up, recording the scene. This will be on the news later.

Margaret looks back to the human sea creatures. She feels herself getting angry. Why are they doing this? Isn't everything horrible enough without this, too?

One of the human creatures gets into the shallows of the fountain and starts kicking up water with their fish feet. The crowd cheers or shouts. The other giant sea creatures don't get into the pool – probably to keep the fabric of their costumes dry. Instead, they roll about the edges of the fountain, or jump onto each other's backs. A couple of fish chase each other in circles, round and round. It's like watching a circus show. Margaret's mouth slips open. There is so much detail in their costumes – silver scales, pink lips, flapping gills. One of the starfish keeps his or her arms up, pointing outwards, like a frozen jumping jack. Like a starfish. The shrimp is coral red, the tallest of the group. It has two long antennae sprouting from its head and what look like pink oven-mitts for hands.

'What the hell is going on?' a man behind Margaret demands in an American accent. She turns and sees a bald white head, pink and shiny from the heat. He speaks again: 'What are these degenerates doing?' There is a very specific expression on his face: that of a person who's stumbled down a rabbit hole and ended up somewhere they don't understand. Margaret turns away quickly, wondering if her face looks exactly the same.

She stands there a while longer, stuck somewhere between horror and fascination. She counts eight human sea creatures in total and decides they must be performers of some kind. Just like the people who made that bamboo pen, everyone wants to cash in. Around her there are parents bending low to children, pointing out the costumed group and laughing. Other people stand with their arms crossed, lips pursed in disapproval. Everyone is transfixed.

Out of the corner of her eye, maybe fifteen full minutes later, Margaret notices a pigeon flying above the crowd. It coasts, haphazard, over the heads and skitters to a halt on the floor by the fountain. It dips its head to the ground, to peck at something edible, and then resumes its jaunty walk between people's legs.

A *pigeon*, she thinks. *That's normal. Just a pigeon, doing pigeon things.*

She shakes her head and pushes out of the crowd, making her way up the steps and onto the bridge. Her legs feel wobbly and she holds the rail as she walks over to Soul.

On the other side she says a quick prayer: *This world is getting crazy. I don't understand it anymore. Send me some strength.*

When she gets home after lunch, she feels low. The sense of normality she was hoping to find through retail therapy hasn't appeared. Even a stack of satay chicken skewers and a large smoothie haven't eased her mind. She wanted to leave her unsettled feeling behind in the suburbs; instead, she found it, double strength, at the fountain.

She makes a camomile tea and forces herself to drink it slowly. Then she tells Roger what happened. He is watching golf on the television, his eyes half-glazed over, and it takes him a minute to refocus on what she's saying. As she talks, his expression gets more quizzical, as if to say, *What the bejesus are you talking about?*

Her cell phone is on the coffee table and she grabs it, searching quickly, muttering to herself and tugging at the cross hanging round her neck while she reads. She finds a KL news outlet covering the spectacle and scans the article.

'Look it, Roger, it says they call themselves "furry fans". I've never heard of anything like it before,' she explains, peering at the screen.

Now she sees the pictures of the human sea creatures again, her heart starts hammering like it did the day she looked up the symptoms of rabies. She can feel heat rising up her chest and back.

Roger leans in and looks, too. 'This is what you saw in town?' he asks.

The article on screen contains pictures from the fountain. Margaret clicks another link, and it brings up photo after photo of humans in head-to-toe animal costumes. She scrolls through them, lost for words.

She flicks back to the original news article. 'These were the ones I saw downtown.' She points at the screen. 'But it seems like people dress as other animals, too. Furry ones, like dogs. Or is that meant to be a fox?' She points again at the second gallery, where there's a giant fluffy creature with orange fur, a white belly and a long whiskered muzzle.

'I think it's a fox,' Roger nods.

She frowns. 'Oh, I don't know. Anyways, the ones I saw today were fish, mostly. There was a shrimp, too, and a couple of starfish. But mostly fish.'

'And what did you say they call themselves?' Roger asks.

'It says they're "furry fans", or just "furries".'

Roger nods, then lifts an eyebrow. 'But today they were "scalies".'

She shivers. 'Scalies! Roger, this isn't a joke. You should have seen the way they were dancing and running around – they must have all been on drugs.'

'But what was the point of them?' he asks.

She gives him a desperate look. 'I don't know – to freak me out?'

She taps on her screen again. 'It says here that "furry fans" are animal characters that display human qualities and emotions,' she reads. 'Oh no, and look here, it says: *Anthropomorphic qualities include human intelligence, and the ability to wear clothes, speak and walk on two legs.*'

'Well, yeah, that makes sense,' he says. 'Humans dressed as animals would be pretty anthropomorphic, wouldn't they?'

'Yeah, but Roger: *The ability to walk on two legs. Human intelligence.* Doesn't that sound like this fish situation that's going on? It's like these kids dressed up today are trying to, I don't know, embrace the fish. Show us what's gonna happen or something.' She rolls her shoulders, closing her eyes briefly. 'I don't like this one bit.'

She goes upstairs to take a shower. She scrubs herself all over, as though she can wash away the feeling of stress that lies beneath her skin. Every day now she wakes up and thinks of fish. They never leave her mind. She doesn't fully understand how she feels about them, but she knows it's not calm, and every day that she doesn't understand them or herself, she hates them a bit more. She can't do anything about them – can't fix that they're here and they're not supposed to be. Can't figure it out. She's useless. She can't ignore them either, like most other people can. Roger acts like nothing's changed.

She puts a Q-tip in her ear and thinks about how Roger's head has always been in the sand. He must be nearly through to Alaska. She pushes the Q-tip in a bit far and pulls it out quickly, feeling like she's just poked her brain.

Two or three women in her church group have locked themselves away to pray for salvation in the face of the oncoming apocalypse – now, that at least is an active response, even if it is a bit dystopian for Margaret to cope with. Jane, founder of the Mission, sends Margaret message after message about sanitation – what if the fish start coming into buildings? What if they get into the water system? What if they get into the brothels? Margaret ignores the messages. If a fish can get into a brothel then it can get into her house, and then she won't be worrying about brothels. She hasn't seen Jane or anyone from the Mission since the night of the storm.

Margaret does wish she could join Roger and everyone else in denial. One of the teachers at school simply doesn't hear the word *fish*. Another church friend just downplays everything. 'It's not a big deal,' she says. 'I've seen one fish, max.' But Margaret can't lie to herself like that. The fish are everywhere – what is the point in denying it?

She could feel better about the whole thing if it were local. If it were just some KL weirdness. She'd feel more confident then that the fish would go away and everything would go back to normal. But it's international; she's seen the news reports from all over the world. She thinks about going home, back to Northern California, and sees fish on the horizon. She considers booking a vacation for Christmas – a chance for the two of them to relax – but then imagines fighting her way along a beach of fish. There's no getting away from them.

She puts pyjamas on for the rest of the afternoon, giving up on the day, and goes back downstairs.

'Let's move to Boulder,' she says to Roger. 'Your old college town. You'd like that, wouldn't you?'

He fixes her with a look of confusion.

She shrugs. 'It's about as far from the ocean as you can get.'

Slowly, he nods. 'You know they have lakes and rivers in the mountains,' he says. 'Besides, KL is our home. You love it here.'

She sighs, to let him know that his rationality is unreasonable, and slumps into the sofa. The strangest thing of all – the thing that lets Margaret know things really have changed – is that she longs to see the marauding packs of macaques. Those ones that she used to fear would be a welcome sight now, with their claws and sharp teeth. But they have disappeared, and she doesn't understand that either. They should be out, roaming the streets and eating the fish. But they're gone.

It's not just the monkeys that have disappeared, either. God is off the radar, too. She's asked incessantly, but He's sent no answers yet about what the fish mean. If she can't find Him soon, she knows she'll go to pieces.

Chapter Fourteen

Cathy

I hear Ephie scream. She is in the bathroom and her short, surprised shriek makes me jump. I turn my ear to the bedroom door, listening. I can hear the noise of the taps running and, beneath that, the hydrogen boiler pulsing.

'You OK?' I call.

The taps stop running. Although I'm not worried that she's in danger – it wasn't an agonising wail, or anything full of terror, more like the noise of a person standing on a spider – when she doesn't answer, I get out of bed.

She appears at the bedroom door, looking like a joey that's been ejected from its pouch: half-undressed, goose-pimpled skin, confused.

'I just – I don't know,' she says. She shakes her head and smiles a little, nervous smile. She points one hand back towards the bathroom.

I feel worry squirm in my stomach. Something inexplicable has happened. The ceiling has caved in or the bath has fallen through the floor.

'You won't believe this,' she says, crossing her arms across her belly. 'And you won't like it.'

The worry in my stomach squirms a bit more.

'It's so bizarre,' she continues. 'I don't know how...'

'Ephie,' I say sharply. 'What are you talking about?'

'Look. Come on.' She pulls on her dressing gown and then holds out a hand.

There are only five steps from bedroom to bathroom in our cottage – two forwards, one down, one left, one upwards. While we traverse them, Ephie says, 'Don't freak out.' Obviously, I feel a bit freaked out.

When we get inside the bathroom door, I find a bathtub full of herring. A fish tank without a lid. I take a step backwards, hand over mouth, and then sit quickly on the loo. The seat is down, fortunately.

'They just – came out,' Ephie says.

I sneak a glance at her, just a quick one because I can barely take my eyes from the fish. She is staring at them, too. She is rolling up the sleeves of her gown. I look back to the tub. It isn't just a handful; there must be fifteen fish in there. Small things, silver and flickering, and quite beautiful, really. But in our bath. In our water. In the pipes.

'What will we do?' I mumble.

Ephie leans over and turns the cold tap on again. 'There can't be that many,' she says, but she doesn't sound certain. 'We'll just flush them out. Wait for the water to clear.'

The water rumbles into the bath and I try to imagine it is the peaceful noise of a jungle stream. I stare at the wall. The fish have made it into the house. I try to enter a stupor, thinking of that stream and a toucan flapping through the low branches of the overhanging trees. I don't look again at the fish. Don't even glance – just focus on the jungle and the jaguar prowling in the shadows. There is a crack in the plaster in the top-left corner of the room, near to where the beams meet the sloping roof. A cobweb, slightly dusty, runs the length of the wall. I want to be back in bed, asleep. There are fish in the jungle stream, and that's OK. Fish live in streams.

Ephie's voice rouses me. 'There have only been two more.'

Looking then, I see that the bath is full. The surface of the water sparkles beneath the grey daylight that comes through the bathroom window, and in the depths of the tank, skittering around between the glittering swirls, are the fish.

'Shall we eat them?' I ask.

She looks at me with shock. That's the sort of ruthless joke she would make.

'We'll put them in the paddy,' she says. 'I guess that's where they came from. And while I'm out there, I might be able to figure out how they got in.'

'Just open the drain. Let them out.'

She shakes her head. 'Then they'll just go to the sewage plant. We may as well save them.'

I shrug and push myself up off the toilet, wondering what exactly about a bacteria-infected fish is worth saving. 'Then I'll go and get the slotted spoon.'

She says she'll put them in the paddy, but I don't want them in there, not with the rice I'm eating most nights. She can take them to the lab and dissect them. To think I used to eat fish, with batter and chips. Despite myself, my mouth waters at the thought.

Of course, you can't catch herring with a slotted spoon. Nor can you catch them with a colander or a small bucket, as it turns out. They are fast, slippery little ladies. We have to wedge a piece of old jam muslin over the drain and let the water trickle slowly through. By the end they are panicking, flipping their silver bodies about in an ever-dwindling reservoir. Can they not breathe air, then, like the rest? I tell myself they could just be normal fish; I try to feel sorry for them, but don't.

Ephie wears rubber gloves to pick each one up and put it in a bucket of water. They turn into fish again the moment they hit the liquid, swimming and using their gills, not gasping in the bottom of my bath. She takes them outside, saying she'll investigate the security breach. I slouch to the kitchen and start making porridge.

'What exactly are you two doing?' I ask of Devon and Cornwall, the starfish on the kitchen window. 'I just don't understand what's going on. Will you be on my window now forever?' We have Dorset now, too, and Somerset, although I can't tell those two apart. The whole of the south-west ranges across the double glazing. I watch them a lot, wondering whether we will get to Wiltshire or Gloucestershire and then on, up into the centre of the country. I hope we never have enough starfish on the windows for my naming to reach the Midlands. Things are unfamiliar to me up there. 'Are you truly landlubbers now, or will you go back?' It's a question I ask them often: *Will you go back?* I should never have named them, though; it's given me a strange attachment to them. I want the fish to go back, the cod especially, but the starfish are OK to stay.

I am watchful as I fill the kettle, running the tap slowly and keeping my eyes fixed on the water. My tea is half-drunk when Ephie comes back in. She's pulled on a bright red fleece to go outside and her thick hair is bunched up around her neck, like a scarf.

'It's miserable out there,' she says. 'Grey and wet. Not cold, though.'

'Could you see anything, then? How did they get in?'

She pulls the fleece off and leans in to kiss my cheek, before reaching for her tea. 'I'm sorry, love, you always end up making the breakfast,' she mumbles. She takes the wooden spoon from my hand, as though doing the final stir will mean she's contributed. 'It must have been the rain,' she continues. 'Did you hear it in the night? It was so noisy against the windows. Anyway, I can't think how else they would have got in, although I still don't understand it. One of the paddies has overflowed and trickled right the way across the garden to the back corner of the house, next to the bench.'

'We have a flood?'

She nods. 'A small one. That could explain how the herring left the paddy. But not how they got into the water system.'

While she serves the porridge, I flick on the radio. A news channel comes out, loud and strong – a formal voice – and I switch quickly to another station, searching for music. Pop stars never have much to say about current affairs.

'I just don't understand how they got in,' Ephie says again, passing me the honey. 'We're on mains water here – it's not like we have our own system.'

I sit down and focus on the honey, swirling it into my bowl and watching it disappear among the oats. No use, though; I can't shift fish from my mind, or the pipes.

'What about the bigger ones?' I ask. 'Some of the ones in the paddy have got quite fat, haven't they? What if they're stuck in the pipes? Dead or dying and wriggling around.' I put the spoon down and fold my arms across my body.

Ephie frowns. 'I hadn't thought of that. Herring do grow quite big – too big to fit through the bathroom tap.'

'Shit.'

'No, come on,' she says, adopting a reassuring tone. 'The water's been coming out clear. The tea tastes OK. We let the last of them into the bath. We'd be able to tell if the pipes were blocked.'

'Listen,' I say, quietening her. The break between songs has come onto the radio and the DJ is talking. Among Ephie's speech I heard the words 'panic' and 'hysterical'. Definitely the word 'fish', too.

She cocks her head for a moment. 'Are they talking about—'

'Shhh.'

Heather in Penryn says they've spoilt the wash. No clean sheets for her. Jack in Swanpool has them in the kitchen sink, the bath and the shower. And St Peter's School in Portmellon is closed

– that's closed, folks. St Peter's School, Portmellon is closed. Apparently, a pipe has burst and the whole place is flooded. Fish suspected to be the cause of the blockage.

'Oh my God,' Ephie says. She puts a hand to her mouth but her eyes can't hide a glimmer of excitement.

I have to say, this is the strangest news report I've ever given. And we live in Cornwall. Things are always a wee bit strange round here.

'We're not alone, then,' I say.

Advice from local council is to run your taps until the water comes clear. Do not catch the fish or try to put them back in the ocean – leave them to it. Just get them out of the pipes and down the drains. Wear gloves. Try not to touch them. We'll be keeping you up to date with the latest on this...

'Well, that explains it,' Ephie says, scratching her head. 'Nothing to do with the paddy.'

'That explains it?' I nearly shout. 'There's fish in the water-works. Fish in the garden, starfish on the window, cod slouching around the harbour. That explains it? Ephie!'

I take a deep breath and run my hands through my hair. I want all this to be over. To stop. To not feel like a prelude of something worse to come.

'OK, it's not great,' she says. 'It's really weird. But at least we know it's not just us. Other people...' She trails off.

'And they're all infected, aren't they? With this bacterium you lot found out about. What does that mean, Ephie? Can we catch it? It is going to infect us?' I speak fast.

'It's not going to infect us,' she says, giving me her 'science knows best' look.

'But why are there fish walking? Why? It's too surreal. Will they mess up every part of our lives soon?'

She sighs. 'I don't know. But I have a feeling this might be the new normal, Cathy. Or at least a sort of hyper-normal. I'm sure things will plateau and calm down a bit, though. We'll get used to it. The world has been changing, hasn't it, for a long while? And we've been ignoring it. But now something really obvious has finally changed, and if we freak out and just want it to go back to how it all was before, that won't help anything.'

I know she's trying to reason with the side of me that's spent twenty years worrying about the state of our planet, the rational part of me that could understand that this might be a strange consequence of everything humanity's done – but all I can hear is: *We'll get used to it*, and I want to scream.

Ephie's phone rings from the other room. She rushes out and I stay where I am, chewing my nails, letting my porridge go cold.

'Hi, Ange,' she says from the lounge. 'Yes, we have. Yes, we've just heard on the radio. Yes, even in Falmouth. I know. So strange. Bloody horrible, really.'

I shut the kitchen door, cutting off the conversation. Angie Wright, our next-door neighbour but one, is the village gossip. She spreads news around like wildfire. It's easy for her to do; she runs the milk service – plant and dairy – with her husband Steve. They visit nearly every house in the village on a daily basis, so she knows everyone and everything. When she's not out delivering, she spends her time looking out of her windows, watching. We often see her waving at us as we walk on the beach. My very first encounter with a cod on land, that day on the shore with David Evans – it seems a long time ago now – was the talk of the pub that night, and well before we even arrived to tell the tale. *That's village life*, Ephie always says. People don't have much to talk about, so they talk a lot and very quickly about the little news they do have. Maybe that's why things have felt so insane around here these last weeks – the fish are a lot to discuss.

Ephie comes back into the room. 'Well, there you have it,' she says. 'Fish everywhere.'

'Eat your porridge – it's nearly cold.'

She picks up her spoon. 'They're sort of transferring me at work, did I tell you? To set up another project team. My group will carry on doing the genetic work on the fish, but Jianyu will take over. The new group will carry on with, and expand, the genetic work on the bacteria. Me and Marianne will be in charge of that.'

I nod, trying not to feel jealous as I see her face light up at the thought of Marianne and their science. 'What will you be looking for?'

'Well, Jianyu's group will carry on taking samples for sequencing, doing global methylation tests for silencing. Anything that can tell us about these mutations that are causing the fish to come on land. And we'll be learning as much as we can about the bacterium. That includes *in vitro* tests with cells from other kingdoms, not just fish. Mammalian cells, for example,' she says between mouthfuls of breakfast.

She looks up from her bowl and smiles. 'We're lucky to have all the departments under one roof and used to collaborating. Without the ecologists and marine biologists, it would all be a lot harder.'

'Mammalian cells?' I ask.

She nods. 'Among others. All in test tubes, of course.'

'It's making people ill in other parts of the world, isn't it? In places they're eating the fish.'

'Yes, they've had some problems in Southeast Asia in particular, haven't they? There's a team of infectious disease specialists looking at that in Exeter.' She scoops the last of her breakfast into her mouth and then stands. 'I'd better get going. I'm quite late. But then I guess half the lab will be late today.'

I wait for her to ask me how I'll be spending my day – what's on my endless self-employed to-do list. She stuffs her bowl in the dishwasher and leaves the room.

'Shall we have chips tonight?' I say to no one. 'I don't want rice.'

Ephie calls me from the lab in the afternoon. She says she's heard that the *wader brigade*, which is what they call the sampling team that go out to collect the fish, are working two bays over from Barvusi today. This is a reasonable distance from their base in Falmouth and makes me worry that the fish near here are particularly worthy of investigation, but she says it's just random.

'They could take them from our beach, though,' I say. 'Then I might feel more like walking down there again.'

'You shouldn't let them stop you, love. They're only fish, after all,' she assures.

'Yeah, but they stare, Ephie. You must have noticed. It's like they have a weird curiosity. Halfway between scared and intrigued.'

'That's probably how you look to them, too. Anyway, it's not like you'd be alone down there with them. There are plenty of tourists now.'

That much is true. The fish are a worrying spectacle, and nothing of a secret. The newspapers and TV channels have run the story far and wide. Our coastlines are invaded and, in response, tourist numbers have been picking up, despite the weather turning towards autumn, the days shortening and the news articles all carrying a warning to stay away. People who've eaten the fish in other countries have ended up in hospital. Local councils here don't want that on their hands, so they've convinced the news outlets to try to discourage visits. It makes no difference. People from the middle of the country want to see this fish phenomenon for themselves: the silver eyes of the fish staring outwards with dead steadiness, the slick wetness of their bodies that never dry out and the hopeless gaping mouths. Some of the fish have such a width to their slack mouths that I almost think I can hear the air rushing in and out of them, like wind through a tunnel. It makes me shiver. They smell, too. A fishy stink. Does Ephie pick these things up when she's in the lab, turning them over and inspecting them? How do they collect DNA from a fish – can you take a blood sample? Or perhaps they just remove a fin?

Because I don't understand all this science, I sometimes find it hard to have the same faith in it that Ephie has. I get distracted by the human response. In the States, homeland of conspiracy theories, the rumour mills are making people do crazy things. It's all an excuse for old divides to come to the foreground: white and black, Christian and Muslim, country and city. Here, too, the Defence League are back on the march, saying it's all about migration – can't we see it's a blight on Britain? I marvel at the human ability to bring everything back to vitriol. I think they're superglued to these soapboxes.

Since Ephie's research centre started looking into the fish situation, they've been partnering up with teams all over the world, including Monterey Bay Aquarium. This is cool, because my brother lives in California, on the banks of the Russian River an hour or so north of San Francisco, and on our last visit, two years ago now, we drove down to visit the aquarium. I've been addicted to looking at photos of sea otters ever since. They are fluffy and beautiful – why can't they be the ones to come into town and start lazing around the streets?

Monterey is connected to some of the best marine scientists in the world, and now to Ephie and her colleagues. She is buzzing with the energy of discovery. I have to remind myself that people *are* doing something. Ephie's doing something. That thought is soothing when I feel too anxious to leave the house. Then I feel jealous that she has these skills; that she can work on figuring out what's going on. She's lucky, to have all that. The only thing I can do is worry – a thing I'm very good at.

When she says she'll be late home, and not to wait for her for tea, I feel the walls of the cottage get a little tighter. I put the phone down and go back to the kitchen window, to Devon and Cornwall, who are silent and unmoving in the top left of the pane.

'Shall I go to the pub?' I ask them. One of Devon's little star legs wriggles a bit. I take that as a yes.

Chapter Fifteen

Ricky

Ricky finds Kyle standing in the surf, shoes soaked, hands in pockets, eyes trained on the horizon as though he's trying to see all the way to Tasmania. As soon as his phone vibrated with an incoming call from Kyle's mum, Ricky knew something must be wrong. They only spoke for half a minute, and then he put his shoes on and walked out to the beach.

'Hey, man,' Ricky says from a metre behind the surf. 'Your feet are wet.'

Kyle doesn't look round. When he came out looking for him, Ricky thought that maybe Kyle just hadn't seen the missed calls or the messages from his mum. Now, looking at him and the way he stares out at the sea, Ricky figures that Kyle's got the news. Something complicated is going on in his friend's head – something Ricky doesn't understand.

'You OK?' Ricky tries.

Kyle sighs. 'Don't want to talk about it.'

'OK. We do have to go, though,' Ricky says. 'Your mum's waiting.'

'I'm not going.'

Ricky's turn to sigh. Kyle's mum said that his dad had been out running on the beach to the south of town when he'd been in some kind of accident. They rushed him to hospital and managed to get him stable. Mary's at home with Kyle's sister now, waiting to go to the hospital. She'd assumed Kyle was with Ricky when she called.

'You have to go,' Ricky says, bracing himself for the response.

'Fuck off.' Kyle finally turns away from the sea. His eyes are red. 'He's only been round once, you know, since he left. And Mum messages me: "Your dad's in the hospital". *Your* dad. As though he's a total stranger. I hate it.'

Ricky doesn't know what to say. 'Your mum said he could have died.'

'Yeah, but he didn't,' Kyle says quickly.

'Come on, I'll go with you if you want. I can talk to him about rugby so you don't have to. Go sports teams.'

That gets a 'Hah' out of Kyle, but no proper response.

'Look, can you just get out of the waves?' Ricky asks, gesturing at Kyle's wet feet.

A long pause, and then he finally does move, taking three steps out of the surf and letting his friend put a hand on his shoulder. 'Come on, then,' Ricky says.

They walk the half-kilometre to Kyle's house and let themselves in through the back door. Kyle goes straight to the fridge and Ricky hears footsteps from the main room. Mary appears in the doorway and he nods briefly at her, as though the two of them are in cahoots. She frowns at her son.

'Where on earth have you been?' she demands. Kyle keeps his back to her and says nothing, instead pulling a carton of juice from the fridge and taking a swig. 'Kyle, you're soaking wet – you're dripping all over the kitchen floor. What's going on? Why didn't you answer my calls?'

Ricky feels awkward, watching this play out between them. He shrinks into the corner of the room, trying to make himself invisible.

Kyle turns. 'Sorry,' he mutters.

'Hannah and I have been waiting for you for hours.'

'I said I'm sorry,' Kyle snaps. 'You should have gone without me.'

Mary glances at Ricky, as though him being there makes a difference to what she says next. 'I'll just be in the other room,' he says, and she smiles at him as he passes, making him feel even more like the two of them are playing some kind of good-cop, bad-cop routine with Kyle. From the sofa he hears them talking in low voices and tries not to listen. A noise behind him turns out to be Hannah sitting at the top of the stairs, eavesdropping. She scowls at him. Her eyes are red, too.

Kyle and his mum both seem to agree that Ricky should go with them to the hospital. They pile into the car, with Kyle in the front, leaving Ricky in the back with Hannah, who starts to cry. 'I want to see Dad,' she moans to her mum. He knows what he'd do with Janie – shuffle into the middle seat and put his arm round her. Hannah's a bit older, though, and a pain in the ass. In front, Kyle looks out the window. Mary mutters, 'It's OK, Han,' once or twice, but otherwise doesn't say a word.

At the hospital Mary pulls up near the doors. 'You go in without me,' she says. 'Just ask for him at reception. I'll park the car and catch up.'

'Let's go,' Kyle says, looking back at Hannah. Her eyelashes are long and wet.

A receptionist with silver hair gives them directions to the ward. The lights in the corridor are white and the floor is sky blue. It's like a clinical version of heaven. Things smell of bleach. Ricky walks behind the other two and they reach a room called Tōtara, with a frosted glass window in the door. Kyle stops outside, studying the sign beneath the room name. 'Your dad would like this,' he says to Ricky. *The Tōtara tree grows on all parts of the North and South Island, and has stiff, spiky leaves. In the past, its stringy bark has been used as splints for broken bones.*

'No one cares,' Hannah says, pushing past him and tugging the door handle.

'He'd bloody love it,' Ricky says to Kyle, pushing him gently over the threshold. 'Here goes, eh?'

There are three beds in the room: two occupied and one empty. Machines and equipment beep all around. Hannah stops, waiting for Kyle. 'Is Mum coming?' she asks, looking scared.

'She'll be here in a min,' he says. Together they move further into the room, stopping beside the second bed. Tony, Kyle's dad, is either asleep or unconscious. His eyes are closed, and some sort of breathing mask covers his nose and mouth. His right leg is elevated in a sling, with a mass of bandages around the foot and ankle. A monitor filled with spiking lines beeps continuously beside him. Tubes come out of his arm.

'Daddy,' Hannah says quietly. She reaches out, and then recoils, scared.

'Shit,' Kyle says. He puts a hand to his head.

A man comes into the room behind them. 'Hello, are you Tony's kids? I'm Nurse Dave.' He looks at the three of them and Ricky mutters that he's just a friend.

Nurse Dave smiles. 'Don't worry, guys. He's OK, just fast asleep. I've got to take his blood pressure and give him his next round of medication. Maybe one of you can wake him up for me?'

Ricky shuffles backwards and Kyle looks away.

'I will,' Hannah says.

After a big sniff, she wipes the back of her hand across her nose – Ricky sees Nurse Dave flinch – and starts gently prodding her dad in the arm, whispering to wake him up. Kyle crosses to the other side of the bed and slumps into one of the two chairs near the window. Ricky follows, standing a little behind his friend.

Tony blinks awake and Nurse Dave says, 'Hey, how're you going? You can take your oxygen mask off.' He then pulls the long green curtains shut around the bed, cutting the five of them off from the rest of the room.

Tony looks around and lifts a hand to his face. There is a moment or two of fiddling and then a raspy, unfamiliar voice. 'Hey, you guys.'

'Dad, you sound weird,' Hannah says.

'Yep, bit of a Darth Vader thing going on,' he wheezes. He lets out a short, breathless laugh.

'What happened?' Kyle asks.

'He was attacked by a fish!' Nurse Dave bursts out. 'Poisoned. Paralysed. It's a miracle he's here safe and sound. Can you believe it?' Ricky thinks he looks absolutely thrilled.

'Right, very funny,' Kyle says.

A slow, rattling breath comes from his dad. 'No joke, mate. Pufferfish maybe. The doctor's closing off the beach.' He ends with a feeble cough.

'No way!' Hannah says.

'You can't be serious. They're closing off the beach?' Kyle asks. Tony and Nurse Dave both nod. Ricky thinks of Kyle standing in the surf.

'Dad, did you see it?' Hannah asks. 'This fish? Was it big? Why did it do that?'

'Didn't see a thing,' Tony croaks.

'You must have felt it,' Kyle says.

Tony pauses, steadying his breath before the story can really begin. Ricky thinks he looks about twenty years older than usual.

'I was running along South Beach, away from town, right? About halfway along I started to feel weird. Like my right leg had turned to lead, and my whole body felt kind of slow and heavy.' He pauses, drawing in deep breaths, then continues. 'I thought maybe I'd just pushed myself too much. I stopped at the end of the beach for a breather. Did some stretches. I couldn't catch my breath, though. I felt wheezy. I guess I collapsed. The doc said I was lucky someone spotted me from the highway.'

'And then what, Dad?' Hannah asks.

'I woke up in here. In the ICU, actually. Figured I'd had a heart attack, but then the doctor started talking about toxins in my blood.'

Nurse Dave is nodding enthusiastically. 'TTX,' he says. 'It's the name of the neurotoxin. You were in a state of paralysis, apparently. Your right leg is where the venom entered. Look—'

He carefully peels back the edge of the bandages on Tony's ankle, exposing some of the skin near his shin. All four of them lean in to see better. The skin is purple and red, and looks sore and angry.

'That's where the fish bit you?' Hannah says, looking horrified. 'Does it hurt, Dad?'

Tony nods. 'It aches and feels itchy now. At the time, it was like I'd just taken a boot to the thigh. Haven't felt anything like it since winter season of... '98, it must have been.'

'Everyone's been talking about it,' Nurse Dave says, nodding. 'Never had anything like this at Claremouth General before.'

'Woah, Dad, you're famous,' Hannah nearly shouts.

'Right, let's do your meds and then I'll leave you in peace,' Nurse Dave says, moving towards the bag of fluid standing next to the bed.

Tony looks from Kyle to Ricky to Hannah. 'I should have known. There was that news article. Saw it in the *Post*. About the fish attacking people in Japan.'

'That was a hoax,' Ricky says. 'Some teenagers trying to get their channel viral. There weren't any fish attacks.'

Tony frowns. 'A hoax? I'm not so sure.' He nods towards his trussed-up foot. 'It could have been worse, you know.'

Kyle sighs. 'Dad, you stood on a fish. It defended itself. It wasn't an attack.'

'But why was it on the beach in the first place?'

'They've all got this infection, haven't they, and it makes them a bit dangerous to eat. And stand on, apparently. But it's not like they're forming an army,' Kyle explains.

Ricky stares at his friend in shock – this is the exact one-sided conversation the two of them have been having, but it's always been Ricky talking and Kyle not paying much attention. Seems like he can be logical about nature if it means disagreeing with his dad, though.

'But they *belong in the water.* Why would they go so far from home?' Tony asks.

Kyle shrugs. 'Why would something leave home? You tell us – you're the expert.'

'OK, let's pause this for a minute,' Nurse Dave interrupts. His voice is calm. Kyle's face is red, his jaw set. Ricky feels awkward again, straying into this new family dynamic.

'Tony, I need to check your blood pressure now,' Nurse Dave says. 'Then we can let in your next dose of steroids and sleeping pills.'

The blood pressure monitor adds another set of beeps into the chorus already sounding through the room. When the medication has been delivered through some kind of syringe inlet in the bag full of liquid, and then into the back of Tony's hand, Nurse Dave says that they've probably got twenty minutes before drowsiness sets in.

'I'll leave you to it,' he says, turning towards the gap in the curtains and giving Kyle one last wary glance. 'But listen, your dad's delicate right now. So, behave.'

'Need to pee,' Ricky says, taking this moment to extract himself. He follows Nurse Dave out and as he goes, he overhears Tony say, 'Where's your mum?'

Ricky goes all the way back to reception to ask them where the washrooms are. They direct him to another part of the hospital, and he idles there for as long as he can, reading the signs on the doors and wondering why adults have to make life so weird and difficult. When he gets back to the room with Kyle and the others, he sits near the door and tries not to listen to them talking through the curtain. He can hear everything, though.

'I don't like the way things have changed,' Tony says. There's a pause and then he adds, 'With the fish.'

'Well, things have changed,' Kyle replies. He sounds angry. 'So we'll all just have to get used to it.'

'Yeah, but maybe it'll go back to how it was before,' Hannah joins in. 'The fish will go back to the ocean.'

'Yeah, maybe,' Tony mutters.

'No. There's no going back to how it was before.' Kyle's voice is firm.

He then says he's thirsty and emerges from behind the curtains. 'Let's find a vending machine,' he tells Ricky.

When they get back ten minutes later, with L&P, Coke and two chocolate bars, Tony's fast asleep and Mary is sitting in one of the chairs next to the bed. Hannah's sitting on her lap.

'You're back,' she says to Ricky and Kyle. 'Let's leave him to sleep. Come on.'

In the corridor Ricky walks behind the others. Kyle hands one of the chocolate bars to his sister, who stuffs it in her mouth, all signs of tears gone. She grabs his arm with her free hand and talks between mouthfuls. 'Oh my God, Kyle. Attacked by a fish! No one at school will believe me.'

He shakes his head. 'It wasn't an attack, Hannah. It was just unlucky.'

'Whatever. Kyle, what will happen next? They'll have to make sure there are no more fish around before we're allowed on the beaches.' She spins round as she walks. 'Maybe they'll, like, send the army in to fight off all the fish. But the fish will fight back and poison everyone. Bam! We'll all have dead legs.'

Kyle actually laughs. 'It's not really the dead legs I'd be worried about, but sure.'

Mary, two paces ahead, drifts down the corridor.

'Death by fish,' Ricky just about hears her say. 'Could be worse.'

Chapter Sixteen

Margaret

'What is this?' Margaret demands. 'Do you think this is appropriate?'

She brandishes the flyer in front of her. Sweat drips down the inside of her waterproof jacket. The vicar raises his eyebrows and then smiles.

'Hello, Margaret. How nice to see you.'

'Take this,' she says, thrusting the flyer into his hand. She unzips her jacket and peels it off like a Band-Aid, keeping her eyes off his face – she's too infuriated to look at him directly. 'Do you really think we should have that sort of thing lying around, Matthew?'

He glances at the flyer. It's crumpled and ragged where Margaret has gripped it in her hot fist.

'Where did you find this?' he asks.

Margaret throws her arms in the air. 'There's a whole stack of them in the foyer. Next to the receptionist. What, are we supporting this?'

He points a finger at the flyer. 'We're not using the word *plague*. But, of course, things happen for a reason, whether we understand His plans or not. All creatures are God's creatures.'

'Matthew, I know the story: on the fourth day He filled the seas with fish and the skies with birds. But there wasn't anything about the fish walking onto land a few million years later.' She pauses for breath and he doesn't interject, so she continues. 'Nothing about plagues of fish at all. I get that people are worked up. Gosh, I'm worked up. Matthew, this is a dangerous route.' She points to the flyer. 'You know I'm from the US. I know what it's like in some places back home. Gun sales are going up right now, and not just on the coasts. Phoney preachers are preying on the weak. They're drumming up fear so they can take advantage of it. They're using the same old lines they always do: *it's someone else's fault, blame the folk that don't go to church, anyone who doesn't fit in*, that sort of thing. It's old-fashioned and dangerous. And this—' she points at the flyer again. 'This is just the same. It's full of hate and anger, and, frankly, it's un-Christian.'

The young vicar frowns.

Margaret takes a deep breath, trying to steady her mind. 'We need to be caring and loving. What do Christians do in times of evil and suffering, Matthew? They help. But I'm just hearing a lot of hellfire and end-of-the-world talk, and I don't like the sound of it. Our church has to be a place of support and safety, right?'

He nods. 'It is and always will be a place of refuge for anyone that needs it.'

She holds out her hand and he passes the flyer back. '*Godless peoples bring threat to Christian civilisation*,' she reads from the front. '*God has sent this plague to curse our valueless society. Christians stand up for purity. Have strength against the atheist masses.*'

Across the centre of the flyer is a shadowy cartoon: a hooded, ogre-like man, bare-chested and hairy, looms above a city skyline. On his hood is the word 'Godless', and in his hands are clutches of fish. Across the bottom of the flyer is a call to action: *Save your soul – pledge your life to God.* Then a list of services by Revd Davis R. James, of the Fire of Light Missionary Baptist Church.

'Look, it's not even a church. It's a soapbox. The services are in one of the downtown parks.' She snorts. 'I'd like to see what the Malays make of that.'

The vicar glances at the flyer. 'We can't censor religious expression, Margaret.'

She sighs. 'For the time will come when they will not endure sound doctrine; but after their own lusts shall they heap to themselves teachers, having itching ears.'

The vicar sniffs. 'A warning from Paul to Timothy. Well done, Margaret.'

'You'll get rid of those flyers, then?' She wants to wring his neck – how dare he *well done* her.

'I hope you're coming along tonight, Marge?' he replies, ignoring the question.

She frowns, thrown off by the change of topic and wondering what it is she's supposed to be going to. Her routine is completely off in this new hysterical world.

'It will be great to see you there,' he presses.

'Yes, oh, I really wanted to,' she lies. 'But we have a… well, a book club meeting tonight. And, you know, with everything so crazy at the moment I think we've gotta try to keep to our routines, don't you?'

He nods solemnly. 'Yes, very good – it's admirable of you to set the time aside for such things. Reading certainly nourishes the mind. I'd love a bit more time to do it myself.'

Margaret gives a weak smile – jumped-up little punk.

The vicar lifts an arm and runs his fingers through his hair. He's wearing his signature black shirt, white collar showing bright beneath a face full of stubble. A crease sits between his dense black eyebrows, and his hair is thick and tactile. Once again, Margaret tries not to look too closely. She doesn't like how handsome he is. It's distracting.

'It will be a shame not to have you with us tonight, though,' he says. 'The Bishop of London is sure to give a very moving sermon.'

'The Bishop of London, right. Well, perhaps we should consider live-streaming some things,' Margaret replies briskly. She wants to end the conversation.

The vicar frowns. 'I'm not sure how that would encourage community spirit.'

She nods. 'Just a thought. Hey, Matthew, I must get on with my prayers. You'll get rid of those flyers, OK? See you later.'

Before he can reply, she turns and walks away, into the centre of the church where pews of glossy Malaysian oak stand out against the white-tiled walls.

On a Thursday afternoon in mid-October, when the rain is falling, the church is usually empty. The placid vicar is mostly out doing his rounds among the flock and, though Margaret has been coming every day for the last two weeks, today is the first time she's been unlucky enough to run into him. He's so unsatisfying. So mild-mannered. Sure, he puts some zeal on when it comes to the crunch – his Sunday sermons are pretty good. But if you catch him any other time... he's so meek.

She takes a seat three rows from the back and tries to steady her breathing. She can feel her heart thumping against her chest – it's been doing that for weeks now. She can't slow it down. Looking at that flyer has started her off again: thoughts of fish scatter her brain, pressing in on each other, one slippery scale after another, until she feels their cold skin press against her own, smells their stench even there, in the church pew. They're weighing her down. She shivers violently, shaking her head and looking around her. No fish. She tugs a hand through the frizzy ends of her hair. No fish. She takes a deep breath in, lets it out slowly. Sweat trickles down her chest, dripping between her breasts.

Come on, Margaret, she berates herself. *Get a grip. Say something. Ask questions.*

But what questions to ask? She wants to find some peaceful advice to help with the nagging feelings at the back of her mind. There are two issues here, wrapped up among one another. The fish, and – that other one. That's the one she's afraid to examine.

It started as a little niggling hollowness in her chest; it sat alongside the anxiety that had come with the fish, and it stayed silent for a while. Then it spread out a bit, then a bit more, until finally it was in her head, too, where it snaked into all of her emotions. Sometimes she doesn't feel at home in her own house. She doesn't feel like she is present when she drives her car down the KL roads she knows so well. She has an empty feeling, and normal things like the mall or church or good food won't cure it. Sure, some days are worse than others. But it's always there in the background – an emptiness.

She looks around her, glancing at the vacant pews as though for help.

For the first time in her life, she feels completely alone. He used to hear all her thoughts, and now it's like He's stopped listening. She's lost it. These past weeks she's just been thinking to herself.

It's the goddamn fish. They're ruining everything. She hadn't meant to get so caught up in it, but somehow she has. She knows about the evangelical movements back home because she reads every news story she can get her hands on, like an obsessive. All over the internet things are popping up, screaming one opinion or another at her. She hates that line, though – that *blame-the-atheists* line. It's so 'them and us'. Her parents didn't raise her as a good Christian so that she could go around hating everyone with different ideas to her own. She's supposed to love and care for people, even if they are different. That's the whole point. *Let's take it out on the fish, not each other.*

She listens to her heartbeat for twenty minutes, trying to slow it down, then gets up to leave. On her way out she goes past the beanbags and armchairs of the Connection Space and into the foyer. At the coffee shop near the church entrance she sees the vicar, chatting to the vendor. She wants to get past without having to speak to him again, but he smiles and beckons her over.

'Margaret, I hope our chat was useful,' he says with concern in his eyes. 'I hear you've been coming in quite a lot these past few days. Was it something specific that's bothering you?'

So the woman who sells the coffee has grassed her up. 'The world's bothering me, Matthew.'

He swallows and she sees his Adam's apple bob. 'Ah. Well, I know it can be hard to see the good during difficult times. Our world is unsettled, but we must have faith that God gives us the strength we need to see us through. Remember that He has a plan for all of us. That everything He does is for a reason.' The vicar shrugs. 'I will admit that I personally find the creatures a bit horrible myself. How do you feel about it all, Margaret?'

She opens her mouth and then closes it again. How is she feeling about it? She cycles through a few words in her head: *crazy, terrified, disgusted, confused.*

'I feel lost,' she blurts out.

His eyes open even wider. He glances very quickly over his shoulder, as though looking for help from the coffee vendor, then back at Margaret. For several long moments they stare at each other, neither speaking. His silence makes it obvious he has nothing to offer.

Margaret wishes she could take the sentence back. *Lost.* It is a very big word to go throwing around in church. She has exposed herself now. With that and the flyer outburst, he'll be putting her on some sort of 'faith watch-list'. She takes a deep breath and shakes her head.

'I'm just having a bad couple of weeks,' she says with a sad voice. 'Roger's been very busy with work, so I've had a lot of time to myself. And this damned humidity is making me crazy. I'm sure things will sort themselves out.'

Finally, he speaks. 'You will never be lost, so long as you have your heart open to God.'

'How helpful you are. I must go.'

She mutters a goodbye and turns away. As she starts to move, Matthew lays a gentle hand on her shoulder.

'Marge,' he says. 'You are never alone. Remember that.'

She sees seven fish on her drive home. She doesn't mean to count them but the number lodges in her mind all the same. Seven days. Seven sins. Seven fish.

They're like the monkeys used to be – they always show up two or three at the same time, as though they take safety in numbers. Packs of fish. They start at the edge of downtown, where the sky-line stops. The first two are on a square of grass at the edge of a suburban shopping mall. They're not big – she probably wouldn't have noticed them if she hadn't been glancing at the hair salon she goes to when her silver roots start showing. But she sees them there, half-upright near the trunk of a small palm tree. Their pale bodies look sickly in the bright sunlight and she looks quickly away, back to the road. The parking lot outside the mall is deserted.

All along the highway, the Prime Minister's eyes follow her. The words are in Malay and English. *Danger of death. Poisoning. Stay indoors for everything but essential business.* The campaign is semi-effective. A lot can be counted as essential business, church included, but the streets are certainly quieter. After the initial bout of hospitalisations, of which there were a lot, they couldn't risk the population making use of the cheap food source. Propaganda was needed. Margaret shivers, seeing those huge irises looking down at her.

Next there are three fish in a quiet side street just off the sky highway. As she takes the exit to drive down into her part of town, she sees them in the road. They're moving around, slouching in their indefinable way, almost gliding. Their mouths are open. Margaret grips the steering wheel tighter, wringing her hands around the leather. Why is it that so many people, Roger included, can completely ignore them, while she notices them everywhere she goes? She sees them and feels watched. Her chest gets tight. She can't think about anything else. She presses her foot harder on the gas pedal.

From her purse she hears the buzz of her cell phone. *Not now*, she thinks. *It's too much.* She gets news alerts from all over – the *LA Herald*, the *New York Times*, *BBC News*, *Malaysia Today*. They give her daily round-ups and notifications of breaking news stories. The *Herald* has changed tack in the last few weeks: for the first month after the fish's appearance on land they were considered a curiosity, happily tolerated because they seemed to drive off the hordes of rough sleepers from the Venice coastline. They brought tourists as well. But then there were a couple of incidents. The fish numbers just kept increasing and tourists started getting too close. A little girl grabbed hold of a large moray one day and lost four fingers. Then an elderly man stepped on something called a stargazer – the pictures of that fish were horrendous; Margaret dropped her cell phone so quickly, it clattered to the kitchen tiles and the screen cracked. Anyway, the man went into cardiac arrest and the paramedics couldn't save him. The fish was poisonous to touch, it turned out. After that they closed off the beaches and now the *Herald* takes a decidedly anti-fish tone. Beach tourism in LA is really suffering.

The *New York Times* and the BBC report on the fish with much more detachment. It's been nearly two months now, so while the fish stories are still there, they're not top of the list anymore. The readers they can pull in with snappy aquatic headlines must have decreased. She saw something about parts of England's water supply systems being invaded by herring, though. That was freaky, and for once she felt relieved to be living in KL, and not a small island where there really would be no escape. At least Malaysia is part of a bigger land mass.

The science reporting on the fish is less now, too. She's heard it said that people lose interest once experts start talking – but that's what she thinks there needs to be more of. The main problem is that no one understands, and on top of that they're not sure if they really need to care. Is it really a big deal? For thousands of people who don't live near coastlines, it's all quite a non-event. The image of the Prime Minister's eyes flashes back into her mind: how could it not be a big deal? She just wants everything to go back to normal.

There are two more fish at the end of her road, and for a second she's tempted to swerve right into them. But she thinks of the mess on the car – of the smell they'd leave behind. When her gate creaks shut behind her, she lets out a sigh of relief.

'You home?' she calls, pushing through the front door. It's only just six and she wouldn't normally expect Roger to be back, but despite what she told the vicar, he's been leaving the office a bit earlier recently. Her husband hadn't done that since her mother died four years ago and Margaret didn't have the energy to leave the house for two weeks. She needed him, then, to pull her out of bed and roll her onto the sofa – to shove a cup of coffee and a grilled cheese sandwich into her hands.

Is she acting helpless again? She shrugs and drops her purse at the foot of the stairs, goes to the refrigerator and pulls out a bottle of Yantai. Roger isn't back. The beer is cold and refreshing, and she drinks it quickly, feeling the bubbles pop in her stomach. When she's finished, she goes to the cupboard under the stairs and starts rooting around for a bottle of Australian Shiraz that she knows has been in there since last Christmas. It's been an age since she enjoyed a decent glass of wine, and she still feels angry about the flyer she found in church. Another drink or two will help.

She hears Roger's keys in the front door an hour or so later, while she sits half-numb on the sofa watching reruns of nineties sitcoms from home.

'Hey, honey,' he calls.

She watches as he comes into the lounge, taking in the details of him and trying to steady his image. He wears dark grey pants and a white shirt with a thin yellow tie. His summer colours – he's worn nothing else since they moved to KL fifteen years ago. 'It's too hot for black and navy,' he said then. He went out and got himself measured up for three new suits that first week in Malaysia – a grey, a brown and a khaki green. That sort of thing suited him then, back when he was sleek and young. Now he looks like a retiree from Florida. She smirks as he walks towards her.

'What are you laughing at?' he asks.

'Just you,' she says, grabbing him gently as he comes within reach. His eyes slip over the two-thirds empty wine bottle on the coffee table. A tiny frown.

'You opened the Shiraz?' he says.

'I just had to.'

The frown a little bigger.

'Bad day?' he asks.

'Shall we go away for Christmas?'

'If you want,' he says slowly.

'Let's go to Myanmar. We haven't been yet. Let's drink tea on the streets of Yangon. And pray to big, fat gold men.'

He raises his eyebrows. 'I've heard that travel is opening up there again. But praying to big, fat gold men? How would *your* guy take it?'

She waves a hand in the air. 'My guy's AWOL.'

Now Roger really frowns. He takes a seat next to her on the sofa.

'Is that why you've decided to drink all your Christmas present?' he asks.

He says it gently, but Margaret can hear judgement beneath the concern. She wants Roger to make her laugh. She wants him to drink the rest of the bottle, and pick her up and carry her upstairs, the way he used to when they were first married. She doesn't want this needling.

'It's just a bottle of wine, Roger. I haven't drunk it all.'

'It's from the winery we stayed at for our tenth anniversary. It's kind of special. I just thought you might have waited for me.'

She rolls her eyes. 'Well, I didn't.'

'Honey, what's up?'

She takes a deep breath and puts both hands to her head, fingers pressing her temples.

'Did something happen?' he prompts.

'Not really,' she says. 'I don't know. I can't explain it.'

'Just have a go.'

She shrugs. 'I went to church. I've been going to church every day. You know, to try to get some perspective. But I don't know – it's a waste of time. I'm getting radio silence, and it's driving me crazy, Rog. No feelings. No reassurance. No signs. Nothing. Then today, I bumped into stupid Vicar Matthew and his goddamn beautiful blow-dried hair.'

Roger chuckles.

'I swear, I just want to get my hands around that scrawny neck of his.'

'What happened?' Roger asks.

'What happened?' she echoes, wondering herself. 'Nothing. Absolutely nothing. He's no use to anyone.'

'But what did he do to upset you? What were you two even talking about?'

She waves a hand in the air and relays the exchange in church, ending with how many fish she saw on her drive home.

He droops his head a little. 'Oh, Marge. I've told you: you've gotta let this go. You've let these fish really get under your skin.'

She stands up quickly. 'I can't, Roger,' she says loudly. 'I can't, all right? It's like the whole world is changing around me and I don't know why. Everything's going wrong and you just say, "You gotta let it go, Marge, you worry too much; you think too much; they're only fish." Well, I don't think too much and I can't just stop worrying by telling myself to stop worrying. There are fish hanging around in the streets. Why am I the only one around here who seems to care? Even God won't speak to me about it.'

She pauses a moment, catching her breath, then rounds on him again.

'And by the way, what do you mean *your guy*, Roger? What are you saying – you've been going along with it all this time?'

He looks alarmed. She's suspected for some years now that his religious fervour is mostly only in support of her own.

'Of course not, honey,' he replies gently.

'Bullshit!' she shouts, waving her hands in accusation. 'I knew you had doubts, Roger.'

Her left hand connects with her half-full wine glass. It tips off the table and smashes to the floor. Red wine splashes between shards of broken glass, like blood seeping from a wound.

'Shit,' she says. 'That's just perfect.'

'I think you should go lie down.' Roger stands, blocking her route to the smashed glass.

'I can clean it up, Roger. I'm not a kid.'

He shakes his head. 'Come on, Marge. You've had a rough day. You're tired. A little drunk. Go lie down. I'll sort this out.'

He moves close to her and puts a hand around her waist, then tries to land a kiss on her forehead. She jerks away from him, feeling patronised, and stamps up the stairs.

When he comes to her an hour later, she's buried deep beneath layers of blankets. The air conditioning is set to sixty and the lights are off.

She hears his clothes rustle and drop to the floor, then feels the mattress compress beneath him as he gets in. His hands reach over to pull her close, but it takes him a moment or two to find her beneath all the covers. Finally, his arms are around her.

'It sure is cold in here,' he whispers.

'I'm a burrito.'

'A burrito?' he laughs. 'Are you really? Human burrito?'

'Yep. With guac and sour cream. And black beans.'

'Hot chilli?'

'And cool salsa.' She sighs. 'I miss California.'

'I'm sorry about earlier,' he says.

'Me too. I wish I could explain it, Roger,' she says. 'I don't know what it is about the fish – I just can't seem to find the words. They just... They make me feel sick.'

'It's OK.'

'And I'm so disappointed with church, Rog. It's always been such a guide to me. But I don't feel like it's giving me anything rational at the moment. There's just hate bubbling beneath the surface.'

Roger sighs and pulls her a little closer.

'But the Anglican Church hasn't even *said* anything much about the fish, Roger. We always respond, right? In times of crisis?'

'We band together in times of crisis, yeah,' he agrees.

She snuggles into him. 'There are literally fish *slithering around the streets*. All over the world. They're closing off beaches. People are getting stung and poisoned and killed. We haven't even set up a relief effort. The fish are like zombies. This is probably just the first thing, isn't it? Who knows what's going to happen next?'

He runs a hand through her hair, smoothing the frizz. 'I don't know what will happen, Marge. But I think you're right to expect a little more support from church, and to hope for some answers. It's your community, after all—'

'Exactly,' she interrupts.

'But who knows,' he continues. 'Maybe this *is* one of those tests that He's always giving people in the Bible. Maybe He's trying to find out whose heart's really in it and whose isn't. Is that possible? Maybe you could speak to your girlfriends from church and see what they think? Hey, start creating some of your own messages. You know as much as the vicar, after all.'

'That's true.'

He gives her a squeeze and lets out a little chuckle. 'Just, you know, have faith.'

Chapter Seventeen

Cathy

Each day is the same. I watch the news. It is a meal for me now; I sit and consume it, chewing laboriously over every bite. It lodges in my throat and brings tears to my eyes. Some stories are quick and easily digested. Others sit heavily in my stomach; I turn them over and over. Some are with me for days. Jim's story is like that.

I didn't know him – I've never known a single Alaskan fisherman – but I can't get him out of my head. They said the orca were infected, of course. Crazed, like the walking fish. Jim came into the headlines crazed, too. His eyes filled with tears when they interviewed him – the rolling banner underneath reading: *Killer Whales Attack and Kill Alaskan Fishermen* – and right in the depths of his pupils I could see the studio lights glaring back at the camera.

I first saw it online. When I read the details under the video, and found out Jim and his son Daryl were from 'a remote part of Alaska', I wondered what that meant. Isn't every part of Alaska remote? I imagined trawling for a living, sixteen-plus hours of darkness in the winter, nothing between me and the great snowstorms of Russia. *Snow and ice*, that was all I could think. I've heard that the US government has to pay people to go and live up there, because it's so bleak. But then I read on and found out what remote really means. They were from Kodiak. I looked it up. It's an island off the south coast of the mainland, mostly known for being home to the Kodiak bear, which is the biggest of all of the brown bears. They're nearly as big as polar bears. So within that land of snow and ice and desolation, there is Jim, stuck on an island with the second largest bears in the world. That's not a home; it's just a slab of wild rock.

Then it got worse. The orca made it worse.

I don't understand the intricacies of fishing. I don't know why I've spent hours now looking it up, trying to learn – but I have. My research started with an episode of *Horizon*. 'An industry in peril', they called it, because the walking-fish epidemic has had such devastating effects on small-scale coastal fishing. There is still plenty of deep-sea fishing going on, though, as there are no signs of infection away from the coastlines. To keep everyone safe, rigorous spot-checking has been introduced to any form of trawling. So a fisherman can go out, bring in a five-ton haul, and if one fish in the spot-check shows signs of infection, the whole lot is lost. I agree with the system, of course. We can't risk it. But it must be hard for these fishermen, like Jim, whose lives depend on the catch. Mind you, trawling isn't good – we banned it off the UK coast probably ten years ago now.

It was Jim's blank expression in the interview clip that really scared me. There was barely a flicker of personality about him, as though his soul had been snuffed out. He'd woken up that morning in a world he knew. OK, so things were weird: there were fish prowling the shorelines of his island, right there next to the bears (the bears won't eat them, we know that now – the wildlife learnt quickly to keep their paws off). But Jim could get away from all that, and the new regulations, by heading out to sea. He could take his son and show him a life that was hundreds of years old. They could fill their trawler net with thousands of slippery bodies, just like they'd always done. Killer whales stalking fishing boats isn't unusual either – I found that out through my reading. They've been chasing boats down in the Alaskan and Icelandic seas since forever. For Jim, there was nothing unusual about that day. It was normal. Until it wasn't.

Jim's a rounded character now, in my head. Not just a headline and a fifteen-minute interview – in my inability to rid my brain of him and his story, I've replayed every bit of his day. I've seen him walk the floors of a large, solid log cabin, one with hunting rifles locked in a chest at the back of the kitchen. The path out to the harbour is gravel leading to tarmac – asphalt, I suppose, if I'm being authentic – and Jim drives along it in an SUV, four-wheel drive needed because the island is thick with snow; it's November, after all. Daryl is in the front seat next to him, with scraggly brown hair curling under the edges of a black beanie that's pulled down over his forehead. That's the boy in the picture, anyway – the one Jim holds up in his TV interview.

Two other crew meet them at the harbour: Rudy, the first mate, and Alexei, a seasonal worker. I don't know what either of them looks like, but all four will be dressed for the blistering cold and the wet. Out at sea the salt-filled air will be freezing – the wind will cut like knives, finding gaps in any clothing and funnelling down them. Jim's had years of it. His cheeks are ruddy with burst blood vessels, his hands calloused.

Their vessel is named *Adrenaline*, and it's a curse that they were out on her that day. *Bertha*, Jim's larger boat, was not seaworthy. Since the storm that brought fish to land, *Bertha* had been dry-docked and under repair. *Adrenaline*, fast but small and vulnerable, is a wreck now. 'She was in pieces,' Jim says in his interview.

I see them next, far out in the Gulf of Alaska: land barely visible, white waves all around and a trawl net cast, its chains taut against the winch. Rudy and Alexei crouch near the stern, sheltering, while Daryl is in the wheelhouse keeping a steady course. Everything is typical. Disastrously cold, but typical. There's a glimmer of winter sun in the sky.

Jim said he saw only one whale at first. She was there, right next to the boat, darting along with them in a playful way. Orca are part of the dolphin family, which means they're intelligent and curious. They have fun. So there she is, black and white, with a fin splitting the waves above a sleek back, and Jim looks down at her and maybe even smiles, because that's the joy of Alaska. Bears on the beach and orca in the ocean. A land of giants. He doesn't even worry about his trawl at that point, because there's only her. But he knows the rest of the pod must be nearby, so he finds his binoculars and then finds the other whales. He's been stalked before, plenty of times, and he accepts it. Who can blame them? It's an easy meal.

There must be a moment in the story where everything tips suddenly into frightening. I haven't managed to pinpoint it, in this sick movie reel I have turning in my head, but there's a moment in Jim's interview where everything collapses. *I tried to save him*, he says at seven minutes and forty-three seconds. At that point something inside him breaks and folds in. By eight minutes I'm only watching the shell of a man.

I wonder if any of them were thinking of that documentary about the captive killer whales that got cabin fever and killed their trainers. That's what I'd have been thinking about. How they could play with me a bit before the kill – toss me about, pulverise the meat some. I hope Jim and his crew weren't thinking of that documentary. I hope they'd never seen it.

Once Jim had spotted the whole pod, he made the decision to turn for home. He told Daryl to keep a steady course, increased their speed a bit and hoped to get back before the whales went in for the catch. They nearly made it. The coast was looming, beckoning to them, when the whales started to ring around the haul and get their teeth in. Jim gave the orders to bring in the net and it came out with a hole in the bottom, fish slipping out of it like sand through an hourglass. I think Jim must have cursed the whales when he saw that. Or maybe he didn't. Either way, that should have satisfied them, that splash of escaping herring. The fish would have fallen right between the whales' teeth, while the gulls screeched overhead.

The whales weren't satisfied, though. They kept on following the boat, two on each side, until they were joined by a fifth – a huge male, Jim said, with a dorsal fin that must have been six foot. I can't imagine how a whale could be that big. How can something with a fin the height of a man swim around smoothly? What must it be like, to find yourself in the open ocean next to such a thing?

The whales ate the fish that slipped from the net, and then stalked the boat right to where the water was shallower. They corralled the boat into a bay, using their five bodies to swim beside it and push it off course. Once it was there, near the rocks, Jim said they started doing barrel rolls. He talked about the way they swam together, beating their tails. His eyes were unfocused but wide as he spoke, as though he was seeing something no one else could see. Only Jim made it back to shore. He was nearly dead. He spent a week in hospital, being treated for severe hypothermia.

This story feels like a turning point. I think that's why it's stuck with me. It must be why I've developed this grotesque obsession with Kodiak Island. With herring fishing in the Gulf of Alaska. With the height of the dorsal fins of killer whales. The last two nights I've gone to sleep with orca swimming round my head.

There's no proof yet that the whales are infected, but some scientists and a lot of news outlets have drawn that conclusion all the same. They'll go out and hunt that pod now. Bring them in dead, for sampling. Or maybe it will all be hushed up. The seafood industry would suffer too much if it were out in the open that the bacterial infection has perhaps now reached the deep ocean.

How long will it be, before everything in the sea turns on us? When they come, I will feel like we deserve it.

Chapter Eighteen

Ricky

'Krampuss, you little prick,' Ricky shouts. 'Not another one!'

Kristopher Krampuss is a large black tomcat who has never quite learnt house rules and, even after four years, still hates their other cat, Checkers. Krampuss pauses on the hearth and looks up innocently. A red fish, nearly the length of Ricky's forearm, hangs from his mouth. The fish's tail flicks back and forth, as does the cat's. There is a stink of ammonia in the air.

'What have you got this time? Krampuss, you know you're not supposed to eat them.'

Ricky grabs a cat treat from a kitchen shelf and shoves it in the back pocket of his jeans, then starts to walk towards the cat. Krampuss sinks lower, head to the ground, ready to run.

'Don't even think about it,' Ricky says. He opens his arms wide and crouches, ready to catch the cat. They study one another, eyes narrowed. The fish writhes again and Krampuss gives it another shake. Ricky drops lower, seating himself on the floor near the animals.

'Krampy, it stinks. And I'm so bored of you throwing up,' Ricky says. 'This treat would be nicer, eh?'

He pulls the Paws Fish Bite from his back pocket – a bit squashed from the quick sit-down, but it'll taste the same – and begins to flatten it out. The foil wrapper crinkles and the cat's ears prick up.

'Come on then, fat cat,' Ricky says. 'This is delicious. And that – what is that, a gurnard? – will make you ill. You know it will.'

He keeps talking, using a low soothing voice to try to coax the cat. But Krampuss is a difficult beast – mean and not one for contact. He wants the treat, but he doesn't want to get too close to Ricky.

'You're thinking maybe you can put that down, have this treat and go back to your fish, aren't you?' Ricky says, crackling the Fish Bite wrapper. 'Well, sure, let's just say that's allowed. Come over here.'

The cat stares for a moment longer and then looks away from the treat. The fish wriggles. Its skin is bright red, almost the colour of fresh blood, and for its size it has enormous front fins, like red-brown fans sticking out from its body. One is caught up and crumpled in the cat's mouth. Ricky watches Krampuss slowly place the fish on the hearthstone. The moment it hits the cold floor, it flips its tail, pushing itself onto its belly, preparing to make a run for it. Ricky feels the hairs go up on the back of his neck.

Krampuss reaches out with a paw and pins the fish to the ground.

'Jesus,' Ricky says, noticing as the red-scaled body begins to thrash that it is missing an eye, and that its tail is split. 'Do you really have to?' he asks the cat.

Krampuss ignores him and begins to play. The fish's mouth, wide open and gaping, seems to scream for help. Its gums are sky-blue and fleshy – Ricky can almost see the whole way down its throat. Its cold wet eyes, black with a rim of yellow, show nothing. It lumbers onto its fins again, wet tail dragging against the floor, the wound oozing.

Ricky stays silent and starts counting in his head. He needs to let Krampuss focus just long enough on this cat-and-mouse game and tries not to flinch as the teasing begins. A paw in front, a knock from behind, a bite on the tail. When Ricky has counted to sixty, and then to sixty all over again, he starts to lean forwards. As he gets closer, the stink of the fish becomes stronger and he wrinkles his nose. Is this thing worth saving?

With another knock of the paw, the fish flops flat on its belly, all strength lost, fins splayed out weakly. Like a fish should be. Ricky stares at it, pretending to pay no attention to the cat. When he feels he's close enough, he swipes violently with an arm and sends Krampuss hissing away, leaving his fish behind.

Ricky hisses back and watches the cat's fur rise along his spine. 'Out!' he bellows, and Krampuss finally runs.

He turns back to the fish, crouching lower to look at it, but is distracted by his phone buzzing in his pocket. When he pulls it out, Dad's face is there on the screen, showing up an incoming call.

Ricky answers. On the other end of the phone Dad's voice is excited and his words tumble out. Something about the harbour, boats and whales. It makes no sense.

'Slow down,' Ricky says. 'What're you on about?'

He listens as Dad tries to explain again.

'Why are you at the harbour?' Ricky asks, confused.

'Getting some breakfast at Trevor's, of course,' Dad replies. 'On the way back from this morning's job. Mate, you've got to come down here,' he says. 'Never seen anything like it.' His tone is mischievous.

'It'll take me ages to get there,' Ricky complains.

Dad tells him to get on his bike.

Ricky groans, but agrees. 'Be there in fifteen,' he says.

He ends the call and puts the phone away. Dad's excitement is infectious. Ricky wants to know what the fuss is about, but he needs to sort this business with Krampuss and the fish first. Get a move on. He turns back to the fireplace and sees that the fish has hauled itself a little over a metre away from the hearth, and is still moving. He rushes over and bends to pick it up, but then remembers Kyle's dad lying in the hospital ward and thinks better of it. He grabs a pair of rubber gloves from under the kitchen sink. Will that work? Can fish venom go through rubber? Is it even a venomous fish? *Shit, just get on with it.*

Now the fish is nearly at the living room door, ready to enter the hallway. Ricky scoops it up with both hands, trying not to imagine that he's getting short of breath, trying to ignore the way the fish squirms about, flexing its long body between his palms. He should take it back to the ocean, to where Krampuss can't get to it, but he doesn't have time. Instead, he runs through the back garden and down the slope to the edge of the beach and puts the fish gently on the pebbles. It can make its own way home. He stops there for a moment and looks around. He feels bad that he hasn't taken more care of this creature, with its broken tail and ragged fins. There are other fish about on the beach – some alive. He can smell that some of them have died. Will this one join them? He shakes his head and turns away.

When he makes it back to the house, Krampuss has returned and is sitting on the hearthstone next to a small pool of vomit.

'Fuck you,' Ricky says. 'It's your own fault.'

He turns away from the cat and runs to his room. His sneakers are on his bedroom floor and he pushes his feet into them, while spraying deodorant under his arms. He glances out of the window, sees grey sky, and decides to pull a sweater over his head.

When he gets to the garage, he doesn't bother to check the bike tyres – they're probably soft; he never cycles. No flats, that's the main thing. As he pedals out of the drive, he thinks of Krampuss, sitting next to his own sick. *Stupid cat*. Ricky feels a twinge of guilt.

With the road peeling out before him, he feels the breeze ruffle the edges of his hair and realises he's forgotten his cap. He hopes there's no one from school at the harbour – he didn't even look in the mirror before he came out. His hair must be greasy. How could he leave without a cap? *Just keep pedalling*. His breathing gets heavier as the road goes on, his legs tired.

The sea is calm today, a quiet rumble against the sand, and it feels like there's sun somewhere nearby, behind the clouds. It's getting warm as summer comes on. Ricky sweats beneath his sweater. When he comes to the first roundabout outside town, he's thankful of a couple of cars pulling out to his right. His back brakes squeak as he slows. Even after the cars have gone, he still pauses, one foot on the ground, catching his breath.

When he's ready, he pedals round to the third exit, leading to Main Street. He cycles past the shops and then turns left halfway down to veer off towards the harbour. No ambulances or sirens, no police cars speeding through the streets. Maybe Dad's having a laugh, or is just bored and wants some company. But the tone in his voice...

Ricky leaves the road at East Street and picks up the path that leads to the footbridge over the Clare. From there he sees that the tide is in. The river is a swollen grey mass of water, no sticky brown mudbanks in sight.

He gets some speed coming off the bridge and takes the final corner too fast, nearly toppling off the bike, back tyre skidding. The clouds shift, letting sun through a crack, and up ahead he sees the ocean glittering. There isn't much to Claremouth harbour, just a small industrial site and a rectangle of water filled with drab fishing boats. Some tourists make it in now and again, their white yachts showing up like pearls, but the rest is just peeling paintwork. Ricky passes Cut'n'Edge Carpets and the Claremouth Seafood Company, before the harbour comes fully into view. He sees a group of three men standing near the water's edge, hands on hips or arms folded. One of them raises a hand and waves.

When Ricky reaches them, he sees no boyish excitement in Dad's face. No grin. He looks sad, almost, or concerned. The other men are jovial, though.

'You must be Ricky,' one of them says, smiling. 'Nice to meet you, lad.' He holds a large, rough hand out for Ricky to shake. 'We've had quite a morning here.'

Dad takes a deep breath, like he's preparing himself for something.

'What's going on?' Ricky asks.

Dad shakes his head. 'Mate, you're not gonna like this. I tried to call...'

Ricky pulls his phone out of his pocket and frowns at the two missed calls. 'I was cycling.'

Dad shuffles from one foot to the other. 'Well, they just all got a bit... overexcited.'

'What are you on about?' Ricky says.

'Come on, then,' Dad says, shrugging. 'See you guys later.' He nods to the other two men and leads Ricky away, towards the boats.

As they turn the corner, the whole harbour finally comes into view and Ricky sees a police car. It's parked up next to the building where the harbourmaster lives and where Trevor, a retired fisherman, serves bacon sandwiches, and fish and chips. Ricky feels nervous. What will he not like?

'Over here,' Dad says, turning left and walking close to the water's edge.

The boats near the harbour mouth, next to Trevor's, are packed tight, but start to thin out as Ricky and his dad walk on. Up ahead, between the gaps in the floating pontoons, Ricky sees a small fishing boat on its side. Its dirty red hull bobs above the water. 'Shit,' he says. 'How did that happen?'

Dad takes another deep breath.

'So, there were these three whales. Tommy reckoned sharks, but they were definitely whales. They got in the harbour. Just swam right in and went crazy.'

'What do you mean "went crazy"?' Ricky asks.

'I don't know – it was like they started thrashing about, slapping their tails, making waves and jumping out of the water, almost. Swimming into things. I called you when they first appeared, because I knew you'd want to see them. Really nice, they were. Sleek. Even if they were crazy.'

'Well, where are they now? Did you get them back out into the main ocean?'

Dad grimaces. 'Two of them just sort of swam out on their own.'

They've nearly reached the far side of the harbour now and Ricky feels worried. Dad isn't telling him the whole story. In the pause in their conversation he hears shouts and cheers up ahead.

Dad stops walking, drawing up abruptly. 'There,' he says, pointing.

Across the water, half-lying on one of the pontoons, Ricky sees the huge body of a whale. Its skin is slick and black, its wide, flat tail drooping into the water. There's a ring of men standing nearby, looking at it. They're animated, each one of them pacing on the spot or talking, with arms waving. Ricky sees one of them walk to the whale and hold out his phone, posing for a photo.

'It's beached itself,' Ricky says, starting to run towards the whale. 'Why haven't they pushed it back in?'

When he's two boats away, he notices that the water on the far side of the creature is red. Ricky slows his pace. As he draws even closer, he sees two metal harpoons sticking from the whale's side.

Dad catches him up. 'Sorry, mate,' he says.

Ricky shakes his head. 'They killed it.'

'Yeah. It was going crazy, Ricky. It turned that boat over.'

'But they didn't have to kill it.'

'It was ill. Must have been. You know, like the fish.'

'Right, well, I'll just go over to the hospital and kill everyone there who's ill, shall I?' Ricky snaps.

Dad raises his palms. 'You know this isn't the same. It's an animal, Ricky. Anyway, when I called you, they'd only just come into the harbour. They were just swimming around, causing some trouble. I didn't know this was going to happen.'

Ricky looks at the ring of men standing near the whale. 'And now they're taking photos to celebrate.'

He feels tears building in his eyes and blinks them back. He wants to go closer – to put a hand against the animal and feel its smooth skin. He's never seen a whale up close before. He'd like to protect it from the cameras and jokes of the gathered men. But he's afraid he'll do something stupid. He'll get angry and start a fight, or start crying in front of them. They'll laugh at him. Dad will be embarrassed.

Ricky sniffs and takes one last look at the red water, the silky black skin, the gashes of the harpoons, then turns his back on it all.

'I hate this town,' he says.

He feels Dad's arm go around his shoulder and for a moment he wants to accept the embrace. But he's not a child. Too old to get upset about things being unfair.

He throws Dad's arm off and walks away. A stone lies on the path ahead of him and he kicks it angrily. It skims over the concrete and pings heavily into the side of the nearest boat, sinking to the bottom of the basin with a plop. *What a waste*, he thinks.

Chapter Nineteen

Cathy

Ephie is out there, floundering around to solve the problem and find the answer. She volunteered for the wader brigade. They go out in a little blue-edged fishing boat. Nothing will stop her. Would she end the research – do it for me? Never. A distance has been growing between us. She's started sleeping in the spare room most nights, making excuses about having to get up early for work. The November rain hits the windows at night as I lie alone.

She is part of a pack of biologists waging analysis against the tide. They sample, photograph, collect notes. They prowl the beaches and brave the waves, then scurry back to their laboratory. They press their noses against the screens of laptops, corroborating their findings. New research, old research. A collaborative partner in Southern Thailand. An infection here, a mutation there, a gene silenced somewhere else. A gene – silenced? What a word. I didn't know such things could chatter. Genes are strings of code – that's how Ephie has always explained it to me, as though each of us is a computer. Strings of code too small for us to see, but there, working their magic. 'Gene silencing – it's like you've stopped listening to a very small section of the code, so the outcome is different. It could be the reason,' she says. 'Identical twins are never exact. Same code, same result. Same code, some parts silenced, different result.' But why did this silencing happen? Who gave the order for quiet? Such metaphors these scientists use.

Ephie is out there studying fish. Fish, fish, fish. They are all around us. The headlines, the talk shows, the emergency legislative groups, think tanks, relief efforts. In some places there is mass hysteria. In my home there is quiet desperation. They are on the beach, in the rice paddy, lolling against the harbour wall. Sneaking through the pipes. I try not to think of them, but they slip through my every waking moment. I have been silenced with the thought of them.

Little else but the fish catches the eye or enters the head now. They dominate. There are still other problems in the world, of course, but we have no thoughts left for them. The world I once lived in, one of starvation and drought and calamitous storms, is still there. None of our previous problems are solved, just forgotten. Hard to see, among the fish, but they are there. I stumbled on one today. Small, delicate, silent. Nameless.

His head is malformed, pushed out of shape by a skull too large for the flesh that fills it. His eyes, rheumy, stare up at the human above, who points a lens at his sorry body. That body is small – oh, it should be small; he is a baby. But it is so delicate. So miniscule that I almost miss it, scrunched up there in the corner of the news. He will die, and most of us will never notice. He is the victim of this world we have loved so intensely, each one of us, just for ourselves. He could use a fish or two. We'd have to remember him first, though, before we could give him any.

Today, I am overwhelmed.

The fish are not out to kill us. Of course they're not – they're just fish. It's our fault they got this way; that seems certain now. So how can we blame them for wanting to wriggle out of this situation we've put them in? There is one real problem here, and it is not the fish. It is us. It is a human problem, twisted deep into our daily lives.

It covers every surface, climbs the highest mountains, sinks to the bottom of the deepest seas. *We leave shit everywhere we go.*

There, I said it. We are rooted in shit. I am as guilty as anyone. There are moments, long moments like this one, when I realise the truth. It can be hard to move on from those moments without just pushing the thoughts away. I don't know how to reconcile my own complicity – all the advantages I have, all the power I've been given to hurt everything around me – with my continuing lifestyle.

Today I saw a photo of a starving baby, three months old. His family are dead. Cholera took them after their island, somewhere between Borneo and Papua New Guinea, was swept almost into non-existence by the storm that started this fish plague. There weren't any relief efforts. We didn't notice. How could we have, when the storm caused disruption here? We were without power for two days. There were floods. Then the fish came. We didn't have time, not a second, to take a breath and realise that we are ruining things.

I could never bring a baby into this. It might have been nice to watch my stomach swell, or Ephie's, in a time when I felt more ignorant. The idea of creating something made from her might have got me through the fear of childbirth. But not now. There's no space in this world for babies. There's just me and her, our new silence, and the fish.

Maybe she feels differently. She is out there, trying to fix things. I can imagine her now: winter clouds overhead, her cheeks flushed and eyes bright as she dips a flask to the waves, collecting samples. The two male biologists she is working with are both in love with her. How could they not be? She has a fervour about her; it fills every cell of her body. Her brain, inexorably curious, moves quickly. She's always five steps ahead, bounding into the surf.

I used to find it contagious, this fervour of hers. Now it's just annoying. I don't know how to focus my mind as she does. I don't have the skills to look for a solution, so I sit here in my studio, propped up on my elbows, with my sewing machine before me, and my phone – the bringer of bad news, the source of that little photo – thrown miserably on the floor somewhere beneath the feet of my mannequin. All I can do is dwell on the problem. I want to take a black biro and draw a hole in the centre of my desk.

I hate the fish. I want them out of my sight. If they were back in the ocean, I could go back to that world I once lived in, where things were slipping but, oh, so slowly. Where the planet was simmering but hadn't boiled over. Back in that world, the starving baby didn't compete with fish – he might have been saved, with a little food.

Chapter Twenty

Margaret

'Why have you abandoned us, Margaret?' Jane demands.

It's been four months since Margaret's last meeting with the Mission. Not since the evening of the storm, when she spent the night in the church, has she been back to the brothels. In that time she has missed three meetings – the first because the fish had arrived and she was scared, the following because she'd had a run-in with "furries", and the last because she just couldn't go. Because church wasn't working.

Now here is Jane at the front door, trying to find out what's going on. Margaret wants to ask what she thinks she's doing, chasing her down at home like this.

'You'd better come in for a drink,' she says instead.

Jane pushes her fine red hair behind her ears and nods, following Margaret inside.

'Hey, Jane,' Roger calls from the sofa. 'Long time no see.'

'Sure is,' Jane replies, with a glance at Margaret. 'How are you, Roger?'

They stick to small talk: work, family, church. Margaret listens from the kitchen, noticing how neither mentions fish. If only she could do that herself – just leave them out.

Margaret comes back from the kitchen with two beers and sees that Jane has settled at the dining table.

'I'm worried about you,' Jane says as soon as Margaret's butt is on the seat. 'We all are.'

Margaret tugs her ear. 'There's nothing to worry about,' she says eventually.

'Then where have you been? It's been months. We miss you. Are you OK?'

Margaret sighs. 'I just... needed a break. I don't feel like I'll be much help to anyone right now.'

'Why not?'

Margaret takes a long swig of her beer, wondering how to tell Jane half the truth but not all of it. 'I feel like I have this weight...' She reaches her hands to her shoulders. 'I don't understand what's happening in the world right now, Jane, and I'm feeling overwhelmed.'

Jane takes her hand. Both women have wet palms from the condensation on the beer bottles.

'Think about the others, Margaret. If you feel anxious, imagine what it's like for the women we're trying to help. They're stuck in these uncertain conditions. They're not as lucky as us. A lot of them haven't found Jesus yet. They have no one to turn to.'

Margaret untangles her hand. She can't help anyone else find Jesus, not when she feels like she's lost Him herself.

Jane continues, 'I know things have changed. The world is very strange right now. But I think it's a sign that God is reaching out to us. He's asking us to have faith.'

Margaret nods but stays quiet.

'I can't afford to lose you now, Marge. The Mission is only as strong as its supporters, and we've worked so hard on it over the years.'

'I'm sorry,' Margaret hears herself say. 'I should've come.'

Jane smiles 'You can come on Wednesday.'

When Jane leaves, Margaret stays at the dining table, wringing her hands around the neck of her empty bottle. From somewhere high up in the heavens, shame presses in on her.

*

By the time Wednesday comes around, Margaret has spent three days trying to find a good reason not to go. In among the excuses and confusion, she does her best not to think about God, or the absence of Him in her life. But even absent, He's become the elephant in the room – enormous and silent.

In the hours leading up to the evening meeting, messages flash up on her cell phone from Chitra and Allison. They both say how much they're looking forward to seeing her – that Jane said she was coming. Margaret sighs, wondering whether she can get away with letting them down. She does miss them both. She misses the comfort of it all, the warmth she always got from the prayer sessions. She feels so guilty for not turning up.

When the time comes round for her to leave, she hangs around in the kitchen, slicing pieces of cheese off a block and slipping them into her mouth. She barely notices how good they taste. Her mind is in a church hall. She imagines Chitra and Allison – Jane, too – delaying the start of prayers to wait for her. She can't ignore them forever; maybe it will be better than she thinks. And it might do her good to spend an evening thinking of someone other than herself. It could be the first step to fixing this whole mess.

Roger isn't back from work, so she leaves him a note on the coffee table saying she'll be back late and not to wait up. She puts *x* three times at the end, encouraging herself to feel loving.

On the drive over she feels cold for the first time in months. She turns the radio off, sighing and shifting in her seat. This will be the first time she's seen the Mission girls since the world turned upside down and emptied fish onto land. She talked about it with them a bit at the start, a few messages here and there, but then she stopped replying. She doesn't really know how they've all reacted. They don't know how *she*'s reacted. Will they be able to tell that she's nearly lost her mind? That God is an absence in her current life? Without Him at the centre of their relationship, it feels like something's broken – like there's a void. She doesn't know how to act around a void.

She keeps her eyes pointedly on the road, determined to keep the fish littering the sidewalks out of her vision. The ones squashed flat on the asphalt can't be avoided, though – they don't get scavenged by birds like normal roadkill.

In the car, outside the church, she idles, pulling the visor down and checking her reflection. In the mirror she goes through her entrance speech, then looks over at the creamy yellow building with its big red cross. When she opens her door, she smells roti canai and chilli from a nearby restaurant. She takes a set of deep breaths and lets the aroma settle her.

Walking into the church, she feels alone. At their meeting room, pushing the door open carefully, keeping her head high, she finds prayers just about to start. *Perfect*, she thinks, slipping into the room. *No time to talk.*

She sits quickly, giving Jane a nod, and tries to throw herself into the singing. It feels strange, alien even, to be back. The room is somehow smaller, the faces less familiar. The words of the first song catch in her throat and she mumbles through them. She keeps glancing around, worried that everyone's eyes are on her – that they can sense her awkwardness. She scratches at her arm, anxiety making her itch. She has missed so many sessions, and with no real excuse. She doesn't know how to be friends with anyone anymore.

When the second song starts, she forces herself to sing loudly, rocks her body a little to try to get into it. It's an old classic. 'How Great Is Our God' has always been a favourite of hers. But despite her efforts, the joy of the hymn evades her. She can't seem to relax – there's no transcendental lift, no pulsing heart rate. She feels like a phoney. She wills herself to keep going, to sing like she used to, but she feels something inside of her breaking down. Without warning, tears well in her eyes and she blinks them back. By the third verse, a sob escapes her. She pulls a hand to her mouth, trying desperately to stifle the cries, but all she can feel is an emptiness opening out in her chest. She looks around the room and realises that no one has noticed her: every woman is in her own place, singing with Jesus. Margaret turns her eyes on each one of them and envies their expressions of connection. Tears drip down her cheeks.

After three songs, the prayers begin. Margaret's hands are cold, clenched tight in her lap. A little three-blade fan in the corner of the room spins monotonously, raising the hairs on her arms. She wants to stand and turn it off, but knows how awkward it would be to get up in the middle of the session. She tries to ignore it, curling more tightly into herself, letting weeks of uncertainty wash over her. *Speak to me, then*, she wills. *Send me a sign. I'm alone in the darkness here.*

She's thankful that Jane doesn't pass the prayer to her – that she's allowed to play the part of spectator. When it is all over, she cuffs a hand quickly across her eyes and straightens up in her chair. She tries to smile but doesn't manage it.

'Thanks to God,' Jane says, standing and holding her arms out to quiet the room. She looks at Margaret. 'And thanks to old friends.'

She moves into logistical details then, reminding everyone of the Mission statement and why they are all there. 'We're getting close to one of the most important days of the year,' she says. 'So we've got these beautiful greetings cards to hand out tonight, and bags of cookies. Let's spread some festive joy, and remind ourselves and everyone we connect with of the true meaning of Christmas.'

She splits the room into three groups, and then tells each one which particular brothel they will go to. Margaret gets put with Chitra and Allison.

'Oh, and Margaret, as you haven't been with us for a bit, you should know that one of the young ladies in your brothel is pregnant,' Jane says. 'We guess about five months. And the last time we went visiting, she was still working, God save us.'

Margaret shudders. 'Can't we do anything?' she asks. 'She shouldn't be in there.'

Jane shrugs, her forehead crinkling into a frown.

'We'd have to get her to tell us she wants to leave – that would be our only chance.'

Margaret sighs. 'OK.'

When she walks out of the church into the sticky night, her legs are leaden. A batch of nativity-themed Christmas cards is clutched in her palm.

They walk past a hardware store, its window filled with hammers and sandpaper and posters for electric drills. Everything is cast in shadow, the street's daytime identity gone.

The brothel is close by, hidden round a corner, away from the eyes of all those who do not wish to see it. A knock on the door – a large wooden thing with a red light hanging above – brings a young man wearing a pair of sunglasses pushed back on his head. Margaret doesn't recognise him. He has lines shaved into both eyebrows and he holds himself as though ready to fight.

Chitra steps forwards. She speaks with the man, telling him who they are and why they have come. Margaret follows some of it. *We're Christians. We visit every month.*

As Chitra speaks, his lip curls into an expression of mistrust. Margaret smiles, Allison unfolds her arms and Chitra raises her palms. They have all practised looking unthreatening. 'We only come to spread the word of God, and give out some gifts,' Chitra says, showing the cards and cookies to him.

He lets them in with reluctance and they step inside, entering a wide, open room with terracotta walls. The floors are covered in threadbare rugs in faded reds and blacks, and three dilapidated couches are pushed against the walls. In the left corner of the room, sitting on top of a long bar, two women eye the group. They sit close to one another and their bare legs swing beneath them, stilettos clicking against the wooden side of the bar. In the right corner at the back of the room, an archway leads into gathering gloom.

'Go on,' the doorman says. He points his finger towards the archway, eyes full of aggression. Margaret forces herself to smile again and walks on.

'He's a stand-in,' Chitra whispers. 'No wonder I didn't recognise him. Yu, the doorman who's usually here, is away.'

Margaret nods. She feels so out of place; she wishes the ground could open up and swallow her.

'Come on,' Chitra says gently.

Much like the other brothels on the street, this one is based around a central corridor with doors leading to rooms. Margaret follows Allison, who follows Chitra, and they make their way along the yellow-lit passage. Some of the women come to their doors to see what is going on. Chitra and Allison stop to talk; they have forged relationships with some, and know them by sight and name. Margaret has been absent for long enough that she recognises no one. She keeps walking, passing two closed doors. Behind one she hears the deep grunts of a man. She blinks, then rearranges her face to make sure she isn't grimacing. How many times before has she done this?

Halfway down the corridor she stops and looks back. Despite being so familiar, there is nothing comforting about the dismal walls, or the hot, musty air of the brothel. It makes Margaret feel old and tired. She lets a breath out, running her hand along the collar of her shirt. Sweat trickles down the back of her neck. Just like in the Rotunda mall, here too she feels round and ancient. In the past she used to joke about it with the others – she'd take on a mother-hen persona, clucking through the brothels. Now that all seems ridiculous. She hates the part of her that feels jealous of these women for being young and beautiful.

Seeing no sign of the pregnant woman, Margaret tells herself she must have been given accommodation elsewhere. She'll be somewhere comfortable, where she can stay healthy during the later stages of her pregnancy.

Margaret is nearly at the end of the corridor when a woman in a red leather miniskirt appears in front of her with urgency. Seeing Margaret, she rushes forwards and grasps her hands. She has high cheekbones and large black eyes, and her hair is chopped short.

'You help?' the woman says.

Margaret hears panic in her voice. 'Help?' she asks.

The woman nods quickly. 'You must help,' she says. 'My name, Jessica.'

She tugs Margaret to the very back of the corridor, where they turn left and enter a shabby kitchen. A woman lies on a mat on the floor, her head pressed up against the edge of a dirty cooker, while a second woman crouches over her, cloth in hand. The woman lying on the floor has a large stomach, swollen with months of pregnancy. Her shirt is stretched tight over it. Rings of sweat show at her neck and under each arm. Margaret takes a step closer, anxious, and sees the woman's chest rising and falling with short breaths.

'What's happened? Is she in labour?' Margaret asks quickly.

The woman with the cloth looks up suspiciously, and Jessica speaks to her in Chinese, before looking back to Margaret. 'She eat fish,' Jessica says.

Margaret feels the breath rush out of her. People have died. She looks down at the woman lying on the floor. Her light brown hair lies ragged around her face. Her skin looks thin and pallid.

'She must see a doctor,' Margaret says, looking around her, searching for answers. No one speaks, but a groan escapes from the lips of the woman on the floor.

'When did she eat it?' Margaret asks. She moves further into the room and kneels, pressing a palm to the woman's head.

Jessica takes a seat on the edge of a tiny table. Her eyes are wide with worry.

'Two hours,' she says. 'The man. Father. He bring food. Didn't say fish. She eat. He leave. Now sick.'

'Has she?' Margaret asks. 'Been sick?' She awkwardly mimes vomiting and Jessica shakes her head.

'Too hot,' she says, pointing at the pregnant woman's sweaty brow.

Dear God, Margaret thinks. She feels utterly useless. The woman in front of her is limp, her body unmoving, eyes closed. Only her laboured breath shows that she is alive.

'How many months?' Margaret asks. Perhaps if she went to the hospital, they could induce her and bring the birth on. The baby might survive.

Margaret sees Jessica counting off months on her hand. She stops at six.

'She must go to the hospital,' Margaret says. She nods, as though to convince herself. 'Stay here. We'll call for a doctor.'

Margaret rushes from the room.

'Chitra!' she shouts. 'Allison!'

She starts down the dismal corridor, pulling her cell phone out of her bag as she goes. She must get to the front of the labyrinth, to have any chance of reception. Chitra and Allison appear from side rooms, both looking anxious.

'She's really sick. The pregnant lady. Ate fish. We need an ambulance.'

Chitra is instant. 'I'll do it,' she says. 'Give me your phone. Allison, you go halfway down the corridor. Margaret, you stay with the woman. You can relay information to me. I'm sure they will ask questions. Margaret, quickly, what's happened? How sick is she?'

Margaret explains as best she can, her words rushing out in a confused mess. 'Fish,' she keeps saying. 'She ate a fish.'

By now every woman in the brothel is present, roused by the commotion and eyeing up the scene. They stand suspiciously in doorways, arms folded. Before Chitra makes it back to the foyer, the man with the patterned eyebrows appears, drawn to the shouting. His hands are balled into fists and he barks at Chitra.

Margaret turns away, too anxious to listen. Will he let them take her to the hospital? Surely he must. As she walks back into the greasy kitchen, she hears Chitra's voice, strong and assertive, and feels a moment of reassurance.

Before the ambulance arrives, the pregnant woman – Lin, the others say her name is – starts to shiver. Jessica and the woman who was mopping her brow continue to sit with her, speaking quietly and watching her with worried eyes. Margaret stands in the background, pressed up against the grimy kitchen counter, and chews her nails. She has no idea how many minutes have passed since the ambulance was called. How many minutes has she stood there, useless? She tries not to imagine the baby curled in Lin's womb, with its small limbs and tiny head. How big would it be? How developed? Margaret has no idea. She has never lain like this, six months on, with a baby inside her. She never got the chance.

When the paramedics arrive, Margaret has drifted to Northern California, rooting herself in a forest of Pacific redwoods that are tall and straight, and high as the sky. It is only after Lin has been carried out of the kitchen that she jolts back into the hot brothel. The Christmas cards she brought are in a neat pile beside her on the counter. *Behold, a virgin shall conceive, and bear a son, and shall call his name Immanuel.*

In the foyer, among the faded rugs, Chitra stands with downcast eyes. She steps carefully aside as the paramedics carry Lin through.

'Thankfully that stand-in doorman had no idea what to do. I told him he didn't want a girl's death on his hands. That seemed to convince him,' she says. 'Anyway, Margaret, I've spoken with

Jane. I'm going along in the ambulance and she's going to follow in her car. Will you come, or shall we keep you updated?'

Margaret swallows, unsure, still thinking of a baby in a manger.

Chitra takes her hands. 'I have to go. Jane's outside. Call me.'

Beyond the open front door of the brothel, Margaret can see the flicker of blue lights among darkness. The smell of the street comes in, sweet and soothing. Chitra disappears into the night.

'I'm going with Jane,' Allison says.

She has appeared by Margaret's shoulder, her blonde hair ragged around her ears, her forehead beaded with sweat.

'Are you coming?' Allison prompts.

Margaret shakes her head. 'I'll catch up,' she manages.

Out of her body again, she could be in another world. It is a place of sorrow and fear, and when the room is empty once more – with Allison gone, the women back in their rooms and the doorman disappeared to God knows where – Margaret finds herself perched on the arm of one of the moth-eaten sofas. Her feet are on the cushions beneath her, knees drawn up close to her body. A dark stain covers the section of fabric near her left foot.

'I want to ask You this one thing,' she says aloud. 'One thing, and I think I deserve it. I haven't asked for much. I've been faithful. I've come to places like this' – she spreads her hands to the room around her – 'month after month, to spread Your love. I've believed. Now I need this one thing.'

She runs a hand across her forehead and over her eyes, willing herself not to cry.

'Please save the baby,' she says. 'He's just an innocent in all this.'

Chapter Twenty-One
Cathy

Ephie is a violent sleeper. When she chooses to share the bed, she crocodile-rolls through the night, every hour edging closer and closer to me. Eventually, I will wake – find myself pressed onto a sliver of mattress, with her glorious face right up against mine. She gets too hot, or too cold. She has a bad dream. Her right arm goes to sleep beneath her. She doesn't wake for any of these things, just struggles through subconsciously. If her body is a ship tossing on the waves, her brain sleeps comfortably in its captain's cabin, beneath a vault of stars. The cabin is intricate: velvet cushioned and wooden-carved, a place of craftsmanship to protect all that intelligence. In our bed the tempest rages on – a heave, a roll, a sigh – but still, her brain sleeps.

I think I am a quiet sleeper. I am considerate of her. I roll slowly, push her gently, when I need to. I don't pull the duvet off the bed or wrinkle it up beneath me. I suffer her discomfort, often, with an hour of wakefulness. She slumbers on, eventually settling, and I grow unhappy that she has woken me. As the minutes pass, I tread a frustrating path, more convinced with every moment that I'll never get back to sleep. I check the time, snarl at the back of her head through the darkness. She's ruined this pre-dawn hour for me. She's disrupted this night.

The next morning she'll say, 'I slept badly; I kept waking up.'

But you didn't, I'll think. You were asleep the whole time.

'And what was the matter with you?' she asked yesterday. 'What were you dreaming about? You were chatting away in the night.'

I was dreaming of fish. I always dream of fish.

The sky is black. I dream in spotlights. Under one of them I move around, searching for a tower block to get inside. No one lives on the ground anymore; it's not safe. There's too much water, great puddles of it everywhere. The skyline is jagged and shadowy, a maze I can't navigate, and I've been left outside. I know it. I feel this rejection like a pain in my heart – why did they leave me? What did I do? I must find Ephie, who is somewhere in this city that could be New York. I've never been to New York. Why did she leave me?

When I find her, she's busy. 'You can't see her,' they say, 'she's working.' But she asked for me. She said I could come. Shadows, all shadows. I don't see faces, don't hear voices. You're the one we left behind – the one that didn't matter. I want to move faster, run to her, but my feet are slow.

When she comes to me – I don't know what work she's been doing but I don't like it; it's a dirty work, a work that fills her soul with soil, but she's good at it – I know it's her without seeing her with clarity. I feel her. A relief, a longing. But she's different. She wears a face that isn't hers. No smile for me, no love. She carries a plant. 'But we don't have those anymore,' I tell her. 'Where did you get that?'

It is a rice plant. A handful of seedlings, pressed close together in a clump of soil. They are so green against the night. 'I saved it from them,' she says.

I have to go. I can't stay – there is no spotlight for Ephie, only for me. She is gone, back into her building. Back to the work for which she wears a stranger's face. There is no time; I am alone. They are coming. The fish are in the garden and I am alone in the house. I must buy milk. I know I must – the fridge is empty – but they are there, blocking the door. 'But the fish,' I say. 'They are here now,' Ephie replies. She's back, thank God. She sits at the kitchen table with her rice seedlings. *They are here now*. They are in the springs of my mattress, half-dead. Spiders crawl from their mouths. They are stuffed, rotting, with the dust that gathers down the back of a radiator. They will wriggle out: the bones, the scales, the webs of their half-dead lives. Their silver eyes. They will put their mouths against my ankles.

They will touch me, here, where I lie.

When I finally wake, I feel as though I've spent hours trying to find my way home from that place. Tossing and turning, half-awake and half-asleep, with only a world of fish to welcome me from a dream of fish. My body is drenched with sweat, duvet tangled, windows dripping with condensation, and Ephie's side of the bed dead cold.

I feel completely unnerved, with a weight like a killer whale pressing on me. It's a straitjacket, an endless useless worry, and before I know it, I've risen from bed and pulled a jumper on over my pyjamas. I want some kind of action. I go to the back door for my wellies and leave the house, picking up the garden shovel as I go. Listening to the blood pulsing in my ears, I finally feel a bit of power.

The wind is fierce on the beach. I pause the tip of my shovel above the neck of a cod. The edge of my blade flashes silver in the chill morning sun. My teeth chatter and my fingers hurt from the cold of the metal handle. My mind is still there, in that dream – in that shadowy city, or trapped in the kitchen, summoning the courage to buy milk. And the nightmares are true. They have killed the Alaskan fishermen and now they are taking Ephie from me, too. Her eyes are barely on me anymore; she hasn't even noticed the way I prowl the house, sewing projects forgotten, no business beyond the fish. How could she notice? She's never there with me.

So I stand still with my shovel, but only for a second. The cod fish looks at me with its watery eyes and then it moves, ready to slouch off, and I feel bile rising in my throat. I bring the weapon down with two hands and all my weight, and it slices through the scales and flesh, and thuds right into the sand beneath. The fish still looks at me. It opens its mouth a little wider, then closes it, as though asking why I've done this.

'Fuck you,' I say to its bloody body, and move on to the next.

By the time one of the villagers finds me, I must have killed twenty. It's Bill the barman, announced by his Border terrier barking at his heels. He shouts my name across the beach and, though I hear it, I continue. I slice tails from bodies and sever fish hearts. Do fish have hearts? Bill catches me up and shouts at me, and then he wrestles the shovel out of my hands. His dog stands a metre away and growls with her lips drawn back. Without the shovel, I know I must look like a lunatic.

'You're freezing, Cathy,' Bill says. 'You're trembling, you're covered in blood and you're still wearing your pyjamas. Come with me.'

I shake my head, 'I'm fine.'

He pins me with a stern gaze, almost the kind he'd use to throw a teenager out of the pub, but worse.

'You've lost your mind,' he says.

Before I can respond, he takes off his coat and throws it over me, then puts an arm around me and walks me forwards, pushing me gently away from the bodies that are scattered all around. I start to cry. I try to keep the tears quiet, let them fall in silence, but by the time we're off the sand, I'm snivelling. Bill holds me close, walking me past my house and up the hill, straight to the pub. He smells like a shed in winter. The keys to the pub are attached to a belt loop on his jeans and he leans my shovel, red-stained and sandy, against the porch wall while he fumbles with the lock.

'Sit down,' he says once we're inside, pushing me gently into one of the armchairs near the unlit fire.

His dog Kelpie, remembering who I am, whines a bit and nuzzles against my foot. She looks up at me with pitying eyes, and I feel like a waif, sitting there on a worn armchair wrapped in someone else's coat. I lean down to her and drag a shaking hand along her wiry back. As I do so, I notice that my wellies are covered in flecks of fish. The scales show up silver between the blue-and-white polka dots. Splashes of blood and wet sand are caked over the toes. I push the dog away with my hand and tug the wellies off quickly, feeling repulsed. My feet are freezing. I'm not wearing any socks.

Bill appears at my side, holding a mug and a port glass full of deep purple liquid.

'Sloe gin,' he says, handing me the glass. 'I know you don't like whisky. Now come on, you'll feel better for that.'

The gin goes down like lava, sweet and hot. I pull my feet up onto the chair so that I can sit cross-legged and press my cold soles against my warm thighs. Bill hands me the mug of tea, along with four chocolate digestives. He crouches to build a fire and I take a sip, feeling relief seep through me as the warm liquid goes down. I almost start crying again. God, there is nothing better than tea and biscuits. They are the taste of comfort.

When the fire's lit, Bill goes to the back of my armchair and shifts the whole thing around with me in it, so that I'm closer to the flames. The legs scrape over the wooden floor and he grunts. Kelpie's still next to me, and Bill scoops her up and dumps her on my lap. She settles into the crook of my legs, head resting on my thigh, and I put a hand on her soft, exposed belly. She closes her eyes, content. She's not afraid I will decapitate her with a shovel.

Bill disappears and then returns with his own cup of tea. He sits in the opposite chair and puts his feet on the hearth rail. When I steal a glance at him, he's staring back. He runs a hand through his hair and shakes his head a tiny bit.

'Fucking hell, Cathy,' he says, laughter creeping into the end of his sentence.

I feel a smile come to my face then, too. He starts chuckling in earnest, shoulders rising and falling.

'I've never seen anything like it,' he says. 'You were like a banshee out there, screaming blue murder.'

'I was screaming?'

He nods, still laughing. 'Like an absolute maniac. Like, I don't know, a samurai soldier or something.'

'Oh God.' I put a hand to my head.

He keeps laughing.

'Don't,' I say, even though I'm laughing now, too, a kind of gentle hysteria that feels miserable and great. 'I don't know what came over me.'

He wipes a tear from his eye. 'Don't mess with Cathy Calathes. She'll take your bloody head off. With a shovel!'

We laugh together for a good, long time then, until finally I can feel warmth in my fingers and toes.

'Thank God it was you,' I say to Bill. 'Imagine if a tourist had found me.'

'Oh, they'd be dead now,' Bill says, trying to keep a straight face. 'You'd have killed them.'

'I would never.'

'I'm not kidding,' he says, smiling. 'It was very hard to get that shovel out of your hand, Cathy. And you know me.'

I shake my head. The laughter has helped, replacing misery with embarrassment.

'I had a bad dream,' I mutter.

'Where's Ephie?'

'Oh, she's at work,' I say, too quickly. I never saw her leave the house, but it must be true. Where else would she be? She's always at work. For a second, I see an image of her watching my massacre from the kitchen window, but not bothering to come to my aid, because she needs to get to the lab. I shake my head to dislodge the idea.

'I thought she worked from home?' Bill asks.

'She used to do two days at home. But she's in all the time now.'

'Oh yeah? Why's that?' he asks.

I sigh. 'She's saving the world, Bill.'

There's a pause. I stroke the dog, watching her eyes close with pleasure.

'Been doing that a lot, has she? Saving the world?' Bill asks.

When I don't answer, he continues, 'Is that why you've been in here some lunchtimes?'

I'm not used to being so alone in the house. I might have been OK, in the past. Before all of my thoughts swam with worry. But now it gets too much for me. 'I want a bit of company sometimes,' I tell him.

I drain the last of my tea. The biscuits are long gone but I can still taste their sweetness on my tongue. 'Anyway, I should go.'

'Are you feeling OK?' Bill asks.

I nod, looking at Bill's thick black eyebrows and blue eyes. He's wearing a shaggy brown jumper, whose weave is starting to bobble. Bill's a friendly grizzly bear. Tough and soft. I feel a wave a love for him.

'Thanks, Bill. I had a bit of a moment, didn't I? I'm glad you were there.'

'See you soon, my lover.'

I pick Kelpie up as I stand and pass her to Bill, who rolls his eyes and drops the dog unceremoniously on the floor. She pads off towards the kitchen and I pull my wellies on

At the door, the cold winter air rushes against me.

'Watch how you go,' Bill calls.

I pause a moment, not wanting to break the warmth between me and the fire, not wanting to go back out into this world. Then I take a step.

Chapter Twenty-Two

Ricky

Ricky's been thinking more and more seriously about getting out of Claremouth. Away from the whale killers, from the small-town views, from Friday nights with nothing to do. It's time to move on. The school year's finished now; he has six weeks of summer freedom, and then just Year Thirteen left to go. One more year. He wants to meet new people – girls, too – and see more than the West Coast. The teachers at school always say going to university is about *meeting like-minded people*, and maybe that's what he wants. Maybe they're right. Who'd have thought it? He should go to university. He doesn't want to stay here, where the fish are the enemy and humans are the good guys. He wants to go somewhere else, where people agree with him when he explains that it's all our fault. He wants to be part of the solution.

In the meantime, though, the West Coast is still home, and it's as much at the centre of the fish phenomenon as anywhere else. Next year they'll be able to go to The Swan, too, without getting kicked out.

He shifts his cap a bit on his head, as he walks through the front door into Kyle's house. Sweat's gathering at his hairline – it's hot, now summer is here. Properly warm enough to wear only his T-shirt out in the evenings. Kyle wears only a shirt about six months of the year, trying to look cool, but Ricky can't be bothered with that. No one pays much attention to him, whether he wears a hoodie or not.

'Hey, Mary,' he says, finding Kyle's mum in the kitchen with her back to him. 'How's it going?'

'Hi, Ricky. You two heading out drinking, are you? Kyle's already begged me for beer.' She picks a large glass of white wine off the kitchen counter and takes a sip.

'Wanna come with? You could get us served,' Ricky asks.

She snorts. 'Imagine Kyle's face.'

He shrugs. 'We could go to The Swan with you there.'

The smirk drops off her face. 'You know I can't go to that side of town, love. Never know who you might bump into.'

She grimaces. Ricky knows she's talking about Kyle's dad and the woman he lives with now.

'Hey, if anyone upset you, I'd beat them up,' Ricky says, balling his fists.

She smiles. 'How's the family? I saw your mum in Countdown the other week.'

'They're all good. Mum and Dad planning a family night out for their twentieth anniversary next weekend.' He sees her smile flicker a little. 'Shit, sorry.'

She takes a gulp of wine and waves a hand at him. 'It's fine. You're thinking of uni, eh? Your mum told me.'

'Thinking, yeah. Not sure if my grades will be up to it, though.'

'You just work hard, Ricky. Get out of this town. You'll be great. I wish you would take Kyle with you.'

Ricky doesn't know what to say. Half the reason his friend says he plans to stay home once school's over is for his mum. Does she know that?

He's saved having to reply by Kyle walking into the kitchen and asking, 'Ready?' He's wearing tight jeans and a baggy white shirt. Signature Kyle.

'When are you going to give up and shave?' Mary jokes, nodding her head towards the fluffy blonde hair that sprouts from Kyle's chin and top lip.

'Leave me alone,' he says. 'It just needs a bit of time.'

Ricky tries not to laugh. 'Let's go, then, eh?'

Kyle nods. He doesn't look properly at Ricky, just keeps his eyes on the middle distance. Ricky wonders what the problem is.

'See you later, Mum. And yeah, don't worry, we'll stick to the road,' Kyle says. Since his dad's hospitalisation, both boys have been banned from the beach. The one in town is still closed.

Ricky says goodbye to Mrs McGill and follows Kyle out the front door. 'Alright?' he says, once they're well away from the house.

'Yep.'

Ricky frowns, sure that the short response means something more. He doesn't press it and instead says, 'Krampuss died.'

'Shit.'

'Yeah. I mean, we've still got Checkers. And she's a much nicer cat. Krampuss was a little twat. If he got any chance, he'd poo on the beds. But, you know, he was kind of a lovable twat.'

Kyle doesn't respond, just keeps walking.

'Guess he just caught too many rotten fish,' Ricky says, filling the silence.

'Hate to say I told you so,' Kyle comments.

'What does that mean?'

'Come on, Ricky. You love the fish. They're rotten – you just said it yourself. But you still get upset when people clear them off the land. 'Cos, you know,' he puts on a voice, like he's mimicking, *'it's not the fish's fault.* The fish killed your cat, but you can't blame them for it. They're sick.'

Ricky frowns. 'Yeah. All that's true. And?'

'And so why should I have sympathy for your stupid cat? If you cared properly about him, you'd have gone onto the beach and got rid of the goddamn fish.'

Ricky stops still. 'What's wrong with you tonight?'

'Nothing,' Kyle says. He keeps walking.

Ricky watches him for a second, feeling himself start to mirror his friend's mood.

'Fuck it,' Ricky says. 'I'm going on the beach.'

He turns around and starts to double back, towards a path that leads down to the shore. He stamps through the pebbles, not bothering to look back. He was in a good mood when he got to Kyle's. Feeling positive. But his friend's attitude has brought him right down. They found Krampuss yesterday morning, body stiff outside the back door. There was a Pacific cod, also dead, lying two metres from the cat's front paws. Ricky doesn't understand how he feels about it all anymore. He's upset with the whole situation, like there's a sense of betrayal. Perhaps everyone was right. Maybe this isn't a new evolution. Maybe human intervention is the only solution. Get the tanks out. Use chemicals, before any more cats or people die. But it's not like they can scoop every fish out of the entire ocean.

Kyle catches him up at the dunes. They don't speak.

When they reach the wet sand, Ricky feels nerves bubbling in his belly. The beach is scattered with silver and grey bodies. They've snaked out of the shallows – infected, poisonous, gasping their way onto land. It's impossible to ignore them. Hard not to look at each one and inspect it. Doubly hard not to recoil when it starts to walk, mouth open wide and gaping.

The sun is low over the sea as they make their way along the sand, stepping over the fish. There's no one else about, of course, just the sound of the waves coming in one by one, each dragging pebbles with it and then scraping them back along the dark brown sand. The sky above is gathering darkness, the beginning of night-time spreading over their heads. Ricky feels the last of the day's warmth on his arms, and he can hear Kyle's steps, a pace or two behind.

'I overheard what you said to Mum. About uni,' Kyle mumbles, as he draws level.

Ricky takes a breath, looks at the ground and says, 'I was going to tell you.'

A year ago they made a pact, the two of them, to move to Melbourne for a while after school. Get jobs in bars, go to gigs, live in a city. Neither of them is that good at school. They're both completely average students, so they just decided to leave. To get out of Claremouth, together. Ricky wanted to see kangaroos. What a crazy animal. But they never really discussed whether it was a proper, serious plan. Then Tony left and Kyle started talking about needing to be around, to get a job after school to support the family.

Kyle shrugs. 'It's got nothing to do with me. It's your decision.'

'Why're you pissed off, then?'

'We had a deal. I guess it doesn't matter now...' Kyle trails off.

'You've been talking about staying. I thought the deal was off,' Ricky says.

Kyle doesn't reply, just keeps walking.

'I guess I thought I might as well try,' Ricky says. 'You know, try and be something.'

Kyle snorts. 'Nice you've got the chance.'

'Look, if you heard me say I was thinking of applying to university then you heard the bit where your mum said she wished you'd go, too. So don't pretend your life's so hard all the time,' Ricky says, not managing to stop his voice from coming out angry.

Kyle stops walking. His jaw's clenched and his eyebrows are low over his eyes.

'You know Dad came round to the house the other night to pick up Hannah. Him and Mum got in a massive fight. She threw a glass at him across the kitchen. They were both so angry.'

Ricky doesn't know what to say.

Kyle scuffs his feet through the sand. 'I just stood there. Didn't do a thing.'

'What could you have done?' Ricky asks.

Kyle shrugs. 'I just feel useless. Mum says I don't understand any of it, but I understand it's a mess and I can't fix it.'

'I feel bad for your mum,' Ricky says.

Kyle shrugs. 'So that's why I can't leave,' he explains. 'Anyway, I wouldn't get the grades.'

'You don't know that.'

'Why d'you want to go to university so badly all of a sudden?' Kyle asks, his tone still bitter.

Ricky sighs, wondering how he can find the words to explain to Kyle what he can't explain to himself. 'This whole situation with the fish. The whales. Krampuss. The climate. I dunno, I feel like I can't sit around and just carry on watching it. I need to figure out how I feel about it, which is sort of outraged but also, like, excited to do something. So maybe I could do a subject that's useful. Help sort this mess out.'

Kyle says, 'As if one person can make a difference.'

Ricky feels like slapping him. 'Maybe they can't. I don't know – I just think I need to be somewhere where people aren't pretending nothing's happening. Your dad nearly died. My cat died. The fish are walking up the beaches and hanging out on Main Street. None of it's normal and I can't just ignore it. I want to try to do something useful and learn from all this, even if I *am* only one person.'

When he finishes, he realises he's been shouting. Kyle's eyes have narrowed, and there's a mix of sympathy and embarrassment in his expression. He reaches out a hand and gives Ricky a shove on the shoulder.

'I'm gonna get left behind,' Kyle says. 'That's all I'm upset about.'

Ricky frowns, feeling guilty, and angry for having to feel guilty.

Kyle lets his hand drop. 'I don't mean you should stay. I wouldn't expect you to stay for me. That would be a dick move.' He shrugs. 'But, you know...'

Ricky nods. He's about to call it quits, crack a joke to lighten the mood, when Kyle comes to a halt.

'What's that?' he says, pointing out to the horizon.

Ricky looks in the direction he points. A thick cloud of some kind seems to have gathered over the sea. It has a silver-blue tint to it.

'No idea.'

'Smoke?' Kyle asks.

Ricky doesn't answer, just shakes his head slowly. There can't be smoke out at sea.

They stand side by side and stare into the distance. Above the crests of the waves, a haze hangs thick. Tentacles of it drip towards the sea.

'It's moving,' Ricky says, squinting.

As they watch, it spreads more widely, obscuring the orange rays of the setting sun.

'Is it another storm?' Kyle says. He sounds excited.

'Maybe. Does it look blue to you? Sort of... electric?'

'Definitely, mate. Maybe it's a massive lightning storm?' Kyle says.

'But there's no lightning.'

Butterflies start up in Ricky's stomach. He's been here before with Kyle, staring out at something they've never seen. Something powerful and natural, but maybe unnatural at the same time. He feels cold all of a sudden.

'I'll look online,' Ricky suggests, pulling his phone out of his pocket. He silently curses himself for slacking off from checking the news. He was so good about it until school ended. Keeping on top of all the developments in the fish story. Watching the way all the different countries reacted. But since the holidays started – since Krampuss – he's been playing video games instead.

It doesn't take him long to find something, four articles down – *Malay Peninsula obscured by mist: fog causes chaos and devastation.*

Kyle finds a similar piece moments later and asks, 'Reckon it's the same mist, then?'

Ricky doesn't reply, just keeps reading. *Suspected plankton blooms, potential risk to airways. Red tide. Stay indoors.*

He goes on social media, searches for 'mist' and 'Asia', and finds photo after photo of dense white fog – the tops of sky-scrapers poking from within it, trees obscured, car headlights fuzzy and refracted.

'I guess it must be,' he says eventually, lowering his phone. He squints into the gathering night. 'It doesn't look the same, though, eh?' He holds his phone out to Kyle, gesturing for him to look at the photo stream.

'You're right. This looks sort of... beautiful?' Kyle says.

Ricky's surprised by that description, but it's not wrong. The haze doesn't look like the fog pictured on his phone; it doesn't have the same depth. Somehow it shimmers.

'Look at the waves,' Kyle says. 'Can you see it?'

Every third wave or so, out at sea, now flickers electric blue. They roll over, iridescent with some kind of neon glow.

Ricky takes a deep breath, brain whirring. 'The alien con-spiracy guys are gonna love this. I feel like we're about to see a spaceship land,' he mumbles.

'Is it getting closer?' Kyle asks. There's an edge of uncertainty in his voice.

'The blue waves are,' Ricky says. 'Look.'

Nearly at their feet, the waves tumbling ashore are crested with glowing blue. The light that seems to shine out of them intensifies as the sky gets darker. Ricky instinctively takes a step back. Kyle does the same and shouts, 'Woah, your feet!'

Ricky looks down quickly, suddenly terrified that flesh-sucking land fish have surrounded his feet, but sees nothing. Just sand.

'Your footsteps,' says Kyle. 'When you moved. They lit up.'

Ricky takes another two steps back and lets out a gasp. His footsteps stay behind for a moment, lit up blue in the sand. As though he's left a print of neon paint, except that it disappears almost as soon as it shows.

'What's going on?' Ricky says.

Kyle's eyes are wide. He shakes his head. 'Whatever this thing is, it's getting even nearer,' he says, pointing.

The haze spreads closer to shore, until each wave breaks against the sand with bursts of glowing blue. Ricky and Kyle are halfway up the beach – they've moved backwards quickly, without thinking – and the mist continues to march on, drifting above the waves.

'We need to go,' Ricky says. 'Look at the fish.'

All around them, the land fish are scrabbling for ground, crawling up the beach. They flip their bodies around with haste. There's an urgency about their movements that makes Ricky scared.

Kyle coughs. 'Can you taste it?' he says. 'It's like there's something in the air.'

The shimmering haze is now nearly at their feet, drifting up the beach. It moves quickly, spreading from the water and settling across the sand.

'Home time,' Ricky shouts.

He feels panicked, chest tight, lost for words. He grabs Kyle by the arm and pulls. They start to run, leaving electric-blue footprints in their wake. The sky is fully dark now and they both stumble, slipping among the dry sand and the pebbles. Ricky hopes he doesn't blunder into any fish. There's a pressure in his throat; he tells himself it's just from running, but maybe it's from something else. The silver haze that's gaining on them. His mind runs wild: *The bacteria must have mutated, somehow become airborne. Maybe it can infect humans. Or maybe it's just a fog. A weird fog.*

He keeps running. Kyle is ahead, his white T-shirt showing up against the night.

When they make it to the top of the dunes, they pause to catch their breath. Below them the beach is white, mist spreading out like cotton wool. The air looks solid. Flashes of vivid blue waves show each time the wind parts the mist.

'What the fuck is happening?' Ricky says. He's breathing heavily, hands on hips.

'You moving to uni seems like less of a big deal now, mate,' Kyle replies between breaths. 'I think we're gonna die.'

Through the darkness, Ricky looks at his best friend and sees the whites of his eyes reflecting this new world of white and blue. He looks scared.

'No way,' Ricky says. 'I can't die yet – I'm still a virgin.'

Chapter Twenty-Three

Margaret

In the foyer of the brothel, Margaret pulls herself off the ragged couch and straightens up. She feels weak. Behind her temples there's a dull ache.

In the street outside, the air is hot and there is an acrid stench. She wrinkles her nose – the smell of fish. She thinks of Lin. How long since she was taken off in the ambulance? Lin, her skin slick with sweat. Her eyelids flickering. The baby in her womb. Boy or girl?

As she gets into her car, Margaret can't help but think back to her second year of marriage, when all the test results came back. Roger couldn't have kids. They'd even bought a crib, soon after the wedding. So hopeful.

She presses a hand to her belly; the loss she felt with the news has never really left her. The knowledge that she would never experience any of it – no muddle of secrecy during the early weeks, no morning sickness or swollen breasts, no growing bump, no kicking feet. The crib stood empty for eighteen months or so, until one day when Roger removed it from the house. Margaret was out. She came back and it was gone, as though they'd never even wanted one.

It was only a few years later that they moved to KL. Her life has been filled with God, more than ever, since then. Now when she thinks of Him, she feels a hollowness she can't face. She pulls her mind back to Lin: did she make it to the emergency room yet?

As she drives to the hospital, the streets are quiet – no gridlocks, like she's used to. Around the orange glow of each streetlight a thin mist hangs, clouding the air, making her question what sort of weather they're in for. Along the verges of the road are fish, silver among the darkness. Before long the smell of them is in the car, like she's driving through a stagnant harbour. She hates these fish for ruining everything; it's because of them that God has abandoned her.

She parks not far from the hospital entrance and slides down from the driver's seat. Nearby, a couple with a baby carrier head towards their car. Margaret watches the careful way the man holds the baby seat. The woman glances at it again and again. A new-born must be in there, safe and warm, and ready to go home. It's a good sign; Margaret lets it fill her with hope. Lin will raise her baby somewhere safe and comfortable.

There is more mist here. It sinks between the cars in the parking lot, swirling around her feet like tentacles. It has a coolness to it, making the hairs on her ankles stand on end.

The man on reception directs her to the emergency room, where she finds Jane and Allison sitting on plastic chairs against a lime-green wall. There is a clean, surgical smell to the room and the lights are bright white.

'Chitra is in there with them,' Jane says, standing and stretching her arms over her head. 'We haven't heard a thing.' She puts a hand on Margaret's shoulder and gently pushes her into the vacated chair.

'There's mist everywhere,' Margaret says. 'Did you see?'

Jane shakes her head, hardly listening, and mutters something about buying supplies. Allison puts a hand on Margaret's forearm and squeezes.

The emergency room is half-full. To Margaret's left, a mother sits with her son, who coughs relentlessly. The mother reaches over every moment the child pauses and pulls at his nose with a Kleenex. Nearby to them a man sits quietly, staring at the screen of his phone. A large bandage is taped onto his forehead. Across the room an old lady stares at her portion of lime-green wall, unmoving. The scarf wrapped around her neck, orange like fire, stands out in the room with a loudness and a warmth, and Margaret finds herself staring. But the head perched above the scarf has no life in it – the old woman's eyes are glazed, staring into the minutes of unknown while she waits to be seen. The scarf might be the only thing keeping her head in place.

Margaret feels out of place. She is too white, and too well. No sickness laces her body, just a tired ache in her bones. Allison's presence next to her is a guilty reminder of how she felt during the prayer session. She shifts in her seat, self-conscious. At any moment, they'll accuse her of abandoning them.

Has she abandoned them? She feels like she is the one who has been left outside.

Jane returns, holding two coffees and a can of Coke. A large chocolate bar is wedged under her right arm. Allison helps to pull the food and drink loose, unwrapping the chocolate and handing out slabs of it. Margaret eats her piece without tasting it and moves on to coffee.

'Any news?' Jane asks. They shake their heads.

After thirty minutes, the waiting is unbearable. Margaret thinks back to the brothel, to the bargain she made. *Save the baby.* She lets her mind gently prod the question that stands so bottomless and frightening before her: *What if the baby isn't saved?*

It is another forty minutes – Margaret clock-watches, desperate for any distraction – before Chitra appears from a door next to a sign reminding patients: *Please use the sick bags provided.* Her thick dark hair has formed a mass of frizz around her head and her eyes are red. Margaret feels a weight in her stomach as she watches her friend draw closer.

'They've induced her,' Chitra says quietly. 'It'll take a few hours. Hopefully, in that time she gets most of the sickness out of her system.'

'Induced her?' Jane asks. 'After six months? Will the baby survive?'

Chitra bows her head. 'There was no heartbeat.'

'Margaret, are you OK?' someone says.

Their voice echoes. Something presses her shoulders.

'Marge?'

December, the oncoming tropical Christmas season, and white hospital lights. No baby. A black hole has opened beneath Margaret. She sits bolt upright in her emergency-room plastic chair and cries. She doesn't want an arm around her – she needs space to stare into this moment of disbelief. The baby has not been saved. She is wordless, and the moment stretches out long. She needs to leave.

She pulls her hands to her head, to press her palms over her eyes, but the room keeps spiralling. Somewhere nearby a baby cries, and she doesn't know whether it's real or in her mind. She closes her eyes. Wants to lie down. To pull a blanket over her head and disappear in darkness.

'Marge, we're here.'

Her name continues to come, persistent, until she can't ignore it. She looks down at her body, sees other people's hands on her arms, shaking. Eyes before her, round like turtle eggs.

'OK, there you are, you're all right,' she hears.

Margaret finds her own arms around herself, fingers digging hard into the flesh beneath her ribs. She eases them a little, pulling one hand to her mouth and stuffing the shaking fingers between her teeth.

The baby is dead.

'OK,' she manages. 'I'm OK.'

She nods her head, trying to smile. She needs to get home – she can't be here a minute longer.

'This is too much for her,' she hears someone say. 'We'll have to take her home.'

Margaret's quiet tears have stopped and now she sobs, loud and breathless. Months of tension, hours of hopeless prayer, days of anxiety. Her worries spread into the air around her like smoke. *I'm not OK*, she thinks.

She stands, pushing herself against the edges of the chair until her legs sway beneath her. A hand reaches under her arm, to steady her, and she steps away from it. She cannot expect support from the places where she used to seek it. All that is gone. She has Roger now, and only him. The thought of him comes to her like bliss, a ray of light in the darkness.

'I'm going home,' she says.

'I don't think you should drive, Marge,' comes a voice.

'You should stay here a bit,' comes another.

Margaret knows that she has lost her mind, just a little. She almost welcomes it. Together, she and Roger will put it back together.

She heads for the door, hiccups escaping, her body numb beneath her. When the green walls end, giving way to an echoey white corridor, she finds she can't walk another step. She sees a restroom and pushes the door, sinking to the floor next to one of the toilet cubicles. She will rest there a while, until something like clarity returns.

Outside the hospital, the world has disappeared. The mist is thick and white, and it has swallowed everything. Fear rises in Margaret, but she knows she can't go back. There is something too painful inside the hospital – a wound too fresh to examine. The only way forward is home.

The mist licks towards the automatic doors, threatening to pour through. It has a weight to it that blocks out sound, making the world muffled. Margaret shivers – the temperature has dropped, and she wraps her arms around herself as she starts forwards.

It's just a car park, she tells herself, peering into the gloom. *It's just weather*. The sound of her footsteps is absorbed. All she hears is her breathing, loud and heavy.

'Is this a sign?' she asks out loud. As though God has felt her pain and made the whole city suffer it, too.

A railing comes up before her and she grasps it, finding the metal slick and cool to the touch. The mist is so thick, it catches in her throat and makes her want to pull her shirt up over her mouth.

It takes a long time to find her car. Her hands are shaking when she finally reaches it and fumbles with the key card. The city is gone – there is no drone of it, pressing in from the suburbs and roads around. The sky is choking white and full of silence. What is out there?

Margaret can feel panic starting to close in on her. It's madness to drive in this, but she can't stay at the hospital another moment. She just needs to go slow and be careful. Roger will be worrying about her. She has to get back.

As she turns on the car, peering through the windscreen into the white world before her, her mind flickers back to the fish, and she knows this is the second part of the plague. She doesn't know how it will end, but she knows God will not help her through it. He has turned His back. If the end is coming, she'll face it from home, with Roger, and his warm hand in hers.

She sees the refracted flash of blue ambulance lights as she leaves the hospital complex. She can just make out the vehicle on the sidewalk, with its bumper crumpled around a lamp post. She tries turning her lights to high beam, but they only reflect more white. Leaning forwards in her seat, as though the extra half a foot will help her to see, she mutters to herself: 'Go slow, it's OK – just go slow.'

Her journey is endless, crawling through suburbs where the roads are thankfully quiet, then onto the highway that leads towards the centre of the city. Two cars speed past her in the opposite direction. She screams as they lunge out of the mist and then disappear back into it. On the highway there is a little more traffic, cars moving here and there. She slows down even more. Someone comes up behind her, lights suddenly reflecting in her rear-view. For a moment she's certain they'll plough right into the back of her and she braces for the impact. Through the fog their horn goes off, one long peal after another, right behind her. She wants to scream. *Are they idiots?* The car swerves past, jerking right out into the middle of the highway. Its horn still blares and then it's in front of her, tail lights swallowed up by the fog.

She'll never make it home in this. Her breathing is shallow. Her eyes strain and her head is pounding. When another vehicle screams past in the opposite direction, this time a van, she closes her eyes and hits the brake. When she opens them again, the van is gone. He was going far too fast. He'll cause an accident. It makes her so angry. *Why can't people be more careful? Why can't they see that the things they do can hurt people around them?*

When she gets to downtown, the streetlights and brightly lit windows make the white mist glow yellow. There is nothing to look upwards to – the skyscrapers are engulfed. Between the shifting fog, she recognises the familiar pattern of the road. Her shoulders relax a little. She must be halfway home. She can make it.

Visibility is almost better on the sky highway. Perhaps the mist is thinner higher up. She can see the asphalt in front of her, and the weak shine of reflectors in the centre of the highway. When she nearly hits two cars spread at an angle across the road, her heart practically jumps out of her chest. She slams her foot on the brake pedal. Her neck snaps forwards, body like a rag doll. Through the fog she hears men's voices raised, barking at each other. She can just make them out, standing among two smashed-up cars. The dummies have had a crash and now they're fighting about it. She could bang their heads together, tell them to get out of the middle of the road.

She takes deep breaths before carrying on, easing her foot onto the gas to inch around the cars. This is the home stretch. Four junctions to go. The mist lifts a little more and she breathes a sigh of relief. Around her she can see the edges of the highway. At home, Roger will have the news on. Her dinner will be waiting. When they wake up tomorrow, all this will be gone. She'll look back on today and say it was the worst journey of her life.

For an hour, just an hour, she's forgotten about the fish. They, too, have been swallowed by the fog. But here on the highway, where the mist is thinner, they are once again visible. Margaret's heart sinks. Still there. Silver bodies on the side of the road. She keeps her eyes off them. It's easy to do; she concentrates so hard on driving. When she crawls around another bend, though, there is a fish right in the middle of the road, only a few feet ahead. It half-walks, half-crawls, flapping about like a dying thing. She doesn't think. Her instinct tells her to miss it, and she swerves. She shouts out, shocked, watching for the fish in the side-view mirror, and though she's still going slow, the jerk of the steering wheel takes her out into the middle of the road. She only has a second to see the car coming straight for her, fast out of the fog, like a bullet. Then everything goes black.

Chapter Twenty-Four
Cathy

I spend an afternoon and a half making myself a veil – a sort of desert scarf that I can pull tight over my nose and mouth. The red tide is coming. We know it; we've seen it on telly marching along the shores of South Asia, Australia and New Zealand. In equatorial regions in particular it has caused massive disruption, grounding flights and causing whole cities to screech to a halt. Lives have been lost. Cars crash, waves swallow, air poisons. I've watched it all unfold on the TV screen, detached. Ephie is full of nervous excitement. In the daytime the tide turns the sea a deep menstrual red that blossoms through the shallows, and at night it is electric blue with phosphorescence. Day and night, it seeps into the shorelines. The direct fatalities have been in places where the plankton bloom – that's what causes the red tide – has been densest. The plankton release neurotoxins. They are never usually enough to do a human any harm, but we know by now that there is nothing usual about these events. What sort of plankton bloom covers the whole globe? This is the first of its kind.

Waiting for an event to begin is stifling. It makes me feel like a rat in a box. It would be far better not to know it's coming.

We all have different ways of dealing with suspense: Ephie thinks. She says, 'It makes no sense why this plankton bloom would be moving around the world in a similar pattern to The Storm.' (That is what we call it now, that first biblical storm that brought on the madness. It is the only storm in my entire life I can remember.) 'It can't be temperature-related,' Ephie further speculates, 'because they're in midsummer over in Australia and it's early winter here.' She rattles through all the science she knows, and a lot she doesn't, trying to understand it all. Rather than admire her, as I have always done before, I stop listening. She's in a world of her own, out there among the experts. She has been with them, and not with me, for months now. I've felt the loss of her feline limbs in my bed most nights as a deep ache.

As the red tide and the thick white mist roll towards us, the local radio tells us to stay indoors. The schools are closed. Messages are coming in constantly from neighbours checking in or wanting to gossip. I grow weary of the communication. I think of Mum, alone at home, and wonder if I should go to her. She sends me a picture of her kitchen counter covered in mince pies – enough to feed an army. She is keeping busy. Through the window I stare down at the beach and harbour, and not a soul is in sight. The fish tourists are long gone. Barvusi is a ghost town.

The plankton that cause the tide only release neurotoxins during the early stage: the 'aerosolisation' stage, they call it. This is the dangerous bit. Once the 'vaporisation' stage has begun, and thick white mist has settled, the tide is supposed to be harmless. I don't want to take any chances. I choose heavy cotton and two layers of refined silk for my veil, to create a three-ply, because that's what the internet suggests when I watch a video about the construction of surgical masks. I want silver fibres to weave through the veil, because I know those are antibacterial. Ephie has a pair of walking socks that contain silver, and I briefly debate using those, but they're far too woolly and they smell like feet, despite the silver. Instead, I settle for a pendant – a silver cross I have never worn – and stitch it into the seam. My fingers trace the edges of the cross and I think of vampires. The fish that have been slouching across our land are not so different from them. They are driven by something unnatural. This white mist that is coming – will it suck the blood from my veins?

When the day comes, it is announced by the birds. The gulls begin at 5am, shrieking and calling and stamping on the roof, and before long the oystercatchers on the beach join in, and then the godwits and the redshanks. Around dawn, I think I even hear the long, ghostly keen of a curlew, which is very rare. Around 8am every one of them goes silent, and there isn't a bird in the grey sky.

By mid-morning, out at sea, the waves blossom dark and bloody. I watch from my studio window. Within half an hour it is at the shore, red crests pushing into our semi-circular harbour. The fish start to move. Each one of them, our entire collection of air-breathers, slouches into motion. Not towards the sea, oh no. My skin crawls as they head inland, possessed by a mad need to avoid the waves. Do they know this tide would be the death of them? They look scared. I watch them go and wonder, after long, slow minutes have passed, if I look the same. I perch at my desk with three layers of fabric wrapped tight around my face. How long will it last, this apocalypse? I hope the seals in the next bay are all right.

I continue to wear my veil. I eat nothing and drink nothing, for fear of exposing my airways. By midday my stomach grumbles and my throat is dry. The red tide washes on.

It is early afternoon and the beach is crimson. I pace the house. I try not to worry about Ephie, away at the lab as always. An image of her frolicking forwards into this crimson abyss, test tube at the ready, replays again and again in my mind, until I almost feel I'm wishing for it. I shake my head, feeling guilty – how can I keep visualising such a thing?

The mist starts to rise off the water, white clouds of it drifting and hovering over the waves, and I finally allow myself a few mouthfuls of toast, spread thin with butter and a hint of rhubarb jam. The crumbs spill onto the desk in front of me. I watch the mist continue to form. David Evans potters along the beach. He stands out even better than usual, yellow mac against red sand. Too far away to see his face, I scramble onto the desk, pushing the sewing machine aside, toast falling to the floor. I press my nose against the glass, hands and knees on the desk, and shout: 'Get off the beach!' I bang on the pane – knuckles, palms, elbows – and it hurts. He doesn't hear. The mist is over the red waves, not yet on the beach, and he walks with slow complacency, every step leaving a footprint the colour of old spilled wine. I scan the beach around him. He is completely alone.

A few steps later and his walk becomes a stagger. I slide off the desk, scraping my thigh and landing on the toast, mashing jam into my socks. Grabbing my veil, I run from the room. By the time I reach the window halfway down the stairs, he is on his knees. From the kitchen window I see him sink to the sand. I breathe hard, veil on, frantically shouting at him through double glazing. It's all nonsense, words muffled, and I'm hot and breathless with the effort of it.

It takes me a long time, far too long, to put on a jacket and open the back door. It is impossible. How can I walk out into a world like that? I don't want to die. But I don't want David to die. I might be the only person who knows he's out there. This filthy, heavy sense of responsibility makes me turn the handle.

As I pull the door shut behind me, the fear is like a weight, plugging my feet to the doorstep. It threatens to overwhelm me, so I run. I plunge into the outside world as fast as I can. Out through the garden gate and onto the steps leading down to the harbour. I get to the beach quickly and stop on the very edge of it. I don't look around but I know I'm alone. I might be in another world. There is a hollowness to Barvusi that's foreign and terrifying. The only sounds are the drum of the red waves against the beach and, nearer, the rustle of fish bodies against sand. I can smell them, too. The air is ripe with them.

I pull my arms around myself, checking I'm still alive. I try not to breathe, terrified to inhale, but all the same I'm quickly surrounded by my own white cloud as strangled breaths seep through my veil and into the December air. In front of me the mist creeps up the beach. A line of fish shuffle before it.

I stand there, idling on the precipice. I tell myself to get on with it; that it will be OK. But my feet are small and vulnerable, and the beach is cursed. I think of David somewhere out of sight along the shore, and the thought of him finally sets me moving. He might be curled in agony, needing a hand to clutch, and I can't leave him there like that. Perhaps I could leave a stranger, but not this man who I have laughed with over pints of Black Rock on a Tuesday evening in the pub. Not this man who was there that first morning by the shoreline.

I don't run on the beach. Heavy footprints might disturb the red colour all around me, and there are too many fish bodies to avoid, so I go slow. Perhaps I want to delay the moment I get to David. Just keep walking. I keep my arms tight by my sides, hands thrust deep into jacket pockets. Just keep walking. I wait for something to happen: a chemical taste in my mouth, a fire in my throat, a twitching pain in my limbs. Nothing comes. My veil seems to work. I breathe a little more easily.

The white mist is so thick by now that I'm swallowed into its opacity. I enter a world of echoing white, where the rhythm of the waves is muffled and distorted, and the house I call home is gone from my view. A new terror seeps into me – that I could die out here and never be found. That the freezing Atlantic tide will sweep my useless body away and Ephie will never see my face again. Maybe the sea would spit me back out eventually – David, too. We might wash up at Land's End: a dreg of a woman wearing a red waterproof and a three-ply cotton silk veil, hand in hand with an old, weathered fisherman with a Welsh name and a Cornish heart. Or I might disappear entirely, no loose ends tied, no marriage saved. To die alone.

I start to cry. The tears stream down my face, and beneath my mask I'm a snotty mess. David finally shows through the mist, a smudge of yellow on top of shifting red ground, and I shuffle closer and closer, until I finally get to him and freeze. The white fog shows me only snatches of him as it moves with the wind. A button down the front of his jacket. A section of black corduroy, patched at the knee. His face, when it shows itself, is white as winter. He isn't breathing; somehow, I know that. There is a stillness in his eyes that is too keen to be living. I'm so cold.

I want to get down, to kneel with him and grasp his hand in mine. That's what I should do. I should be there for him, properly, but I can't bring myself to move any closer to the red sand under my feet; to let any more than the soles of my shoes touch the tide that has brought him to this end. He lies on his deathbed, and I just stare.

I wipe the tears from my cheeks and manage to take another step until I'm standing right over him. I lean over, rigid as a board, calves aching, and manage to brush my fingertips across his cheek. I recoil. He's cold. Dead.

I call Ephie then, no thought for how miraculous it is that I remembered to stuff my phone in my pocket before leaving the house. My fingers are shaky and clumsy on the touchscreen, and when the dial tone sounds, I'm certain she won't answer. Her own phone will be on mute, shoved into a lab coat pocket and forgotten. I know I'm alone here, in the depths of the fog, and she won't come to me.

'Cathy, are you OK?' she asks in a rush.

'No.'

Some time later, I don't know how long, she comes to me. She brings two paramedics, who bring a stretcher and a silver emergency blanket. They wrap it round me, and it crinkles like tinfoil and doesn't feel at all warm. I think of Bill the barman that day on the beach with my shovel, and the heat of his musty jacket.

David is loaded onto the stretcher, sou'wester in pocket. Ephie and the other two both wear serious-looking gas masks – probably her idea, nicked from a fume cupboard in the lab – and their words as they speak to one another come out muffled. Before David is carried away, my wife does the thing I couldn't. She kneels and embraces him, holding on for a long moment before letting him go. When she turns back to me, her eyes are wet.

'Let's go home,' she says.

Then her hand is round my waist and we are walking. The mist is thick like cotton wool. The occasional silver fish body flickers in and out of view among the cloud. None of them moves. Everything is still: dead or dying. Except for us. Ephie's hand is warm against mine.

At the kitchen table, my whole body shakes like a foal. She tells me I'm in shock, and that it will pass. She makes me a cup of tea and asks me to eat a huge wedge of chocolate while the tea cools a little. I follow her instructions. I'm numb with exhaustion, chewing the chocolate like it's a marathon event. She kneels next to me and reads my vital signs. A thumb on my wrist and a hand on my forehead. The foil blanket is long gone, replaced with thick wool that is heavy over my shoulders. I drink my tea from between wobbling hands, and she barely takes her eyes off me. She has irises the colour of bronze, and she watches me with her cat gaze, cautious and intense.

Once the tea is drunk, I'm bundled to bed. She creeps in next to me, wrapping me up with her limbs like leaves around an unopened bud.

After a long sleep you expect to wake up refreshed. That night I surface, at ten in the evening, and feel lobotomised. Ephie is gone, her side of the bed cold, and I'm too numb to call her. I stare at the ceiling, where light from the bedside lamp splashes an orange glow into the darkness. The room is nearly silent, only the steady roll of waves permeating the quiet. I try not to hear them.

'Hey, beautiful,' she says, appearing at the bedroom door.

She is wearing her red dungarees – a black jumper underneath so that she looks like a ladybird – and when her eyes meet mine, she scrambles to the bedside. I must look awful.

'Did you have a good sleep?' she asks, propping herself next to me.

I nod, curling into her. I feel embarrassed to find tears coming and press my face against her chest.

'You were so amazing today, Cathy,' she says, running her fingers through my hair. 'You went out there when no one else did. Who does that?'

I can hear her smiling. 'You're brave, and stupid, and the best person I know,' she says.

I shake my head, nose rubbing against the ridges of her corduroy.

'I didn't help,' I mumble. 'I just stood there. I was too scared to move.'

'No one could have changed it, my love. But you did help.'

'I was pathetic.'

She nudges me, shifting us both so that she can lie down, and cups my face in her hands. She brings me close until our noses touch and my whole world is her brown eyes.

'You wandered out into the depths of hell. For a friend. What's pathetic about that?'

She kisses me, a slobbery thing mixed up with my tears.

'You silly Sasquatch,' she says, smiling.

I wake up, having slept another ten hours, and grey light filters through the curtains. I make it out of bed and dare to look outside. White.

In the living room I click the local news on. Advice to stay indoors, make only essential journeys. Do not go to work, or school. No long-term danger from breathing in sea mist, but potential for irritation to airways, particularly among the young, elderly and vulnerable. Visibility extremely low. Emergency services overwhelmed with responding to traffic accidents.

No mention of a dead man on Barvusi beach, or anywhere else.

I spend the day curled near the fire, rising only once to help Ephie make a batch of flapjacks. I measure the oats out like an automaton, and she watches me from the corner of her eyes. 'You need to keep talking,' she tells me, and I nod.

'What happened with David, Cathy? How long were you out there with him?'

'He was dead when I arrived.' I tip the oats into the saucepan and there is quiet while Ephie stirs.

'In a few days this will all clear,' she says, trying to sound chirpy. 'And then everything can get back to normal.'

I shrug. She puts an arm around my shoulder and with her free hand passes me the wooden spoon.

'Can you press it into the tin?' she says, squeezing me. 'I'll put the kettle on.'

As the day goes on, a little mobility returns to my limbs, until by bedtime I can't keep still. Ephie is closer to me than she's been in weeks, but I'm anxious. I wait for the moment she'll tell me she's going back to the lab. She must be itching to work. There are secrets in the sea mist; I can practically hear her brain whirring.

We go to bed together early, after three large glasses each of rum, and I almost feel light. She runs her fingers up and down my back before she falls asleep. After two hours of wakefulness, I get up and pace the house. It's 3am before I'm finally exhausted, my brain dead with worry.

This morning, once again, the winter sun sits above the mist and shows us our cotton-wool world. Like the stars on our kitchen window, the cod that lived on the shore are all dead. They lie, stinking, around the edges of the beach. I can smell them.

I am making tea and eating flapjack for breakfast, when Ephie comes into the kitchen with her coat on. I know this is the moment; she has stayed with me, babysitting, for long enough. Work is calling her.

I open my mouth to speak, to beg her to stay, but no words come out.

'I'm going to pop out and get some milk,' she says. I wither, dropping onto the nearby chair.

'Are you OK?' she asks, coming closer.

Tears threaten again but I hold them back, feeling my face crumple with the effort of it. 'I thought you were leaving me,' I say.

She squats next to me and takes my hands in hers. 'I'm never leaving,' she says with a frown.

I must look unconvinced. 'Why would you think that?' she asks.

'You have to work. Find the answers. I thought you'd be back to the lab.' I'm whimpering. She looks surprised, then upset.

'You've been having a hard time,' she says at last. 'And I've been ignoring it.'

I don't say anything, and she loops her fingers through mine. 'I won't do that anymore. I'm having a couple of weeks off from the lab. They're fine without me. You're more important.'

I nod, tears rolling down my cheeks. She sits sideways across my lap with her arms around me until I stop crying, and then puts on her mask and goes out for milk.

I build the fire, a great roaring one stacked high with logs, until I am sweating in my jumper, and I lie down on the floor and stretch. 'You should talk about it,' Ephie said while the flapjacks cooked. 'Don't become withdrawn and over-thoughtful. That sort of thing can lead to depression,' she insisted. 'Don't turn in on yourself.'

Devon and Cornwall have shrivelled and died; Dorset and Somerset, too. Their orange limbs have curled up. They have finally become what I always suspected them of being – satsuma peel. They have fallen from the kitchen window and lie withered on the floor at the bottom of the house. I would go out and see them, if I weren't so afraid that I would join them there.

Two days ago I saw a dead man. Before they carried him off, the paramedics tucked his sou'wester into the pocket of his yellow jacket. For safekeeping. Except there is no one to keep either his hat or his clothes safe for anymore. They took him away, and now he's gone.

The heat from the fire bakes the upper half of me all down my length, so I roll onto my side to let my back cook, too. I am encased in this white box of a world and the air inside the house grows stale, but I would rather have stale air than suffocation. Ephie is out there in it, taking shallow breaths in her search for milk.

I watch the clock. Thirty-five minutes since she left. Too soon to worry, but I can't help it. The floor is hard under my hip. I feel now – with the loss of David, with the death of the fish – that I have woken from a coma. The world, white and toxic, is before me once again. I wrestle with a love and a hate of it. I'm terrified and relieved.

As I feel sweat trickle under my arms and listen for the turn of a key in the door, I try to focus my mind on one thing: Ephie. Her cat eyes are back on me, and that makes me feel like we might just prevail.

Chapter Twenty-Five
Ricky

Ricky sticks his feet in the lake. He's got blisters from trekking the Tongariro Crossing yesterday. It took eight hours and it rained over lunch. The sulphur smell was cool, though: it made him think of a time when all the volcanoes were active, and the skies were filled with ash clouds – when dinosaurs, or at least the giant birds that came after them, were around.

Their summer holiday is nearly over. Another week and he'll be back at school for one last year. The fish are gone from the land now, almost as though it never happened. The strangeness of it still bleeds into everyday life, though. Like the world is living with a sense of suspense, everyone wondering if and when it could happen again. While he's stuck in that suspense, Ricky's trying to decide between biology, marine biology, ecology, conservation or biodiversity. There's a lot to figure out, and everyone he talks to has a different opinion about what he should do. He thinks Janie will be an anthropologist or a historian when she's older. They went to the Taupō Museum and read all about the Māori history of the region. She came away with sparkly eyes, imagining every story was about her own grandpa. She must have forgotten that Grandpa lives in Ngāruawāhia, and is a retired postman, not a god.

The clouds are piling up on the horizon and the smell of barbeque makes his stomach rumble. Not far away, Janie's helping Dad flip the burgers, while Mum works on her latest knitting project. Ricky takes his phone from his pocket and scrolls through the pictures he took on the trek yesterday. The phone vibrates in his hand with a message from Kyle.

What up. Going to see Dad this aft.

Ricky replies, *How's that gonna be?*

Kyle sends back a picture of someone throwing up. *He wants to be 'friends'*, he writes.

Weird, Ricky types. *How do you feel about it all?*

Since that night on the beach, when Kyle and Ricky argued about what they'd do after school, and when the phosphorescent tide came in and they thought they were running for their lives, Ricky's been trying to be better at talking – to Kyle, especially. Ricky sought advice from his mum, and she told him that the best trick she'd learnt in life was just to ask people how they felt.

Kyle replies: *Dunno. Nervous? Bit hopeful maybe. That we can start to move on.*

Ricky waits a minute or two, but Kyle doesn't say more.

His foot all fixed now? Ricky asks, pulling his own feet out of the lake now they've gone cold. Last time Kyle mentioned him, his dad was still limping around.

Think so, yeah. Honestly the most exciting thing that's ever happened to him. Maybe he'll write a book about it.

Ricky suggests a title: *The Fish That Nearly Killed Me*

Puffer In The Sand, Kyle says.

Finding Puffer.

Fintastic Adventures: Running With The Fish, Kyle suggests.

Yes! That's the one, Ricky types. Behind him, he hears Dad shout that the food's ready. *Gotta go eat. Let me know how it goes.*

He turns his phone on mute and puts it back in his pocket. The closer he gets to the barbeque, the more his mouth waters. Mum's laid the picnic rug out on the grass and Janie lies right across the middle of it, perfectly still, with the binoculars trained on two pūkeko pecking around in the shallows. Their old camper van's parked up back, by the road.

'Home tomorrow, then,' Dad says, looking disappointed. He carries the plate of burgers to the rug and Ricky nudges Janie with his foot, telling her to get out of the way.

'Any schoolwork left to do before next week?' Mum asks, looking from Ricky to Janie and back again. They both shake their heads, both lying.

'Ah, come on, let's not talk about work,' Dad moans.

'Let's hope this year is a bit less weird than the last one,' Mum says.

'No fish?' Janie asks.

'No fish, or whales in the harbour. Or hospitalisations. Or massive, weird storms,' Ricky says.

'Probably get another cat, eh?' Mum asks, looking sad and taking hold of Janie's hand. Her daughter nods.

They start eating and Ricky can't help but wonder how long it will be before the next big storm. How long before the next lot of floods.

The pūkeko screech, their black bodies shimmering in the sunlight, and further out in the lake, where the water gets deep and turns navy blue, a fish jumps. It makes a great slap against the water. Ricky sees a flash, and then the ripples spread across the smooth surface, wider and wider.

Chapter Twenty-Six

Cathy

The Saturday paper lies on the dining table, its headline – *Fishteria!* – implying a lighter tone than the article beneath. It is an overview of the world we live in; a round-up of the major global events that have occurred since the storm in July; an exposé of destruction and death. It is a eulogy, with the entire third page filled with stories of lives lost: an Australian girl struck by lightning, a Cypriot father caught in a forest fire, an elderly Japanese woman poisoned by a fish, an American expat in Malaysia killed in a car crash... The list goes on. I would have taken the exclamation mark out of the headline, if I were the editor.

The first page covers the current best theory for what the hell happened. It is proposed by the UN, and the paper has a stab at naming a few people to blame. But on a global scale, who can you really blame – everyone? No one? Ephie says the theories are good but there are a lot of gaps. The marine experts have only just made a start; there's a lot they still don't understand. The UN points to literature from the 1990s about ocean acidification – suggesting it's a story that's been unfolding under the water for decades. But now the fish and the red tide and the white mist have all gone from our coastlines, Ephie thinks her lab is unlikely to get the long-term funding they'd need to see their research through to a decent resolution. It will be like the viral epidemics of the past – pushed from our minds and purposefully forgotten. Until it happens again.

'Are you nearly ready?' Ephie asks from the bottom of the stairs. She wears one of the plum-coloured silk bridesmaid dresses, with the fishtail and low back, and she looks like royalty. That wedding was cancelled back in August. The bride cried on the phone when she withdrew the order – said she wanted to get married on the beach and it couldn't be surrounded by fish.

'Do I look OK?' Ephie asks as she comes into the room.

'You're spectacular. David would be speechless.'

She shrugs, arms dangling. 'Are you sure it's not too much?'

'Everyone's dressing up.'

She frowns at me, still in my dressing gown with a hot-water bottle on my lap and halfway through a cup of tea. 'We need to leave in half an hour.'

David Evans's funeral had to be delayed. While we waited for the white mist to clear, Cornwall County Council urged us all to take an extended Christmas break: to spend it at home, to avoid travel, to stick to higher ground and to keep away from the beaches. More deaths were reported in the days following the arrival of the red tide. They were elderly people, for the most part, and I felt nothing for them. I'm numb. There are probably no tears left in me.

It has been a month and three days since David died. I needed to find some way to mark that period, the way people light candles in churches – to remember. I considered what we'd shared, thinking of the hours I'd spent with him and others in the pub, pints of Black Rock all round. It was a tempting idea: a pint a day. Sometimes I might need to drive the car, though, and sometimes I might want a gin and tonic. I had a good laugh about that, discussing it with David in my mind. *Don't be drinking too much, now, Cathy*, I could hear him say. *Remember me in an easy way.*

Of course, I've settled on chocolate digestives. It's easy to eat one a day. I think of the moment David left me on the beach with the walking fish just gone, and the fluidity with which he went back to his biscuits. He was something obscure and special. The biscuits send me back to my morning in the pub, the terrier on my lap, and I have to focus on the warmth of Bill and the dog and the fire, and not the shame I was feeling for my fish-killing spree. The digestives come with some difficult feelings, I admit, but they are delicious at least.

One biscuit a day, for David. Ephie has one, too. For the week after he died, I couldn't make it through the biscuit without sobbing. The mist was still pressing in on us then and my mind was still a haunted house.

Now it is mid-January, with blue skies and hilltop frosts, with snowdrops showing and a curlew calling. My wife stands in the doorway with her cheetah limbs stretched long, watching me, and I feel guilty when I smile, because David is dead, but I still smile, and I savour the last crumbs of the biscuit, half of which is lost and floating in my tea.

'*Agapi mou*, how are you feeling?' She comes over to me and leans close, nuzzling her nose into the left side of my neck.

'Nervous. How about you?' I push my chair out from the table and pat my lap, inviting her to sit down, but she shakes her head and holds out her hands to pull me up. Ever the timekeeper.

'I feel weird,' she says. 'The only funeral I've ever been to was Yia-yia's in Athens. It was all very Orthodox, and there was a sense that she'd come to the end of a long life. I'm not sure what today will be like.'

'Nor me.' I take her hands and stand. 'Ephie, everyone knows I found David. Are they going to ask me about it?'

'I don't think so. They've had plenty of time to do that already.' She puts her hands on my hips and squeezes. 'Go and get dressed.'

We are at the door, piling into coats and hats and scarves and thick socks, when Bill arrives to pick us up. He eyes us both: half-dressed for a wedding and half for a winter woodland burial, and I look back at him in his black wool suit and feel a lump in my throat.

In a field fifteen minutes away by car, down a drive with a sign welcoming us to Coastal Peace Natural Burials, there is no view of the sea. There is a north-east wind that makes my lungs hurt, and there are no trees. I decide David would like that; without their branches, it's exposed and bitterly cold, and anyone who spent any time in that field would end up with chapped lips and ruddy cheeks, like him.

'At least you can hear it,' Ephie says, reading my mind.

I close my eyes and hold my breath, and there it is, the rumble of the Atlantic. It must be raucous when a strong westerly is blowing.

Nine of us stand around the hole in the earth they have dug for him. Bill, Ephie and me, the village gossips Steve and Angie Wright, a fisherman from Mevagissey who says he has known David since they were kids, and three folk singers, there on Bill's request to sing a shanty. They are part of a group called Bait Box Buoys, and I can't help but laugh when I hear the name. They're young men, all three of them, and I admire the sincerity in their expressions. They stand with their hands clasped in great solemnity.

Bill says it is such a loss, but that David died in the place he loved – Barvusi, right next to the sea – and will now rest in peace, always dreaming of fish. I feel sick for a moment, eyes on Bill, but realise he is talking of fishing, normal fishing, not the land fish or the mist or the red beach that killed David. I dig my fingernails into my palm and remind myself to concentrate. Bill goes on to tell the story of the time he put David's yellow mac to dry near the pub fire, but too close, and the hood got singed. 'I'd never seen him so angry,' Bill laughs. I feel tears in my eyes and blink them back; I have cried enough this past month. We pass round shots of whisky.

Ephie reads a poem, one she agonised over choosing, complaining that she didn't understand poetry anyway. She stares straight down at the screen she reads off, never looking up, and I know it's because she will cry if she makes eye contact with a single one of us. Again, we pass round shots of whisky.

I feel the fiery warmth of the liquid spread within me. He is gone, and he was just a friend; not the best, not the oldest, not the most important, but a friend. I feel a great relief to stand in that freezing field with others. Today, thank God, my sadness is not alone. I can mix the last six months of fear and worry in with it, and I can stand in this field and breathe it all out into the cold north wind.

They sing 'The Farewell Shanty', and it's a funeral march, slow and sad and Cornish as can be. Ephie starts to cry beside me, and that's too much. I blub until my throat hurts, trying to keep my focus on the field we stand in, and not the red beach in my mind. Bill takes my hand into his, so warm, and Ephie takes the other. The men sing as though it might be the last song they ever sing, as though we might be the last audience they ever perform for, and they're lovely but I want them to stop. When it's over, we stand in silence for a long time, listening to the wind. We pass round more shots of whisky. 'You won't be fit to drive,' Ephie tells Bill, only half-joking.

When the hole is filled in – when there's no way we'll ever see him again – a staff member from the burial site hands Angie a pack of wild-flower seeds. It feels like a wedding, each of us taking a handful to throw. Ephie reads the outside of the packet – 'You'd think they'd choose a mix for sandy soil, at least,' she says – and I dig my elbow into her side. 'Just scatter the bloody things.'

I release the seeds with the sun right above us, weak and beautiful, and six gulls in the sky. *Goodbye*, I tell him in my head. *Enjoy the biscuits.*

We have some lunch at home and Ephie checks her emails. Most of the village will be in the pub this afternoon; there's no rush for us to be there.

'Will you really just stop the research?' I ask.

She looks confused and I parrot what she said, about how they'd never get the funding they need.

'Oh, well, long term it will be a challenge. It's unlikely there'll be more funding cycles focusing on this now. I could be wrong, though,' she says.

'So will you have to stop?'

'Not right now. It's a two-year grant and we're only three months in. And it is important to carry on.' She scratches her head. 'Our *in vitro* testing with mammalian cell lines was completely superseded by real life, once the whales started getting infected. That is quite worrying. We quickly need to understand the molecular pathways of the infection. Really, we don't know a thing.'

'You don't know a thing?' I ask, anxious.

She smiles. 'We know a few things. And I know *everything*, of course.'

'Of course.'

'I was talking to the fisherman from Mevagissey, when you and Bill went inside to thank the staff,' she says. 'Lowan, his name was. He said Cornish fishing is done now. It's been on its last legs for years and now it'll never recover.'

'It mentions the fishing industry in that article.' I point at the newspaper. 'They reckon it will be years before demand gets back to where it was. Because who wants to eat fish now? But with the spot testing for infection, too, the industry's ready to collapse. Millions of people all across the world will be affected.'

She shakes her head. 'It's a mess.'

I stare out of the kitchen window at the cloudless blue sky. 'I do miss Devon and Cornwall. I got so used to them being there.'

'I think you'd be very worried if they came back,' she says.

On the walk to the pub, I think of everything that's happened since that drive home from Ephie's parents. Only a few weeks have passed since the mist cleared, but journalists now talk about the walking fish in the past tense, and I find myself believing that it's all over – that things are back to normal. Part of me wants this, too.

'I'll clear the rice stems tomorrow,' Ephie says, half to herself. 'Spring will be here soon, and then it won't be long before we can get the seedlings going.'

The heels of her boots click against the cobbled road. Her Victoria-plum fishtail sticks out beneath the bottom of her long coat. I take her hand and put it, along with mine, into her coat pocket.

'I feel guilty, just carrying on. Going back to normal, as though nothing's happened,' I say.

'But you're not going back to normal. Things have changed. Cathy, my entire work focus has shifted. There's no way I'm forgetting about this.'

I nod, close to tears again.

She squeezes my hand. 'It will get better.'

When we push open the pub door, the warmth and noise of a whole village greets us, and a scraggy terrier runs over and starts nosing at our ankles. From the bar, Bill waves, a sad look in his eyes, and then he shouts, 'Cathy, your shovel's still out there!'

Ephie looks at the bloodstained shovel, propped up in the porch, and then at me.

'I'll tell you later,' I say. 'Can you get me a pint? I'll be there in a sec.'

I let the door swing shut and step back out into the road. The Atlantic rumbles on and there's a fresh, crisp smell of salt in the air. An oystercatcher calls, then another, and I picture them scuttling up and down the sand, fluffed up and fat in the winter wind.

Somewhere in the background, in a quiet corner of the harbour, David's little boat rocks from side to side. Out at sea, fish swim. My wife waits inside, to hold me in her warm bronze gaze. I take a deep breath and go in.

Acknowledgements

I researched the novel's settings to the best of my ability, partly drawing on my own experiences of travelling to Malaysia and New Zealand. Any inaccuracies in the depictions of those cultures are my own. Thanks to Tom and Katie, for helping me answer difficult questions like 'what are roofs made of in New Zealand?'. Thanks to Sasibai, for welcoming me in Kuala Lumpur and taking me out to buy *lemang*. I hope that Margaret's love for the city is a good reflection of how much I enjoyed my stay there.

I would like to thank everyone who has talked to me about fish. There have been a lot of you – and a lot of puns – and I'm very grateful for the support, enthusiasm and humour.

Particular thanks to my fellow writers, who have been reading and helping me to improve drafts since day one. I will especially name Ruby, Polly, Alexia and Trenna, who give excellent feedback and are lovely to be around.

Thanks to Mum, for suggesting I try a writing course. Sam Harvey, for pushing me to make the early drafts better. Hannah and Tim, for being halfway-through readers. Laura at Fairlight for taking this on and editing it with me.

Finally, thanks to Dan for being unfailingly positive and generally great.

About the Author

Joanne Stubbs lives on the edge of the Cotswolds. After growing up in Staffordshire, she studied biochemistry at Wadham College, Oxford. She has since worked in a variety of roles in science communication and engagement. Joanne holds an MA in Creative Writing from Bath Spa University. *The Fish* is her debut novel.